CW01209401

Ascension

Queen Of Ages Trilogy:
Book One

PAULA ACTON

COVER ART BY
Debra @DACreations

No part of this book may be reproduced in any written, electronic, recording, or photocopying without written permission of the publisher or author. The exception would be in the case of brief quotations embodied in the critical articles or reviews and pages where permission is specifically granted by the publisher or author.

This is a work of fiction. Names, characters, businesses, places, events and incidents are either the products of the author's imagination or used in a fictitious manner. Any resemblance to actual persons, living or dead, or actual events is purely coincidental.

© 2017 by Paula Acton

All rights reserved.

Dedication

Sometimes you make friends in the strangest of ways, this book was inspired initially by a game on Facebook, and by the characters each of the players became on there. We started with alter ego's but true friendships that will last a lifetime were forged, many of us have since left the game but we remain in touch, supporting each other through the highs and lows from all corners of the globe.

To the friends and allies with whom we smashed walls, raided and pillaged, you forever have my respect and friendship.

To my beloved Black Roses, those who were with me for years, and those who came and went, I shall forever cherish the nights spent in laughter and craziness during some of the darkest times in my life. In a world where so much is uncertain, where you can be let down by those closest to you, strangers on the other side of the planet can become your greatest support network, the people you can be yourself with, share your fears and worries without fear of judgement, and, if you are really lucky, they become more, an online family as dear to you as those connected by blood.

Special thanks to Dave, Wendell, Susan, Ids, Damien, Larry, Andrew, Priscilla and Stuart for loading the trebuchet, and to Anna, Heidi,

Rhonda, Debbie, and Sharon for your never-ending support when I doubt myself, to Debra for creating the amazing art work for me and to all my friends who have been there during this long journey, I wish I could mention you all by name but I am blessed by knowing so many wonderful people.

Contents

Part One; 7
What Must Come to Pass 7

Chapter One 9

Chapter Two 22

Chapter Three 35

Chapter Four 46

Chapter Five 56

Chapter Six 68

Chapter Seven 82

Chapter Eight 92

Chapter Nine 101

Chapter Ten 115

Part Two; Point of No Return 120

Chapter Eleven 122

Chapter Twelve 129

Chapter Thirteen 143

Chapter Fourteen 154

Chapter Fifteen 168

Chapter Sixteen 187

Chapter Seventeen 197

Chapter Eighteen 205

Chapter Nineteen 217

Chapter Twenty 232

Chapter Twenty-One 239

Chapter Twenty-Two 252

Chapter Twenty-Three..................................262

Chapter Twenty-Four....................................270

Chapter Twenty-Five.....................................293

Chapter Twenty-Six.......................................308

Chapter Twenty-Seven..................................326

Chapter Twenty-Eight 337

Chapter Twenty-Nine....................................340

About The Author   352

Also By This Author   354

Part One; What Must Come to Pass

Chapter One

She pulled her cloak tighter around her, the soft fur brushing against her cheek. She was alone now. She would stay here the full night, paying her last respects to her father until the flames died to smouldering embers. Despite the warmth from the fire itself, she could see her breath as she exhaled.

The night was clear and the moon shone brightly. It illuminated the courtyard with a comforting luminescence despite the acrid smoke which drifted away from the pyre on the slight breeze. She turned her gaze towards the sky, picking out the constellations she recognised from her childhood lessons. Finally, she settled on one series of stars, concentrating her gaze on it. She picked out each individual pinpoint of light that made up the shape of *The Archer*, it had been her favourite, ever since, as a small girl, she had seen a shooting star streak across the heavens, as if it had been shot from the celestial bow.

Each star she looked upon seemed brighter than the last. She knew the *Celeste* represented the Goddess, The Lady who watched over them. She could not help but wonder where the Goddess had been earlier, as her father had fallen.

As children they were taught that the Lady controlled all their destinies, yet tonight she felt she had been abandoned. How could the Lady have let her father be slaughtered? Immediately she felt guilty at such thoughts, it was not her place to question what destiny had in store. She turned her attention back to the stars, forcing her mind to safer thoughts.

Childhood lessons talked of each star being as big as the land she walked upon, home to those who had departed this realm. It seemed as unbelievable to her now as it had as a child. She wondered how far away each one really was. How did anyone know what they really were? Surely if one series represented the Goddess then others must acknowledge those who had departed this life. Was her father there now? Was his spirit one of those brilliant lights looking down at her? She found herself going dizzy at the thought of the insurmountable distance between her and the stars. She lowered her eyes back to the ground.

As the flames flickered and danced before her eyes, she allowed her mind to drift back over the last few hours. Everything had happened so quickly, yet she herself had felt as though she had been moving through water, as if she were viewing the events from a distance, watching her own reactions taking place in slow motion.

The men had carried her father's body back from the battle. They had borne him aloft on a stretcher created from shields lashed together through the walled city to the castle gates. Word had reached her swiftly, arriving on faster feet than those bearing their heavy load. She had raced to the entrance to meet him, not believing that it could be true, hoping to be scolded for the fact she was not properly attired, that she had come running barefoot like a peasant.

Only when she saw his body with her own eyes had she been forced to accept he was gone.

It was reported they had fought valiantly, and on pure skill should have been victorious, but it had not been skill which had determined the outcome, other forces had been involved. The few warriors who had returned had described strange circumstances occurring during the course of the skirmish. She hadn't been able to comprehend it all, as those had been with her father, gave her reports of magick and confusion on the battlefield. Most seemed unsure about what exactly had occurred, the only thing they all agreed on was Wend Y Mawr had powers they had not been prepared for. She did not doubt their words but so much was left unexplained.

Her father was... no, he had been one of the best warriors they had. It seemed unreal he should have been slain as he had. There would be time for the stories to be retold in the next few days. She would piece together the fragments to try to discover the truth but first the formalities for her father must be performed with the solemnity they deserved.

Her father had been a bear of a man, tall and broad. She had gained his height but had inherited her mother's willowy build. In her memories of childhood, he was alternately the kind loving father who lifted her into his lap and regaled her with stories of wolves, and witches, faerie folk and elves, or he was the strict ruler impressing upon her and her younger brother the importance of their future roles.

Her first memories of him, she remembered not even reaching past his knees, she would reach up tugging on his tunic to get his attention. He would tease her, pretending not to see her, before sweeping her high into the air. She had felt safe there in his arms, it hurt her to think she would never know that sensation again.

He had been a strict taskmaster on the training field. He taught them to wield various weapons both on foot and later from horseback. He forced them to practice for hours, even though their arms ached and they had reached a point through weariness where it was all they could do to lift the huge broadswords. He had impressed upon them the need to practise every day no matter what the weather.

She recalled standing in the rain, her clothes clinging to her body as she swung the weapon towards the target dummy. Mud had weighed her down as her feet sank into the earth, tears streaking her face. His voice had scolded her when she failed to connect, however, it was the praise and pride in his voice with each blow landed that she remembered most. She had wanted him to be proud of her. He rarely expressed his emotions with words. Rather it was a gesture or a look that sealed his approval.

A brief smile escaped her lips at the thought. She bore him no ill feelings for the fact the hours training had far outweighed the precious hours of stories. She understood why things had been that way. It had been his way of preparing them, not only for the battles to come, but to face life in general.

Life even without war was hard. The line between survival and death was barely perceptible at times. She had witnessed many stray across it by the smallest of margins that had been unable to claw their way back over the divide. The harsh training had ensured her memories of those evenings curled up in his lap, listening to him tell tales of wonders, were all the more special. The smile faded as the realities of the warrior life returned, as she thought of the lifeless body carried back through the keep gates. Without his spirit, the body had seemed smaller.

Now she would take his place as the leader of their people, and would be expected to lead her troops with the same bravery and skill as he had. Tomorrow she would take the crown and her brother Arth Dwyn would receive the heir's diadem that now sat upon her chestnut tresses.

He had been carried with great ceremony into the great hall, and laid upon a large wooden trestle table in the centre of the room. The men had backed out of the room, leaving the women to assist if their presence was required. Jacantha had dismissed them, fearful her feelings would overcome her. She did not wish to have witnesses to her grief.

She and her brother had washed his body, preparing him for the next stage of his journey. She had removed his torn battle dress; several times she had stopped, needing to soak the cloth that had become embedded in the dried blood of his wounds. She tended each of the wounds as lovingly as she would have had he been alive to feel her touch.

As she had washed the blood from his hair the water had run ruby. The sight of it had almost been too much, her knees had buckled and she had held onto the table to steady herself. She had wept as she saw the wounds which had taken him from them, her brother silent, struggling to hold himself together as he tried to assist her.

The metallic smell of the blood had made her nauseous, she had smelt it before on the battle field and when tending the wounded but somehow this had been different, maybe because this was the same blood that flowed through her. She had done her best to stitch the edges of the larger wounds disguising the severity of his injuries. Then they dressed him in his finest furs. He almost looked like he was sleeping, yet the pale hue to his skin, made it impossible for her to fool herself.

She had combed through his mane of hair, braiding it in same the traditional style he had worn when he had left for his final battle a few days earlier. She had placed his favourite sword in his hands, closing his fingers round the hilt one final time she leant over placing a final kiss on his brow. Her hand had been shaking as she placed his crown in its rightful place one final time, and knelt before him, saying her own private farewell before the others entered the room.

Then the men had lifted him up, carrying him as gently as one would carry a new born babe, out into the courtyard and placed him atop the pyre that had been built there. The whole tribe had gathered for the funeral.

A feast had been hastily thrown together while she had been closeted with her father's body, and now the courtyard was filled with people eating and drinking. She did not feel like touching any of the dishes laid out on the long tables, but food was passed to her, and well-meaning whispers in her ear had reminded of her of her duty, and the long vigil ahead. She had eaten a little, and joined in the toasts to her father as the men told the stories that were expected at this time, tales of his past victories, his courage and valour.

It had been midday when his body had been carried from the hall, now as the sun began to lower in the sky, the final toast was raised before those gathered grew subdued and the next part of the proceedings began.

They had filed past his body paying their last respects as the Guardian had said the words to usher her father's spirit on his journey. As he finished he stepped forward and lifted the crown from the head of the fallen sovereign, it would await the next male heir.

She had wielded the torch to set the pyre alight, burning her father's mortal remains, so they may be turned to ash and dispersed on the winds freeing his soul to move on. Her hand had shaken as she held the torch to the kindling and the fire flickered into life.

After an hour's silence, the majority of people had drifted away, gradually returning to their own dwellings around the enclave, until only she and her brother remained. Her brother had lingered with her for a while, but in the absence of their mother it was she, as heir, who must complete the overseeing of her father's final passage.

Now she sat alone, a silent vigil that would last until the fire had burnt away. With the last dying embers, the reign of Lord Athair Dwyn would end, and the reign of Jacantha Dwyn of Sabhailte would begin.

A sound in the distance made her start, her hand flying to the sword by her side. Tradition demanded the gates of the walled city, and the castle itself, be left open at this time to allow her father's spirit to be freed unhindered. She had questioned the wisdom of this given the recent battle, but had in the end, put her trust in the Guardian. It had always seemed strange to her that his spirit should require an open gate when it could soar to the heavens, but she had learnt early in life that customs must be upheld, without question, and respected, whether they seemed logical or not.

She rose slowly to her feet, raising the sword, peering across through the flames. Her eyes locked with those of another, returning her gaze with intensity. For what seemed like an eternity she held her breath, unable to move, her senses seemingly enhanced.

The stench of burning flesh from the pyre overwhelmed her senses. When the fire had first been lit bunches of herbs had been placed within the logs, but they had long since burnt away. Waves of nausea swept over her, threatening to drive her to her knees. She could hear movement in every direction, footsteps within the castle, horses moving in the stables. She realised she could even hear the cattle in the field beyond the outer walls. All of these noises were present beneath the sound of rugged breathing from the creature now facing her.

Then the spell broke, the wolf raised its eyes to gaze to the heavens, and let out a blood curdling howl, which was echoed in return from the forests beyond the walls. She took a step back, uncertain. Gripping the sword tighter, she waited for it to spring. It dropped its head forward, looking towards her one last time, its eyes penetrating her soul, before turning its back and disappearing into the night.

She looked around the courtyard as if waking from a dream. She could see a few candles had been lit in the windows of the castle. A few shadowy movements suggested her encounter had been observed, but no one had moved to join her.

Many of the families lived in their own homes, nestled between the castle walls and those that her father had built up to surround the city. Some chose to live within the castle itself, many of these were the families of the city guards, preferring the safety of the thick walls, while the guards on duty bunked down in the barracks. Between stints on the outer walls they would join their loved ones in their private chambers and in the communal living areas.

Only should they come under attack, would everyone fall back within the thick inner castle walls.

She thought now of the walled city, its streets bustling, as people arrived daily from out laying regions, fleeing the ravages this war had brought to their peaceful hamlets and villages. She had concerns about how they would cope long term if she could not bring this war to an end. Although, at the minute they had food aplenty, if the numbers continued to increase as they were, it would not last more than a few months. They had cleared meadows round the outer walls, ploughing the land and planting crops. Everyone, peasant and noble, worked alongside each other, trying to cultivate enough food to sustain them all.

She turned her gaze back to the flames. Already the body of her father was no longer recognisable. She let her thoughts drift back to the past, memories of standing by her mother's pyre before being led away, leaving her father to sit his own lone vigil. Her mother's death had rocked her father. The queen had fought alongside her husband, only staying away from the battle when carrying her and her brother.

The terrible accident that had taken Aythera, coming not on the battlefield, where all warriors expected to end their lives, but here in this very courtyard. A horse being broken in had reared and thrown the rider, her mother had rushed to help the fallen man, and the hooves had crashed down upon her. Her mother had not died straight away. Her brother was delivered the same night but they could not stem the bleeding. The Guardian had tried his best to invoke the spirits to intervene, but to no avail. Her mother lasted a few days until her husband returned from his foray. She smiled as his son was presented to him, then she simply slipped away.

For days after the funeral her father had locked himself away, his own grief too overwhelming to recognise that of others. Her brother had been placed with a wet nurse, while she had been left to the care of one of the other warriors. Then on the evening of the fifth night, he had come to her room as she lay trying to sleep.

She heard the door open and closed her eyes, fearful of a scolding for still being awake. She instinctively knew it was her father standing there, then she heard him speak, words which had remained with her from that day since.

"And so the prophecy begins."

The next day her father had taken her out into the courtyard to begin her first lesson. She had been only five years of age when she lost her mother and her training began in earnest. She had tried to broach the subject with him of what she had heard, but he merely gave a sad smile, reassuring her it was a dream, the subject had never been brought up again.

As she sat here now, in the silver moonlight, she wished she had pressed the matter as she had got older, demanded answers to her questions. What if she had a destiny she was unaware of? What if she wasn't up to the task?

She looked around the courtyard again, looked at all the windows behind which her people lay sleeping. They would be led by her, dependant on her judgement, what if she let them down?

Travellers arriving from distance lands told of a new Liege Lord, rising in power many miles away. Kingdoms were swearing allegiance to him, and he in turn gave them protection by deploying the troops under his control to settle any disputes. If he were closer she might have considered this as an option, though she knew in her heart her father would never have allowed it had he still been here. Though she was not convinced an army of any size would defeat Wend Y Mawr.

Their army outnumbered his several times over, yet it had been to no avail. It would take more than sheer force to defeat him. His attacks on their lands continued unabated and no matter how many times they drove him from their lands, he returned with increased ferocity. The responsibilities she was about to take on pressed down on her, an invisible weight settling on her chest.

An urge to run, to follow the wolf through the gates into the night, came to her suddenly and instinctively. There were others who were more skilled on the battlefield than she was, others who were wiser. She sat paralysed by the fear of the future, desperately her mind urged her to movement, yet she knew she would never run. It was not only her duty; it was in her blood to protect those around her.

Whatever prophecies may or may not have been made, this was her destiny. Whatever fate may have in store for her time would reveal.

The hours passed slowly as she watched the moon progress in its journey across the starlit sky. A noise startled her, she looked round. It had sounded like a door creaking, though she could not be sure. She studied the shadows of the castle. At first, she could see nothing. Maybe the noise had come from within but she could not be sure.

The silence of the courtyard made each sound seem louder, more encroaching. The crackling of the fire drew her gaze back. She tried to listen to the individual noises from each log as it burnt, trying to seek the source of her discomfort. Again, another creak, this one definitely coming from behind her in the direction of the castle. Then in the shadows she saw the figure, the long robes, a glint of light cast from crystal topping the long ceremonial staff.

Celdwady Llwny, the current Guardian stood in the shadows watching her. The sky was already beginning to lighten, a few more hours and the prophecy would begin to gather momentum. He knew where it would lead her though not the path which she must walk, and the importance of her success for them all. He would guide her as best he could.

If only Athair had allowed him to begin her training for what was to come. Athair had wanted her to learn to live and to fight believing it would be enough. Celdwady hoped it would not be too late to give her the mental strength that would be needed. He gave her a brief nod of acknowledgement then turned and walked back into the castle to prepare for the ceremonies ahead.

Chapter Two

Wend Y Mawr sat in his throne room surveying the scene before him, the banqueting tables had been set and his men were already filling themselves, a celebratory mood filled the room. The hog turned on a spit in the huge fireplace. A haunch of venison had been carried in from the kitchen along with numerous other dishes. Those too young to be of service in other aspects of court life, ran back and forth filling flagons with ale and delivering up more food from the kitchens. He stuck his knife into a chunk of venison and devoured it, alternating mouthfuls of food and drink.

He had felt drained on their return; the magic he had needed to ensure victory had taken its toll. Maybe this was why he had not pursued the enemy from the battlefield and completed his triumph over them. That was not the whole reason though, if he were honest with himself, he knew they would never willingly surrender; to subjugate them to his will would take more than slaughter on the battlefield. They were fearless warriors, even the women. He looked round those present in the hall, the women here were concubines, fit only for pleasure, at the minute they were helping serve food and drink to his men, soon they would provide other services.

There were, of course, other women. There were a few older women, kept solely in the kitchens, the sight of their aged, wrinkled faces offended him. If he could have done without them he would, but food must be prepared, therefore while they were capable of work, their presence was tolerated. Then there were those chosen to breed with, kept apart from the others.

Those he felt worthy to bear the next generation of his warriors, chosen for their looks and physical attributes, all children were removed from their mothers as soon as they were weaned. Boys were sent to live in dormitories behind the stable blocks, to begin their training, when they came of age they would be brought before him to swear their allegiance and enter his service, those who were not loyal or capable did not survive that long.

He controlled the matches. It would not be prudent to allow any one of his men to gain too many sons, not that they would know. He was careful to ensure the women were kept locked away, so no man would ever be sure if his attempts at impregnation had been successful or the number or sex of any offspring he may have created. The girls were taken to the kitchens to serve until it was seen how they would grow. Once they were old enough, regardless of looks, he enjoyed breaking them in personally, the prettier ones were kept to serve here in the castle, those who did not match his tastes, served the men in the barracks, they rarely grew old enough to make it back to the kitchens.

He knew his men's loyalty was held, partly through fear, and partly through the benefits his power provided. They were not as skilled on the battlefield as their opponents, and although they lacked any real ambition, they were greedy. Wealth and a supply of women to obey their darkest desires kept them from forming any thoughts of obtaining power for themselves. He himself took full advantage of the concubines, but up to this point, had never felt the need for an heir, what was the use of an heir when you had immortality at your fingertips.

Instinctively, his hand closed around the bloodstone set into the hilt of his sword. He felt the energy course into his hand. It was not the source of his power, rather it stored surplus energy which he could draw upon as required, the blood of his enemies, felled that day by his hand, had charged the stone. The energy released by the fallen flowed from their bodies with their blood. He had enchanted the bloodstone to draw their life force into its core, just as he had others to store other forms of energy he could syphon from those around him. Now that energy passed, from the stone to him, as he commanded.

He pondered about her whereabouts. She normally fought at her father's side, why not today?

He had spotted Athair across the field of battle; cutting down those who came between them, until they had stood a few feet from each other. They had looked into each other's eyes, pure hatred flowing between them, then they had launched at each other ferociously. He smirked at the recollection of the look on Athair's face as blow after blow had failed to meet their mark. His shield spell causing the sword to glance off his armour without leaving any trace. As he had struck home the fatal blow he had looked around for her, ready to complete his conquest but to no avail.

Athair's men seeing their leader fall had not crumbled in their resolve as he had hoped. They had regrouped themselves and swarmed towards him, grief giving them renewed energy. His men had been forced back allowing his opponents to reclaim their King's body and bear it away.

No matter, in the end, the outcome would be the same. His men had been eager to follow them and attack when they would be vulnerable during the death ceremonies, but that did not suit his plans. Although Jacantha would never be his willingly, he planned to force her to submit to him, one way or another. He smiled as he wondered just how far she would go to protect her people, he knew she would fight for them, even die for them, but would she lie down for them, and give herself to save them.

His attention turned back to his men, they were starting to get a little rowdier. Time to put on the floorshow before his men got carried away. He needed their full attention in order to draw their energy for what he had in mind. Normally, a trick such as this would have been nothing, but coming so soon after the battle, he required the extra power to sustain the illusion he wanted to create.

He nodded his head to a warrior hovering by the door, the man turned on his heels and disappeared through the heavily draped archway. Wend Y Mawr rose to his feet and banged on the table, immediately the room fell silent and all eyes turned towards him.

He looked around at the expectant eyes. Rugged and uncouth, his men hardly filled the ideal image of courtiers but their depravity matched his own. Somewhere far beyond the castle out in the darkness, Wend heard the faint howl of a lone wolf.

The prisoners were dragged in; there were twelve in all, nine women and three men. They had been cut off from the main battle in a separate skirmish earlier. Taking them alive had been difficult. He had had to intervene casting a spell to stun the group for a few moments to give his men the chance to disarm them. Blood and bruises marked the features of the men. The women had marks upon their bodies from being roughly handled, but as he had ordered their faces remained unmarked.

The men had been fitted with eye masks of his own personal design. The mask fitted tightly over the face, buckling behind. Each mask had a series of small hooks around the eye area. Onto these hooks the men's eyelids had been impaled, rendering them unable to close their eyes to what he was about to do. These three would be the witnesses, sent back to testify to his power, and to take a personal message directly to their new leader.

He looked around seeing the excitement in his men's eyes. The lust at the sight of the women, their lean, taut bodies, browned by hours training all year round. They had been stripped of their armour, leaving only the scant leather clothing they wore beneath it into battle to allow maximum movement. He stepped down and walked in front of the women, inspecting them as one would livestock. He made a great play of choosing, squeezing a breast on one, then the next, pretending to compare the two. He could feel the energy starting to build in the room as his men became more aroused at the prospect of what was to come. He had ordered his men the female prisoners should not be molested when they were captured. Inspecting them, it would seem his orders had been respected. The men knew they would receive a share of the prize, patience however, was not always a virtue they were capable of.

He found himself standing in front of a woman in her early thirties, older than Jacantha. but sharing her build and long flowing hair. His hand reached out towards her, she struggled, futile given the grip his man had on her. The fact this one still had some fight in her stirred his desires. That she had spirit would increase his pleasure, and make his fantasy all the more real. The others had stood placidly, resigned to their fate, determined to show no emotion. That would change once his own performance had finished, and his men had their turn. The women would not be able to remain silent for long.

He motioned to his men, his eyes locking with the woman's as she was dragged from the line. The pure hatred he saw there only enflaming his passions further. A shiver of anticipation ran through him, he wanted to savour this. He only hoped once the transformation took place, he would be able to control himself. He had fantasised so often about what he would do to Jacantha once he had her under him. Even though in reality, he would know it wasn't her, he hoped he would be able to remember that once the illusion was created.

Two of his men wheeled a large device to the centre of the room. The woman's eyes widened as she saw it, and she began to struggle as she was hauled over to it. It was a rack like device, again of his creation, an oval of metal suspended in a large wooden frame. It had taken several trials to get it just right. The metal ring pivoted from the centre of the frame. The ring could be turned in a full rotation, leaving its occupant hanging upside down should he desire. Leather straps with cuffs attached were fitted to hold the subject in place.

The woman was now being strapped in. She was trying to resist with all her strength but her captors held her firmly, as the restraints were fitted one at a time. The men stepped back, falling into the circle which had formed round her. The male prisoners were being dragged to the fore. They were to have a front row seat at this show. The number of men holding them had doubled as they now struggled. Hands gripped their hair forcing them to keep their heads facing what was to come.

Wend Y Mawr stripped off his shirt, revealing his muscular chest, and stepped forward towards the woman. For a brief second she let her head drop backwards, and then threw it forward releasing a volley of phlegm at his face. Smiling he wiped it away with the back of his hand, then struck her across the face. The woman hung dazed from the impact.

Wend pulled his sword from the scabbard. For an instant those present thought he would strike the woman down. That she had insulted, and provoked him enough to preserve her dignity, though not her life, but he held the sword in front of him, one hand closed over the blood stone and he began chanting. The room shimmered around the onlookers. A fog enveloped the centre of the room. Lights seemed to fluoresce within it. Then there was a flash and the fog dissipated.

Wend still stood in the same position, but to those looking on, they no longer saw the prisoner hanging there, a transformation had taken place. Instead, they saw the body of Jacantha, stretched before them on the cruel contraption. Wend smiled, even her father would not have been able to tell the difference. The charge of energy within the room increased. Wend began to harden at the prospect of what was to come.

He stepped forward, the woman was now barely conscious; all the better. He had not heard enough of Jacantha's voice to be able to add that to the illusion, but he did not want the woman shouting out to break the spell. He undid his belt, removing his dagger from it before letting it drop to the floor.

He stepped up to the woman, and slowly began cutting away her remaining clothing. Savouring each moment as he uncovered Jacantha's body. He allowed his hand to trail across the exposed flesh. He caressed her breasts, a parody of affection as he freed them from their covering. Almost tenderly, taking his time, rolling the nipples between his thumb and forefinger, before cruelly pinching them bringing a yelp from the woman.

He knelt before her. Sliding the dagger under the leather near her ankles, he cut up each leg in turn, until the leggings lay shredded on the floor before her. His eyes drinking in her naked flesh as he uncovered her, revealing the silken hair between her legs. His hand trailed across her stomach slowly, savouring each moment, as she squirmed beneath his touch.

He moved behind her, enabling himself to take in the audiences' expressions. The look of horror on the faces of the captives, desperately trying to turn their heads away, their eyes staring unwillingly. The men's eyelids had started to rip as they struggled to close their eyes to the sight before them. The women trembled and silently wept, eyes downcast, despite hands grasping their hair to hold their heads high.

He looked to his own men. Other than those focused on holding the captives, their excitement was visible. One or two had already grabbed concubines, ready to relieve them once things got started. It didn't matter if they started before the show was finished, their energies would only help to sustain the illusion.

Wend Y Mawr kicked off his boots, untying the thongs on his own leggings and allowing them to drop to the floor. He stepped out from behind her, naked and ready for action. At well over six feet, broad and muscular, he was an impressive sight, he knew this. Even the men in the room could not help but admire his physique. For a moment, he wished he was alone with her. That he could take his time just savouring her body, and imagined what it would be like to have her hands wander over his body.

A slight shift in the room drew him back. He knew he must keep his focus; he could not allow his concentration to waiver from the task at hand. There would be time enough for his fantasies once he had the real Jacantha in his power. For now, it was important he maintain the illusion, and deliver his message.

He stepped round in front of the woman again. He pulled her face to his, forcing his mouth on hers. He drew away laughing as she cursed him. He grabbed her behind the thighs, tilting her backwards slightly. He heard a scuffle behind him, as one of the male captives again tried to break loose.

He adjusted his position slightly then thrust into her, driving his full length into her. Holding onto her hips, he began to plunge himself into her in long slow deliberate thrusts. She was biting her tongue, determined not to cry out. He dug his fingers harder into her flesh. One hand now clawed at a breast as she struggled to refrain from crying out in pain, he leaned forward and sunk his teeth into the flesh he had been clawing, careful not to break the skin, he was rewarded by a half-suffocated scream escaping her lips.

Behind him he heard the wailing begin and smiled. He was careful to control his lust. He wanted this moment to last. Not only for his own pleasure, but to gather the energies from those watching, and ensure the captives would have this image ingrained in their minds. He felt his pace quickening. His body determined to fulfil its own desires. He withdrew and stepped back, throbbing with lust still.

He stepped behind the woman. For a few minutes he gathered himself, allowing his hands to wander over the women's body. He pinched her nipples, then grabbed her breasts in turn squeezing them hard. Angry red marks appeared in the wake of his touch. His other hand straying between her legs spreading her, displaying her to those watching. He trailed his tongue down her neck, revelling in the ripples of disgust he could feel pass through her body.

The captives now were broken wrecks. The women had forgotten their determination to stay silent and were openly weeping. The men holding them already taking advantage of their position. Breasts had been exposed and were being groped. Hands worming their way between legs. The women knew, without a doubt, they would share their sister's fate.

The male captives also had tears streaming down their faces, but they were silent still. Faces set in grim expressions of pure hatred. They had ceased struggling, but Wend could read their thoughts. They were waiting, hoping for an opportunity to avenge the honour of their new queen. They had taken in the illusion completely, and could no longer recall that it was not her hanging there.

Several of his men were now engaged in various acts with concubines. Some merely receiving a helping hand, while others chose a willing mouth. He felt an explosion of energy as one released himself over the breasts of a small blonde concubine. He watched as the man grabbed a dark headed girl and forced her to lap his seed up, while he rammed a hand between her legs. Wend redirected a small amount of energy back to him and watched as he hardened again immediately and forced the blonde's mouth back onto his re-erected penis.

Wends hand wandered to his own manhood, time to finish the show, he could not hold back much longer. He moved closer to the woman, pressing himself against her. She whimpered, despite her determination not to, and tried to pull away from him. He did not want the illusion to end before he was finished.

He positioned himself between her firm buttocks, then he reached round, grasped her hips and tilted her forward slightly. Even in her confused state, the woman began to struggle again, aware of how he was about to violate her. He looked directly into the eyes of the male captives. Wend placed himself in their minds so they would share this next action. They would feel the sensations as if it were their own bodies committing the act, and he rammed himself into her. His domination of her complete.

The women's eyes flew open as a scream of pure agony escaped her lips. For a second he was distracted and nearly lost the illusion. He grabbed her hair, and pulling it so tight it threatened to come out by the roots, held her silently in place. Wend stared straight into the male captive's souls as he drove himself into the woman again and again. He sent a message to them, his voice echoing inside their minds, it was simple *'I will win, there is only a question of how. Tell her she can avoid this. If she comes to me willingly, she will be my queen, and be treated as such. But, if I have to, I will take her, just as you have seen, and all the other women will meet the same fate. Your daughters will meet the same fate, and maybe even your sons…'* At their reaction to this he smiled.

The look on their faces told him the message had been understood. Wend quickened his pace, plunging deeper into the body in his grasp. He could feel her flesh ripping as he violated her body. She started to scream again. The sound of pain in her voice spurred him on, and with an explosion of energy, he came deep inside her. At the same time, the hand grasping her hair twisted, snapping her neck and silencing her.

The light in the room seemed to dim for a second then returned to normal. The illusion was broken. The woman hung there, limp, transformed back to her own image. He looked at her with distaste. He stepped back, the signal for the men to take their pleasure.

The female captives were dragged to the centre of the floor, hands grabbing and pulling at them. Their remaining clothing was ripped from their flesh as they met their fate. Their screams echoed around the room as they disappeared beneath a writhing sea of bodies. The sounds muffled as hands were clapped over their mouths, or body parts were inserted by force. Death would be their only release.

The male captives were dragged from the room. They would be taken and dumped close to their own castle. He had nothing to fear from them. The slow acting poison which had coated the hooks was already coursing through their bodies. They would live long enough to deliver his message, but they would take no part in the future of either kingdom.

Wend gathered up his clothing and returned to his throne. He motioned for his cup to be filled. Maybe in a little while he would take part in the proceedings, but for now, he chose to close his eyes and remember the feeling of his flesh pounding against hers.

It was only a matter of time he was sure of that.

Chapter Three

Jacantha stared out across the embers of the fire. She had watched the moon journey across the clear sky, and now, on the horizon, she saw the first rays of the sun, rising to signal the start of the new day.

Around her she could hear the castle come to life. Movement and footfall, as people scurried along passageways, beginning the preparations for what was to come. Each person would be getting up, going about their duties as they would any other morning, except this morning, there would be no friendly greetings, no teasing, or scolding, only silence. She knew many had foregone their own homes last night, to be sure everything would be ready for the ceremony to come today.

The traditions were strictly observed by all, from the lighting of the pyre to the crowning ceremony, nothing must pass their lips, not food or sound, though no one expected those under half a dozen summers to manage to remain silent. The only exceptions for eating being those too young, or ill, to survive without nourishment, babies would be allowed to suckle at their mother's breasts and the sick and elderly were fed a thin broth. The Guardian would only speak to perform the ceremony; she and her brother would only open their mouths to reply, when the ceremony, required responses.

She allowed a smile to form on her lips as she thought of the women in the castle who would find the silence hard, those who thrived on gossip, and the interaction they shared speculating on everything, from who was with child, to how many eggs a certain fowl had laid. The trivialities of their chatter annoyed her at times with so much more serious issues at hand, but, she had come to realise that, it was the continuation of discussing these insignificant matters, which kept her peoples spirits up. It was the sense of normality they clung to, and fed their belief, that one-day things would return to how they had been.

She thought for a moment about the people she would soon be leading. The brave, noble warriors, those who would follow her now into battle, who would place their lives in her hands. She thought of those who would remain sheltered in the castle walls the young, the old and the sick, trusting her to bring their loved one's home safely. She wondered if her father had known what fate had in store yesterday, when he had insisted she remain behind. She had protested of course, but, he had been determined. She had pointed out that she had been at his side in other battles. That should they both fall, Arth was of an age where he could take the crown, but he would listen to none of it. She must remain here at the castle.

She now pondered the hours her father had spent locked away, the night previous to him setting out, for what would be his final battle. He and

Celdwady Llwny had disappeared as soon as dinner was over. She had tried to follow but her father had closed the door on her. Had the guardian told her father something? Had he had a premonition? Of course, it did not matter now, the dice had been cast in this game by higher beings than she, and events had played themselves out. Fate could not be changed, even with hindsight.

She heard noises, muffled by the thick stone walls. She presumed they would be coming from the kitchens where the feast for after the ceremony would be prepared. The whole tribe would fast until she had received the crown. For the first time she was aware of her own hunger, not a morsel had passed her lips, or those of any others, since her father's body was brought home. Her mouth watered at the thought of the food being prepared, the meat roasting on the spit, the fresh bread baking in the ovens. Piles of fruit, a rarity in these days of war carefully prepared into a sumptuous banquet. She considered how hard the hunger would be for those working in the kitchens, surrounded by the food they could not yet eat.

She stood and stretched, her body weary from her long vigil. She was tired, her eyes felt heavy. She would sneak away after the feast she decided. She would try to grab a couple of hours sleep before beginning her meeting with the council of elders that would take place in the evening. She saw movement around the edges of the courtyard, people heading for the stables. She knew some would be heading out of the castle to hunt more game for the feast table, not that there was not plenty hung in the larders already, but as a way of passing time. If she had been able to she would have joined them, to sit waiting was not the warrior way, action was always required in some form.

She knew many were eager to return to the battlefield, to avenge her father's death. She too felt that need to draw her sword and strike down those responsible, however, she also knew that she needed to think this situation through carefully, not rush in. Skill and valour had not been enough. They faced an enemy so different from those they had stood against before. She would need to discuss the situation with the Guardian. There must be a way to counter the magick. Athair had not been one for fully believing in the ways of the Guardians. He had trusted to the sword in his hand, and his own abilities, to overcome their foes. He had believed in the Lady because tradition taught him he should, but he had not been a true believer.

She looked back at the fire. All that was left were the embers, soon the ceremonies would begin. Nothing remained of her father other than, a glint here and there, in the last flickering flames, of a buckle from a belt or boot. She felt tears well up in her eyes. She had cried when she had first seen him borne back into the castle, but had kept her emotions in check since, as was expected of her.

Her father had taught her the importance of always appearing strong. She recalled the times she watched her brother scolded for weakness. Her father's bitterness after her mother's death, always directed towards her younger brother. She wondered how he had slept last night, whether the images of their father's body had haunted his slumber. For so many years she had tried to shield him, to be the mother he had never had, but yesterday, she had seen his eyes age as they washed away the blood.

She felt a hand on her shoulder. Celdwady Llwny was standing behind her. She turned to face him, studying his face as if she had never really seen him before, his long white hair and beard flowed over his robes. Today he wore his full ceremonial robes rather than the drab brown full tunic he normally wore. Furs hung round his neck, intricate patterns were sewn along the hems of his tunic and leggings. What he had looked like as a young man?

In truth she wondered if he had ever been young. In her eyes he had always looked the same, unchanged from her childhood. He had not aged from her first memory of him. Still in silence he nodded, gesturing towards the castle, it was time. With one last look at the remains of her father's pyre, she turned on her heels and followed Celdwady Llwny into the castle.

He led her through the corridors towards his own chambers. She thought this a little strange. She had assumed she would be taken straight to her own chambers to wash and dress for the crowning. He opened a door and gestured for her to enter. She walked into a room she did not remember having ever visited before.

As a child she had wandered round the castle exploring. She had prided herself that she had seen every room, even those she was not supposed to have seen. She had been caught in his potions room many times, fascinated by the bottles that held a myriad of coloured liquids and powders, she had ignored the official labels, branding them with her own whimsical interpretations of their origins based on the colours and way they sparkled as she held them to the light. Celdwady had always scolded her but in truth it was a half-hearted chastising, never enough to stop her sneaking in again. This room however was darker, and as she looked round she realised contained no windows. Scrolls were piled on every surface, the illumination came from candles encased in metal cages, she guessed to stop the risk of the flames igniting the abundance of parchment.

"Sit!"

The word echoed round the room. Jacantha was startled. Tradition stated that no one should speak to her until the ceremony itself commenced, yet the Guardian was breaking the very traditions he normally rigorously upheld. She looked round, saw a stool close to an empty fireplace and sat upon it. She opened her mouth to question what was happening, but Celdwady Llwny raised his hand to silence her.

"There is not much time" he began "and much I must tell you before the ceremony, that is why I have chosen to break tradition. You must listen and listen carefully. What I am about to tell you is of grave importance, not only to you, but for the future of all who dwell here."

He picked up a chair and moved it so he sat facing her. He studied her face for a moment as if searching for something. Then he began to speak once again.

"I know, many years ago, you overheard your father mention the prophecy. We do not have the time now to go into everything, but things are moving quickly and it is imperative you understand the wheels that fate set in motion hundreds of years ago. I do not say fate cannot be altered, but should fate be altered, so must the outcome.

In the time of your ancestors, a woman arrived in the village, as it was back then. She was heavy with child and her health was fading fast. She was the most beautiful woman they had ever seen. The legend says she was of the faerie folk, whether this be true or not I cannot say, but her beauty bewitched all and she was given shelter and food. The priests of the time did all they could to try to cure her malady, but to no avail. Finally, the time came for the child to be born, those present soon realised that the woman would not have the strength to survive the birth. Many doubted the child would live either, however after several hours a daughter was delivered to the woman, a fine healthy babe.

The woman, exhausted from the birth, requested to speak with the priests. This was not viewed as unusual given the woman's condition. It was assumed that she wished for prayers to guide her in her journey beyond this life. Instead when the priest drew near to her, she reached out with every last ounce of strength she possessed, and gave the prophecy.

She told him that this child held the future of the tribe in her hand. That she would be the queen who would be the mother of sons, until such a time as the tribes need was greatest. Then she would be reborn, to right the balance against the darkness that threatened. Then looking straight into the priest's soul, she gave him the charge which has been passed down through the years. That he would be the Guardian of the child, and of the future generations to come, until the end of time. As soon as she had finished her charge to him, she lay back on the bed, closed her eyes and passed over, it was said, as she did, she smiled as if greeting an old friend.

Of course, her words were dismissed as the ramblings of a delirious, dying woman trying to find protection for an orphan child. The woman had never mentioned the child's father. No one had ever pressed the issue and questioned her. The priest took it upon himself to honour the woman's wishes, in so far as making sure the child was cared for. He found a good family to raise her and he took care of her education.

She grew to be the image of her mother, but she lacked some quality that her mother had possessed. She was beautiful, but without that otherworldly presence that had held all spellbound. None the less, she attracted suitors from a young age, and many times a match was talked of, but in the end it was the son of the tribes' leader who won her heart. It was an unusual match, in that there was no gain from it. He had been expected to be bound to a neighbouring chieftain's daughter to secure better bartering and trade.

Despite this, the match went ahead, a true love match. They were blessed with many sons, all of whom were strong and healthy. The story of her birth was discussed with each child she bore. It became a story all knew and, when she passed away without having borne a daughter, it seemed the story itself would pass also. However, when her sons made matches and failed to produce a single daughter, the story resurfaced. The priests began to consult with each other as to the possible meanings of the woman's words. And so it went on, through the seasons, each generation of her descendants producing only sons. The prosperity of the tribe increased with every passing year until your grandfather's time.

There had always been skirmishes over land especially over the border areas, but mostly things had been peaceful. Your ancestors fought when it was needed, but it was not their way to fight for the sake of fighting. The same was true of most of the neighbouring lords. Then from the north came Wend Y Mawr."

At the mention of the name Jacantha's eyes widened. A look which did not go unnoticed by Celdwady. He held up his hand to silence her as the question formed on her lips.

"I do not mean he who killed your father. I refer to his grandfather. He was a greedy man but lacked foresight, he ravaged the land and laying villages to waste. He took what he wanted to satisfy his immediate needs, not considering what may be required in the future. He destroyed his own kingdom with his inability to rein in his own need for instant gratification, and then he turned to his neighbours.

Many to the north and west of him fell. Then he turned his attention southwards to us, and the war began. It has continued ever since with many losses on each side. He died under what were considered mysterious circumstances, his son had already died and his grandson took command of his lands.

We hoped that there would be an end to their warring ways but instead it appeared the grandson enjoyed battle even more, his men however were weak and for a while we fought them back to their own boundaries. But then there was a change, suddenly we were losing skirmishes we should have won with ease and it became apparent that dark forces were at work. Your grandfather fell and your father become king. He was already bound to your mother; within his first year of rule you were born. The first daughter in any generation since the prophecy had been made.

Your father did not want to believe in the prophecy. He was always reluctant to believe in anything he could not reach out and touch with his own hands, but there is a final line to the prophecy one which he would not accept. He loved you too much to contemplate it. The final line was that, *when she has most to give, she will sacrifice herself for those she holds most dear.* It does not say what form this sacrifice must take, and as much as I have consulted the runes and called to the Lady for clarification I cannot see this part clearly.

I have watched you grow from a child, and I love you as I would my own child. I can understand your father's reluctance at the fate destiny has in store for you. If you will be guided by me I promise to do all I can to help you but you must put your faith in me. I know this is a lot to take in. I can see the questions in your eyes, but for now we have no time for them, you must prepare yourself for the ceremony ahead."

Celdwady rose to his feet and moved towards her, he held out his hand. Jacantha placed her hand in his and stood, he gazed into her eyes seeming to search her soul.

"You will be ready child, do not fear, you will not face this alone. We, the Guardians will be with you. I am but the latest in a long line of Guardians, each of whom have sworn to protect the chosen one for all eternity. I know there are difficult choices ahead of you, but I know you will do what is required. I see the strength in you, you were born to fulfil the prophecy but I sense you will do more. You will create a new one, your reign may be short but will shape the future of your people forever."

Jacantha stood trying to take in everything that had been said. The thought of what was expected of her weighing heavily in her heart. Celdwady gestured towards the door, it was time to prepare for the ceremony. In a daze she left the room and hurried back to her own chambers.

Celdwady Llwny stood in his room staring at the fireplace, as he did so the kindling combusted and flames burst forth. Although he had told her much, there was so much he had held back. There was also so much unclear even to him.

He turned, walking to the table in the centre of the room. He emptied the runes out of their pouch into his hand and cast them onto the table. He leaned over them, his finger trailing over each one as he deciphered their meanings. He was sure he must be misunderstanding something, the message they spread out before him made no sense. He turned to the bookshelves and took down a heavy leather-bound volume and settled down in a chair by the fire. He studied each page of parchment, searching for the answers which eluded him.

Chapter Four

Wend Y Mawr woke to see the sun already high in the sky. He had left his men hours ago, still engaged in a drunken orgy. Their energies had revitalised him. He allowed his mind to drift back to the previous evening's proceedings. The memories aroused him as he thought of the image of Jacantha hanging in his power. He rolled over, his current favourite concubine, lay sleeping at the edge of his huge bed. He grabbed her roughly, hauling her across the mattress, barely allowing her time to wake before he mounted her. He took her brutally, there was no pleasure, only the need to gratify himself.

As he drove himself into her, he looked at her face, it was devoid of emotion. He felt himself anger towards her, partly because of her lack of response, but mainly because she was not Jacantha. He closed his eyes and thought of her and his illusion from the previous evening, his climax came quickly. He rolled away from the woman and barked at her to get out. Only once he had heard the door open and close did he open his eyes again.

He lay back against the pillows. He could not understand his obsession with Jacantha. She was desirable, that was obvious, but it was more than that. He needed to possess her, to have her submit to him totally. Maybe it would be like when he was a child. He had always had strong desires. When he wanted something, he wanted it immediately. Once he had possession of the object he desired, he bored of it, destroying it for failing to live up to his expectations. He hoped this would be the case, this obsession was beginning to prove a distraction. If it were not for the need to have her people submit he would have taken what he wanted by force and had it done with.

He recalled as a child the city here had been thriving. Tradesman of all types had successful businesses, all that could be needed was made and sold here, the markets had filled the streets around the castle. People had flocked from all over the kingdom to barter and buy what they had wanted. Nobles from other courts had travelled to enjoy the hospitality of castle life.

Their apparent shock at the debauchery had not stopped them immersing themselves in the pleasures it accorded. He laughed as he recalled how many had sent their wives and daughters to continue on their journeys, while they stayed on to discuss business. He, of course had merely taken what he wanted from the ones whose protectors had not possessed the forethought. Who would argue with the King's favourite grandson?

Then the stranger had come and things had changed. The man had brought magick to the castle and a promise to share his secrets in return for sanctuary. He had loitered in the shadows, watching as his grandfather had learnt the man's secrets. His grandfather had become lazy after the strangers' appearance, he had begun sending troops out to take what he wanted rather than paying, it had not taken long for the prosperity of the land to decline. He quickly realised that if he allowed his grandfather or father to possess this knowledge, his chances of coming to power were slim and there would be little left for him to reign over. Action had to be taken.

First, his father, a weak man, had met with an accident while out hunting. It had been easy to manage. After all, with his grandfather still in power, he had nothing to gain immediately, and it was well known his father was not the best horseman. His grandfather proved a little harder. He was constantly surrounded by bodyguards. There was no chance of removing him without it being known he was the culprit. Too impatient to wait for a covert opportunity, he decided to begin his reign the way it would continue, with a sea of blood.

He sought out the stranger, making a pact with him, that he would teach him the secrets rather than his grandfather. He promised him a high position within his new court, but insisted the man continue to instruct his grandfather until he was ready. Of course, the instruction would be now focused on weakening the old man, rather than strengthening him. Looking back, he still wondered why the stranger had been persuaded so easily.

He began to examine those in the court, seeking out those whose loyalty could be bought and who lacked a conscience, noting those would stand in his way of, attempting to interfere what was to come.

He found more men whose loyalty was for sale than he had expected.

It was at the feast, celebrating his Grandfather's birthday, that he decided to put his plan into action. As he stood to give a speech, he had moved behind his grandfather's chair, placing a hand on his shoulder in a mock show of affection. Then suddenly, he had pulled out his dagger, and slit the old man's throat before he had a chance to realise what was happening. His newly bought supporters had swiftly dispatched his grandfather's bodyguards, and those few courtiers who moved to intervene. Most of those present had stood rooted, by first shock, then by fear. They quickly surmised they had only two options, to stay and serve his reign, or to sneak away in the night.

Several would flee in those first few hours, he did not care, most left behind them the majority of their belongings, which he would claim as his own.

He recalled the screams, coming from his mother at the sight of her father, his body lying across the table in a pool of his own blood. She had cursed him, cursed the day she had ever borne him as he had given orders for her to be hauled away and locked in her room. For the briefest of moments, he had questioned his actions, but it passed no sooner had it formed in his mind. He had picked up his flagon, despite the blood which had splashed into it from his grandfather's throat, and drained its contents in a long satisfying draught.

For a few months, things had continued to run in the castle as they had before. He spent more time and more time closeted away with the stranger, while his supporters quelled any thoughts of rebellion. He learnt all the man would teach of the strange magicks he had brought to the kingdom, soaking up the knowledge.

He had always been a lazy student, yet now he threw himself into his new studies with enthusiastic zeal, he asked questions constantly, always questing for more information. Ironically, it was during these lessons, he learnt how to rid himself of the stranger, and take his power into himself. He chuckled to himself at the man's naivety, of his warnings about the dangers of abusing the powers he was starting to possess. How little had the stranger realised the use to which those powers would be put.

Wend stretched out on the bed. He felt restless. He knew he would have no reply from last night's proceedings for a few days. It was a day's hard riding to border of the two kingdoms, and was a further day's travel on foot to the outlying villages, where the prisoners could hope to find faster passage, to the main city. He had instructed his men to take the prisoners as far past the border as they could, but he doubted they would travel far into Jacantha's kingdom.

Sabhailte was the closest kingdom to Diafol yet it had been one of the last he had turned his attention to. The other kingdoms to the north and west had been easier targets they did not possess the same skills as Jacantha's warriors had honed throughout the generations. In hindsight that had been a mistake, he should have taken out their strongest enemy first, but, had he achieved that his prize may never have been born.

He had destroyed those with whom he had the closest links first. He did not wish word of the powers he now possessed to spread. Outside of the castle walls only the news of his power need be known, other aspects of the magick he had learnt were a carefully guarded secret. Over the years he had slain those surrounding him who suspected the full extent to which he had mastered the very nature of life and death.

His men would most likely be content to sleep off last night's ale and make their own amusement for a day or two. After that, he would have to find a diversion to keep them occupied while he waited for a response. He rose from the bed and pulled on leggings and a tunic, a quick survey of the room revealed his boots protruding out from under the bed and he set out striding through the castle's corridors.

The castle itself had known better days, he took in the furnishings as he passed through the corridors. A sense of neglect was evident everywhere he looked. The heavy curtains threadbare and faded. The skills to produce new ones lost along with many other skills as he had trained men for war rather than trade. There were newer hangings in the great hall, plundered from surrounding kingdoms as he had conquered them. It was unfortunate, the bloodlust he had imbibed in his men meant that no one survived to be brought back and put to work. That would be different this time. As much as he wanted Jacantha for his own personal desires, he wanted her people, with their skills, to work as slaves within his kingdom. They would not need them all, but that could be taken care of later, once he had her, and them, in his power. Then he would weed out those surplus to his requirements and dispose of them.

In his reverie of the past he had lost track of the present. He realised he had reached the great hall. He stood in the archway and surveyed the aftermath of last night. The woman he had violated had been taken down, another now strapped into the device in her place. Her body covered in bites and bruises, she hung there, still clinging to life. The broken bodies of the other female prisoners were strewn across the room. She was the last survivor, although he had no doubt his men would amend that situation once they awoke. Most of his men had retired to their own quarters taking a concubine or two with them. A few however, having consumed too much ale, were slumped around the room. He spotted the captain of his personal guard, unconscious between the legs of a concubine, her breasts forming a pillow.

Nadredd was the closest thing he had to a friend. Not that he trusted him with his secrets, but his loyalty was unquestioned. Nadredd had been a mere boy when he had found him and he had given him the opportunity to gain wealth beyond his wildest dreams. The irony that it was now Nadredd who looked the older of them did not escape him.

As he strode through the hall he passed close the woman hung in the frame. She lifted her eyes and looked at him. He expected to see hatred, instead he saw pleading. A desperation to be freed. There would only be one escape and they both knew it. He walked over to her, her eyes lighting up for a brief moment as she thought he would end her misery. Instead he turned and walked over to Nadredd, he woke him with a couple of nudges of his boot.

Nadredd woke with a start, jumping to his feet reaching for his sword before realising he was naked. Wend let out a bellow of laughter, he turned and pointed to the woman hanging there

"Can you not finish a job properly?"

Nadredd looked confused in his hung-over state, then realised that she was still alive. A smile slowly crossed his face as he understood what was meant. He started stroking himself to hardness as he walked towards her. She would get her release just not as quickly as she had hoped Wend thought to himself. He watched for a moment as Nadredd tipped her forward to force himself into her mouth. The proceedings of the night before had taken all the fight out of her and she suckled on him like a new born babe, resignation and the desire to avoid any further pain her only thoughts.

He left Nadredd to deal with her. He withdrew a large key from its hidden niche behind a loose stone, it was obscured by a tapestry, he unlocked the small wooden door set into the wall next to it. Once in the room he locked the door behind him. This was his sanctuary; the place his powers were most concentrated. The room was mostly bare. Candle stands formed a circle within the room, alternately they held either a candle or a large bloodstone, each one the size of his palm. He moved round the room lighting the candles. In the centre of the circle, on a pedestal, stood a large orb crafted from an immense bloodstone. Once the last candle was lit he walked over to it and removed the cloth which covered it.

He placed his hands on its surface and stared down deep within the orb. Slowly images began to appear, vague at first slowly gaining clarity. There were several women rushing around the room, a hive of activity, surrounding their queen, who stood regally in the centre of them. He watched as her dress fell to the ground and she stepped out of it, only for a second did he glimpse the firm flesh.

Immediately she was gone from sight, obscured as her attendants began the process of bathing her and preparing her for her coronation. He stared intently hoping to catch glimpses of her as the women moved around her but, by the time they stepped back, she was robed in her ceremonial dress. It did not matter, he had watched her enough times to be able to visualise every inch of her body, as his display last night had shown. Looking at her in her flowing gown, she looked so different from how she did in the battle dress he normally associated with her.

Seeing her this way only fuelled his fantasies more, he imagined sliding the fabric up over her thighs and pulling her onto his lap. She turned and walked towards the mirror bringing him back from his daydream. She looked straight into it. For a moment, it seemed as if she were staring straight into his soul. She appeared to shudder, he sometimes wondered if she sensed that there was an extra presence in the room with her, but then she turned and left the room. He moved his hand over the orb again and the room disappeared.

Wend stood staring at the blank stone, he had never in all his life felt this mixture of feelings. He couldn't understand why this attraction he felt for her was so strong. It was more than simple lust, somehow, he felt their destinies were entwined. The problem with that was, he believed you made your own destiny, he certainly had so far. His hand strayed to a nearby smaller bloodstone, he felt the tingle as the energies connected with his own. Maybe his men weren't the only ones who needed a distraction for a day or two while he awaited the response to his message

Chapter Five

She stood looking into the crystal mirror. She was now dressed and prepared for the hours to come. She studied her face looking for signs of what had passed in the last day. Outwardly she could see none, but she felt so different inside. She struggled to understand how the knowledge that had so recently been imparted to her could have made no difference to her appearance.

She thought about the carefree girl she had been when she found this mirror, it had been during one of her frequent explorations of the castle. Her father had said he remembered it hanging in his mother's room, it had been there when he was a child, but for some reason it had displeased her own mother and had been banished to an unused chamber. She had spent hours polishing away the layers of dust before hanging it here. That girl was gone now, a ghost consigned to the shadows by duty and destiny.

A knock on the door announced the arrival of her escort to the great hall. With one last glance in the mirror, she turned and walked to the door. Ready or not, she must step forward and assume her place. She must accept the role she was born for in more senses than one.

The guards stood lining the corridor, all dressed in their finest armour. As a child she had loved the pomp and ceremony of court. She had looked on in wonder, seeing everyone in their finest outfits, the impractical plumes on the helmets that would never see a battlefield. She looked down at her own dress, floor length, floating linen, dyed the palest of blues. Hours had been spent sewing the tiny flowers. She had known, that round the fire in the great hall each evening, women toiled over the cloth that she would one-day wear. Before her father died, it had been expected that the material they so carefully worked upon would be used for a wedding gown. Now, instead, the embroidered cloth had been used to make the gown for the coronation.

It was so different from her normal everyday wear of leggings and vest, clothes selected for practicality rather than the way they looked. This dress was so fragile she had feared it would tear as they tightened the laces of the bodice. As they had dressed her, she had imagined the looks on their faces if she had acted as she wished and attended her coronation in battle armour and boots. They would have been horrified, but even in the heavy armour, she would have felt more comfortable than she did now. She knew had it been her brother to be crowned, he would have been allowed to wear furs such as those they had laid their father out in. She would fight alongside the men, dress like them in combat, but she felt the unfairness keenly, that she must wear a dress such as this to be crowned their queen. Her hair had been left flowing, rather than braided as she would normally wear it, the only concession being the two slim braids one at each side of her face that held the rest back.

She took a deep breath and nodded at the captain of the guard. The first four guards stepped out to lead the way, the rest would fall in behind. Other than the sound of leather on flagstone, silently the procession began.

When they reached the entrance to the great hall, the huge wooden doors stood ajar. She could see into the room beyond, and that it had been filled with as many people as could fit in. Others spilled out into the chambers that stood to either side; everyone jostled to gain a better position from which to view the proceedings. Candles had been lit and flooded the room with a warm glow. Garlands of flowers were strung across the rafters, their fragrance sickly sweet as it mixed with that of the wax. She knew they had been hastily gathered in the early hours by the women, an attempt to dispel the memories of her father's body lying here only hours ago, and of course to cover the smell of death. The effort that everyone had put in was evident everywhere she looked.

Now, they all stood waiting for her entrance. Through an aisle create between the bodies she could see Celdwady Llwny waiting for her. His apprentice Brawd Y Blaidd stood beside him. It seemed strange to her that he should have taken on an apprentice when she could not imagine Celdwady being absent from the castle.

The apprentice had appeared at the castle gates only a few weeks ago. No one knew where he had come from or why he had appeared. Only Celdwady had not been surprised by his appearance, it had almost been as if he were expecting him. The ways of the Guardians were strange and secretive. No one questioned their word nor asked for explanations. The young man was quiet, and seemed naturally shy. Several times he had seemed uncomfortable in her presence, or that of other woman. The only thing Jacantha knew for certain was that only one Guardian was ever present at court at any time, the arrival of an apprentice did not bode well for the future.

She walked forward towards them glancing round at the faces in the crowd as she passed trying to read the expressions on their faces. There were some she knew who doubted her ability to lead them. Not that they doubted her heart or her ability in battle. Jacantha knew that in whispers they would have questioned her age and, of course, the question of her unmarried status. Her father had always dismissed discussions over her match, saying she was too young to think of such things. In the light of this morning revelations, she now wondered if there had been more to it.

She caught sight of Trwyn Sron as she passed. He stood close to the front, he smiled as their eyes met briefly. He was highly born and, given the lack of suitable matches in the surrounding kingdoms, the first choice of many to be bound to her. She had considered many times whether she would like that match. They had grown up together, in many ways she felt closer to him than her own brother. Lately things had changed.

When they sparred with each other she knew he was trying harder to overpower her, to prove himself to her. He had never been able to defeat her, even as children when he had the advantage of two summers growth, and, the extra height and reach they gave him. She had teased him over this, but lately she realised, though she may be the better warrior it was not his fighting skills she loved him for. Her feelings had grown as she learned to value his loyalty and his friendship. She just wished he would realise this.

Jacantha reached the front of the room and stood before Celdwady. A glance to her right revealed her brother stood pale faced, ready to take his place in the chain of succession. She reached over and squeezed his hand. She must prepare him for the future as Celdwady would prepare her. His destiny was tied up in hers. If she failed, he may have no future. If she succeeded, he would need to take the reins of power sooner than he thought, and as everyone in the room could see, he was nowhere near ready.

"Do you come here of your own free will?"

Celdwady Llwny's voice broke the silence of the room,

"I do"

Jacantha's reply sounded strange to her ears after her night vigil. In front of her was a low wooden stool, carefully lifting her dress so that she did not catch it, she knelt upon it, her head bowed forward.

The ceremony began with prayers for the departed before moving on to the part which required her responses. To every question Jacantha answered in the affirmative. To put her people above herself, lay down her life to protect them. She promised to guide them with wisdom through the journey they were about to embark on together. Celdwady then turned to her brother, asking his oaths to support his Queen, to prepare himself for standing in her stead. She listened to the fear in his voice as he answered, she knew without looking at him that he was trembling.

She wondered, not for the first time, how Arth would cope were she not here to guide him. At that moment she decided, no matter what else the future held, she must find him a strong wife to support him. She would find someone to tutor him in taking command. Possibly Celdwady read her thoughts, because at that moment his eyes found hers and gave the slightest of nods, imperceptible to anyone else in the room. She glanced over as the diadem that she had worn at court for the last fifteen years was placed on her brother's head. She knew it weighed next to nothing yet his knees seemed to sag with the weight.

Celdwady now turned back to her. More questions and affirmations, but this time the trimmings of ceremony accompanied them. The rowan staff to confirm that she would honour and protect the woods that surrounded them and gave them fuel for their fires. The sheaf of corn that signified she would honour the earth in return for a plentiful harvest. The moonstone sceptre to declare her protection for all living things within her realm. A promise that no animal would be killed for sport, only those required for feeding her people would be killed. A vow that they would live in harmony with the other dwellers in the kingdom no matter what their creed.

The image of the wolf last night flashed into her mind. She had always been taught that they were all linked as part of the earth, every living thing had its place and all were part of each other. Finally, the crown. Not the one her father had worn, but one that had been prepared years ago when she became heir. She had assumed that it had been made because her fathers would have been too large, but in the light of what had been said this morning, she now questioned this.

The crown was wrought from gold and had intricate carvings round the base. The front distinguished by a single point, embedded into which was a moonstone. Jacantha dropped to her knees to receive the crown. She lowered her eyes as the final vows were made that sealed her future as Queen. As the crown was placed on her head she felt her emotions well up. She took deep breaths to compose herself. Then finally, came the moment when she must rise and face her people.

Fear swept through her at the enormity of the task ahead of her. She looked to Celdwady for reassurance. He smiled and gave her a nod. She stood, taking a moment to compose herself, then turned to face her people for the first time as their queen. A chorus of cheers broke out in the hall. Jacantha allowed a smile to cross her face, for today at least she would enjoy the moment.

After the fighting of the last months she recognised a need in herself, as much as anyone else in the hall, to relax and celebrate. A scramble of activity began as tables and benches were brought into the hall to lay out the feast. Jacantha found herself being hugged as people made their way forwards, partly to make room as the food began to arrive and, of course in the contest to be amongst the first to greet their new leader. Blessings came at her from all directions, she could barely keep up with acknowledging each speaker. She surveyed the crowd looking for Trywn. She caught sight of him just as he ducked out of the room into an antechamber.

She worked her way across the room, accepting the congratulations and condolences, given in equal measures from those she passed. On entering the room, she saw Trwyn staring out the window, lost in his own reveries. As she approached him he turned, his eyes filled with tears. He looked at her and smiled.

"My Queen" he bowed his head to her.

She placed her hand under his chin and lifted his head "Why so sad?".

"You looked so beautiful up there. You cannot be unaware of my feelings for you. I love you, I always have, but now, we both know you will make a match for the kingdom. I have nothing I can offer to compete with that."

Jacantha reached up and put her hand to his cheek, a smile on her face

"You idiot. I will be bound only to one who can make me happy. My father always told me that I would only enter into a match with someone who I could truly love. He loved and respected you, he believed you would be a good match for me when the time was right. I do not need to look at other kingdoms to find love, it is here standing before me."

Trwyn pulled her to him, his hands winding into her hair as he leaned down to embrace her, his lips seeking out hers. She leaned her body into him allowing his arms to envelop her, her hands following the curves of his muscular back.

Until now she had been unsure of the intensity of her feelings towards him, but at this moment she knew, she would take no other. His hands explored the contours of her body through the thin dress. She felt herself awakening to feelings that were strange to her. She wondered what it would be like to feel those hands on her body, to be one with him, to nestle her head against his chest and fall asleep in his arms.

He pulled back and stood looking at her as if seeing her for the first time. She knew they must return to the feast before they were missed, but still she grabbed him, and drew him back to her for one more embrace. This time it was she who took the initiative, kissing him passionately. She pressed herself into his body until she felt as if they were the only ones who existed. Then, realising that if she did not stop now they may not be able to, she stepped back. She straightened her dress down, then offered him her hand, allowing him to lead her back into the hall.

The tables were laid, dishes of succulently prepared game, piles of fresh baked bread covered each available space. The aroma from spices and herbs filled the air. With a squeeze of his hand Jacantha left him to take her place at the head of the table. No sooner had she taken her seat, the toasts began. Each lord raising their glass to pledge their loyalty to her.

Once the formalities had been taken care of, the feast began. Jacantha ate ravenously, piling her plate high with meat and fruit. She drank slowly, careful not to allow herself to consume to much ale, knowing she needed to keep her wits about her. It was not the feast of her childhood memories with ale and wine overflowing, but a more restrained affair. All knew the need to remain vigilante, no matter the nature of the occasion. The dignitaries from neighbouring kingdoms were not present. War made travel perilous, and those who had once resided at court had long since returned to their own lands. While the joy and celebration was genuine she knew each person in the room was moderating their merrymaking in reflection of the hostilities which could recommence at any time.

The gates which had stood open last night were now heavily barricaded. Guards stood look out on the ramparts, although they had left their posts briefly to watch her crowned, they had returned immediately afterwards. These men were aware of how vulnerable they were at this time, but also knew how important the traditions were. Jacantha had not had to order anyone to forgo the feast, they had volunteered, for which she was thankful.

The evening passed quickly, whenever she spotted Trwyn through the crowd his eyes were fixed on her. She could feel the longing radiating from them, but she knew there would be few opportunities to be alone together for the next few days at least. She wondered if she had done the right thing encouraging him. She did not doubt that she wanted him every bit as much as he wanted her, but would it be possible. Would it be fair to him?

Celdwady's hand on her shoulder announced it was time for her to leave the feast and meet with the elders. Normally in times of peace, this would have waited until tomorrow evening, but under the circumstances, it had seemed prudent to arrange it as quickly as possible. She followed Celdwady through into the council chamber.

Two seats remained round the table, which she and Celdwady took, making up the full complement of eighteen in the circle. She looked round the table. Celdwady's apprentice sat next to him. The fifteen other seats were filled with the elders of the tribe. A mixture of those representing the eldest families and those who had distinguished themselves through battle made up the council. She was the youngest person in the room. Many of those present had watched her grow since birth, now they were expected to accept her rule.

The meeting was to decide the next course of action, many pushed for immediate retribution. With Celdwady's support she needed to persuade them that this was not the best course of action. In normal circumstances she would have agreed, and would have been ordering the horses saddled, she knew that, had several amongst them not been witnesses to the manner of her father's defeat, they would never have considered yielding to her. The descriptions from those who had been on the battlefield alongside her father persuaded them that powers other than the strength of their arms were at play.

Trwyn's father, who had stood alongside her father, described the way the clouds had gathered overhead. The heavens had rained down fire upon them which avoided Wend's troops. He talked of the way that the weapons refused to hit their targets, glancing off even when they should have delivered a death blow. Then he described the way her father had fallen. Jacantha could barely bring herself to listen.

She had seen her father fight, the description of him she now heard was something she had trouble accepting. That Wend Y Mawr had stood with his guard down, giving her father an easy target, yet his blows failed to connect, only proved to her that greater powers were at play here. She swallowed down the bile that rose in her throat as she thought of his return home, of the blood running in the water.

Finally, it was agreed that they would wait a few days to give Celdwady time to consult his books, and try to find a way to counteract the dark magick of Wend Y Mawr. In the meantime, Jacantha ordered all warriors attend extra training sessions. They did not need extra training, but she knew that they needed to feel they were doing something. At least the physical exertion of training would occupy their minds, along with keeping their bodies in shape.

As she rose she realised how tired she was. The journey back to her room was a blur. She had no memory of undressing, and no sooner than her head hit the pillow she was asleep.

Chapter Six

Wend rose at first light. He had allowed his men to spend the previous day indulging themselves round the castle. He had watched, absorbing energy from them but had refrained from pleasuring himself.

This morning he felt restless, he had dreamt of her again last night. Images of what he would do to her when he had her in his power had flowed through his mind. He was having trouble thinking of anything else recently. This feeling bothered him it was like an itch he could not scratch, constantly working away on his nerves. As much as he wished to invade and possess her body she in turn seemed to have invaded his thoughts his dreams the previous night more realistic than ever before. He wondered if it was a side effect of the show the other night. If so surely if he kept busy it would wear off, that was why he had decided to take his men out on the hunt this morning.

His scouts had returned with reports of a group of travellers passing through his lands a couple of hours ride out. Three caravans loaded high with goods was too good a target to let pass. It would provide the diversion he needed while waiting for her reply. He strode out into the courtyard and gave the order to mount up. He climbed upon his own horse, a fierce black stallion. As always the horse bristled for a moment spooked by him climbing into the saddle it seemed to sense that he was not what he seemed. He projected himself into the horses mind, calming it before digging his heels into its belly and leading his men out of the castle at full speed.

As the wind blew through his hair, he had a flashback to being a boy. Before the magick had come he had wanted nothing more than to be a horseman spending his days in the saddle galloping across the open fields. As a member of the royal household it was the only time he had experienced real freedom from prying eyes determined to report any indiscretion back to court in an attempt to gain favour. Not that his father or grandfather had really cared what he got up to although the felt the consequences of their annoyance when he got caught. It was never the action for which he was punished only his failure to cover it up adequately. After his grandfather's death he had total liberty, he answered to no one. He barely recognised himself as the boy who had wanted nothing more than to ride any longer. That was so long ago, in other lifetime.

The miles passed quickly beneath the flying hooves. As they neared the area where the travellers had been spotted they reined the horses in. Wend ordered them to dismount and leave the horses tethered in a copse of trees. They approached on foot creeping cautiously through the undergrowth.

As they crept closer they spotted the travellers. They had constructed a makeshift camp, tents had been created by throwing blankets over low hanging branches. A pot hung over a campfire, from the aroma drifting towards them Wend surmised they had been planning some form of stew for their dinner. Rabbit skins stretched, pegged out it the ground attested to the fact they had only recently caught their meal. Silently they assessed the numbers, not that it made any difference the outcome would be the same. They counted a dozen men and four women. They were all older, probably in their fifties Wend decided.

He raised a gloved hand and gave the signal and his men moved in on their prey. The men never stood a chance they were slaughtered where they lounged around the fire but at least their death was swift. The campfire spat as blood splashed into the flames. A stray foot lashed out and the meal spilt across the floor one of Wend's men cursing as hot liquid scolded his leg.

The women would provide sport for his men for a little while. He watched as one of his men grabbed some rope tying one of women's hands together then threw the rope over a nearby tree branch. He strung her up so her feet hardly touched the ground then another woman was tied to the same rope. Each time one tried to pull away she dragged her friend into the air. Nadredd took at his whip laughing as it flicked through the air causing the recipient of its stinging tongue to leap in a macabre parody of a dance. As the rope slackened for those few brief seconds the woman would leap back away from their capturers. They were unable to control the automatic reaction which they knew would exact pain from the woman attached to the other end as it snapped tight again ripping her arms from the shoulder socket.

The women held no attraction to him, their saggy breasts being exposed as his men toyed with them. He turned his attention to the contents of the caravans. A few of his men were already dragging out the spoils from the back of the vehicles for him to inspect. At first glance there was little of value, some cloth, and other household wares but he would make certain before his men filled their own pockets. He would take the caravans back and inspect them properly at his leisure then distribute the bounty between his men once he had taken his pick.

The sound of a twig snapping caused him to spin round he studied the undergrowth. He was about to look away when there was another snap then a flash of blonde hair moving quickly away from where he stood. He smiled, a chase was just what he needed to amuse himself. He left his men at their tasks and ran after his quarry.

The girl realised she had been spotted and that he was coming after her. She bolted upright and started running for her life. Hitching her skirts, she was running quickly as her legs would carry her. She crashed through bushes, brambles scratching at her bare flesh. She was no match for him, with each stride he gained on her. She panicked as she heard him gaining on her. As she was almost within his grasp, she tripped on a tree root. She fell to the ground, her momentum carrying her a few feet away before he pounced on her. He rolled her onto her back to get a better look at his prize. She lay in his grasp struggling to regain her breath.

She was young maybe seventeen at most he thought. Although she had womanly curves, her expression was that of a frightened child. Wends gloved hand stroked her face he felt her stiffen beneath his touch. He assured her if she stayed quiet and didn't fight him he wouldn't hurt her. The look in her eyes told him that she didn't believe him, rightly so he mused. He had no intention of hurting her anymore than was necessary for his gratification. He had other plans for her. One so young would make a nice addition to the concubines back at the castle.

He leaned over her and kissed her, forcing his tongue deep into her mouth. She tried to push him off but his weight pinned her to the ground. His hand moved down her body, tugging at the laces of her bodice releasing her breasts. They were small but pert, against her will, her nipples hardened under the touch of his gloved hand. She looked up into his dark eyes, her body trembled under his touch. She could feel his bulging muscles as his body pressed against her. It only added to her realisation that escape would be impossible even if she got away he would catch her again. He was handsome but the lines of his face were hard despite his soft words, she tried to calculate his age, thrown by the feeling his eyes were so much older than the rest of his face.

His hand moved lower grasping at her skirts, pulling them up to her waist. As she tried to protest, he kissed her harder, while at the same time moving his weight forcing her legs apart. He reached between them undoing his own leggings releasing his weapon ready to impale her upon it. The resistance he felt upon entering her confirmed she had been a virgin.

He lifted his head and looked at her, tears rolling down her face. How easy it would be now to consume and destroy her but he knew to create the perfect concubine was a slow process. It was not enough they lay there and endured, they must revel in the degradations performed on them.

He reached down to a pouch on his belt and withdrew a small vial. He pulled the stopper out with his teeth and prised her lips open emptying the contents into her mouth. He held her head steady until he was sure she had swallowed the contents. The draught was a concoction he had perfected for breaking the concubines in, it relaxed them and made them subservient.

He lay still on top of her talking to her gently, reassuring her until he saw her eyes begin to glaze over his sweet words masking his true intentions. He moved his head down to her breasts taking each of them into his mouth in turn. Her gentle moans showing him the potion had taken effect upon her making her body respond and dulling her senses. His hands slipped under her buttocks lifting her legs and spreading them further apart.

He drove into her deeper, meeting no resistance this time. She groaned as he slid his full length into her. As he pushed into her over and over again he was rewarded with her thrusting her hips up to meet his. He smiled, he was right, this one would make a good plaything. He rolled over onto his back, pushing her upright. He grasped her hips and controlled her rhythm as he bounced her up and down, pulling her down harder onto his manhood each time. He felt his climax approaching, the potion also had the effect of ensuring that the concubines could not conceive but it took a few doses before that took full effect. He lifted her off him and spun her round, flipping her over onto her back.

He knelt over her, his knees either side of her head. He adjusted his position slightly then he thrust himself deep into her throat. She gagged at first but he continued ignoring her hands trying to push his hips away. He buried his head in the soft downy hair between her legs his tongue probing her most intimate parts. He spread her with his fingertips lapping at her exposed delights. He felt her lips tightened round him as her body responded to his touch. Her body convulsed as he found the secret place that brought her to a climax just as he released himself down her throat.

He rolled over again and lay on his back. He looked over at her she lay panting, her breath rugged after her new experiences. Her face and chest flushed from the rush of blood that had coursed through her body. It was tempting to stay here now, taking his pleasure with her but he knew that his men would coming looking for him. He stood and rearranged his clothing, then he hauled her to her feet. In her drugged state she did not register her breasts remained exposed. He did not bother covering her up, modesty was something that would no longer be necessary for her. Wend grasped her by the arm and led her back through the undergrowth to where the caravans were.

As he approached he could see a mass of bodies under the tree. All four of the women had been strung up in pairs facing away from each other, now and his men were taking their pleasure with them. They were doubling up with rear and frontal assaults on each woman to optimise the opportunity for pleasure that each man received. The only noise that could be heard was the laughter and taunts from his men. Wend was surprised the women were not crying out in pain as his men abused their bodies.

As he got closer he realised why the woman no longer screamed. Blood ran from their mouths where their tongues had been cut out. The severed appendages lay discarded on the ground trampled by the men's boots. The men noticed the prize Wend pushed before him and moved towards her but he motioned for them to stay back. She was his for now, once he had finished with her they would get their chance to take their pleasure with her.

She froze at the sight of the women. He presumed she must be related to at least one of them. Even in her drugged state the panic began to rise in her. He grabbed a handful of hair and dragged her nearer to them. He watched moving her round so each woman saw her until noticed one woman began to thrash wildly at the sight of the girl in his grasp.

"Your mother?"

The girl nodded tears welling up in her eyes. He began to laugh, he whispered in the girl's ear that if she disobeyed she would meet the same fate.

He pushed her to her knees and called Nadredd over to them. Nadredd approached, his manhood already erect as he had waited for his turn with the other women. Wend tipped the girls head back so their eyes met and ordered her to take his friend in her mouth. Wend moved over to where the girl's mother hung. The girl's eyes did not leaving him as she hesitated in obeying his order. Wend pulled a dagger from his belt and grabbed the woman's breast. He held the dagger as if he intended to cut it off, the sharp point releasing a trickle of blood which ran down the woman's ribs. The girl threw herself against Nadredd taking his full length into her mouth. Wend watched as she sucked on Nadredd mistakenly believing that she could save her mother by obedience. Nadredd pulled out, holding her hair, he released himself over her face. Holding her still by the hair he turned her so the mother witnessed the daughter's degradation.

Wend ordered the girl be bound and placed in one of the caravans. She protested pleading for her mother's life to be spared. Her begging irritated Wend and she felt his fury as the back of his hand made contact with her cheek. The men took advantage of the opportunity for a grope as they manhandled her into the back of the wagon. He ordered his men to finish taking their pleasure of the women and to slit their throats quickly.

One of the men had been dispatched to retrieve their horses from the trees. Wend mounted his horse gesturing the others should do the same and they set off towards home leaving the corpses of the women swinging in the breeze. The men were in a jubilant mood as they rode back. Although the action they had enjoyed with the women was not the best they had it satisfied them for the present. The prospect of loot from the caravans more than made up for the fact the women had been older. The acquisition of the caravans and horses excited them. Each man was convinced it would be his turn to be rewarded with the prize pickings.

Upon their arrival back at the castle, the girl was handed over to the other concubines. They would clean her up and prepare her for Wend to take his pleasure later. He turned his attention to the loot. After closer inspection Wend claimed the caravans themselves. He had no real need of them at the moment but once he had Jacantha in his power they would be useful for collecting taxes from her people. He found a supply of cloth in one caravan that would be useful that he claimed for himself the rest he divided up. The horses were beasts of burden rather than warhorses. One or two were serviceable and these he gave to his most loyal supporters. The rest of the weapons and goods he distributed to those who needed them. Most accepted their share without complaint but one voice was heard muttering of discontent. Wend spun to look at the person daring to utter dissent.

The voice came from an older man, Wend glared at him. He was getting old and had not fought well in their last few battles. Now he had the nerve to complain about how small his portion of the spoils was. Wend drew his sword. Everyone else fell back silent they knew what would follow. No one questioned Wend's authority, they all knew that. To challenge his word meant death. The man protested his innocence, apologised, finally he looked round for support or somewhere to bolt to, realising too late the folly of letting his mouth run away with him. Wend closed the ground between them in a few strides.

The man, realising he had no choice, drew his own sword. The man knew he stood no chance but was determined not to go down without a fight. As they clashed the sound of metal on metal rang out in the silence. No other noise could be heard. The rest of the men remaining hushed as they waited for the inevitable outcome. The swords collided over and over again. Lunges and parries as steel whirled through the air glinting as the last rays from the sun reflected from their blades. At first the man held his ground but his age took its toll with each swing of the heavy sword.

Wend toyed with him. His victory was never in doubt yet he allowed the man to appear to gain the upper hand and believe he had the chance of winning. The man grasped his sword in both hands, and swung it high above his head, his movement laboured and slow. Wend seized his moment and drew his sword across the man's stomach. A clatter rang out around the courtyard as the man's sword slipped from his grasp and fell to the ground. The man slumped to his knees. His guts spilled from the gaping wound across his midriff, he clutched his hands to the wound trying to hold them in place. Unable to stem their exit the man watched as they slid upon the ground before him as a pool of blood spread across the flagstones where he knelt. The man lifted his eyes and looked at Wend, the man's stare glazed over and his lifeless body fell to the floor.

Wend strode over to the man's body and looked down upon it with distain. He reached down and grabbed a handful of the man's hair. A single stroke from his sword was all that was required to separate head from body. He bore the head aloft, a cruel smile spreading across his lips. He mockingly stroked the hair as he walked toward the entrance to the castle, he stopped at a row of spikes set jutting from the walls either side of the doorway. Grasping the head firmly with both hands he impaled it upon one of the spikes, a reminder to all that ingratitude and disobedience would not be tolerated.

He let out a low whistle and from deep within the castle came the sound of something moving towards them. As the noise grew louder claws could be heard scraping on the flagged floors and individual snarls and yaps. His pack of hunting dogs careered into each other as they burst through the door just as he opened it. Trained to obey his every command they halted directly in front of him awaiting further instruction. The smell of fresh blood filled their nostrils driving them into frenzy it was taking all their training to resist the instinct to investigate. He walked back to the headless body, the dogs watching his every move, and kicked it over with his foot, rolling it so the open wound faced the sky.

"Dinner!" He announced to the dogs with a sneer on his face.

Wend stepped back as the giant beasts approached the body. The first, the alpha male, sniffed the ground around the body before devouring the spilt entrails. Then as one the pack, following his lead, fell upon it tearing flesh from bone. The dogs turned on one another as they fought for the tender soft flesh. Growls and snarls flew through the air as they pulled the carcass back and forth between them. Blood mixed with saliva flew from their jowls as they shook their huge heads ripping mouthfuls from the cadaver to be swallowed down whole. The men stood by watching horrified with the sound of bones crunched and ripping sinews echoing in their ears.

No one dared to move now until Wend gave the word for fear the dogs would turn on them. The dogs made short work of the body, ripping limbs from the torso. One lower ranking dog ran back from the group, an arm hanging from his mouth. He took his prize away from the others to enjoy it in solitude. He settled down in front of where the men stood ensuring they had a view of the ease in which he stripped the flesh from the bones.

Wend signalled to the rest of the men they should follow him inside. At the sound of his voice the dogs stopped their feast and watched as the men filed past them nervously. As he surveyed their faces he was in no doubt that they understood that the same fate awaited each one of them should they cross him. The energy from this afternoon's entertainment and from the blood he had just shed coursed through him as he strode into the great hall. He had learnt how to absorb others energies from the stranger. The sexual energy seemed to last longer but now he felt a shift in the energies in the room caused by the men's unease. Having reminded the men what the perils of dissent were he felt their nerves.

At clap of his hands the room began to fill. Concubines bearing food and ale appeared immediately serving the men, other who had not been part of the outing that morning began to appear unaware of what had passed in the courtyard. The tales of the days sport began circulating the room. The imbalance in the energies began to ease as the concubines set to work. Wend took a long draught of ale and sat back watching as his men resumed their usual resting activities.

Wend looked about him looking at the room itself rather than the activities which were under way. Once he had control of Jacantha's skilled workers he would restore the hall to it former glories. He closed his eyes and allowed his mind to wander to the orgies he would throw in the restored hall, ideas for new instruments of torture and pleasure flooding his mind.

Chapter Seven

It felt good to be back in the saddle and feel the weight of the sword in her grasp. After two days confined by tradition and duty, Jacantha felt the need to throw herself into physical exertion to shake loose the tension that she felt through her body. The swords they used this morning were covered with leather sheaths in order that no one was injured in the training but there was no holding back. Swords were swung with full vigour. Blow after blow crashing down with a ferocity that could shatter bone. She had decided this morning that she would practise on horseback. She controlled the horse's movement with pressure from her knees while holding her sword in one hand and shield in the other. The exercise was designed to perfect balance while engaging in combat while on the move. She turned to charge down yet another opponent, her brow glowing with the soft sheen of sweat from her exertions.

In battle the horses would usually be corralled together, forming a group protecting each other's backs. The horses would be heavily armoured at the front and underneath protecting them if they reared. Each rider shared a bond with their horse, almost a telepathy which tuned both horse and rider to the slightest change in the other. Man and beast needed to move as one in a perfect symbiosis, in the clash of swords the spoken word was drown out.

They had been out practising since just after dawn. It was now approaching lunchtime, the smells from the kitchens drifting across the courtyard. As she fended off a blow with her shield, she swung her sword catching her opponent under his sword arm. The blow caught him in his ribs knocking him from his horse. She could have happily continued with the training but she sensed the others being distracted by the thought of the meal awaiting them. She gave the signal for them to break for lunch. They would resume training in the afternoon when she planned to work on hand to hand combat.

She dismounted and led her horse back to the stables, and into his stall. She looked across the stalls her father's mount standing patiently awaiting him even though they both knew he would never come. She would assign him to someone else in time, but knew they would never feel the same bond with the horse that her father had. She shook off the melancholy that threatened to descend and turned her attention to her own steed a magnificent chestnut stallion. She had him chosen when she first learnt to ride. He had been far too big for her, the men had laughed when she chosen him.

She had been seven, a tiny wisp of a girl and he a huge two year old barely broken in but the bond had been immediate. They shared a wilful temperament and she had been thrown many times in the power struggle between them, both as stubborn as the other. Eventually she had overcome and the horse now trusted her judgement implicitly. While other horses bore the scars of battle hers remain unscathed. She rubbed him down feeling the powerful muscles beneath her hands as she worked over his flanks. His ears pricked, and he whinnied, she spun to see what had attracted his attention and saw Trwyn stood watching her. She filled the manger with hay for her horse before leaving the stall and approaching him.

    Trwyn had been training with a different group this morning. She had not had chance to speak with him since their encounter last night. She saw the apprehension in his eyes, his fear she regretted what had passed between them. To silence his fears she pulled him towards her, her mouth seeking out his. The morning's exertions rather than tiring her had left her feeling energised. Adrenalin coursed through her body urging her to action. He responded forcing his tongue into her mouth, his arms drawing her closer lifting her from her feet. She felt a strange heat spread through her body from the contact between them. She could not understand how she had gone from being unsure to being so desperate for him in such a short time. She had heard others talk of love and lust but this was the first time she had experienced the latter. She knew that they must wait until bonded to consummate their match but her body ached for him. Her hands clutching at his back and from the hardness she felt pressing against her she knew he felt the same.

    Silently he lifted her carrying her into an empty stall and laid her down upon the straw. The risk of being caught added to the excitement. His hands sought out her breasts, a sigh escaping his lips as his hand found its target beneath her bodice. She trembled at his touch, a mixture of fear and expectation racing through her. His mouth moved from hers down her neck towards her newly exposed breast. She moaned as his tongue flicked her nipple, her hand moving to his head burying her fingers in his hair. She knew she should stop him but her body betrayed her.

    She arched her back forcing her breast towards his mouth. She felt his teeth close in on her nipple gently nibbling on it, awakening feelings in her she had no experience of. Her body had taken on a life of its own over which she had no control. Her legs wrapped round his waist pulling him closer to her, her hands now clawing at him trying to pull him into her. His mouth now closed over hers again muffling the moans that were escaping her lips.

    Through their clothing she could feel his desire for her. She slid her hands down his back trying to push away the cloth that stood between them and their union. She knew she must not, she should not want this but she could not stop her hands movement. Her body and mind worked against each other as she abandoned herself to the moment. He grabbed her hands holding them in his above her head and began to grind his body against her. Her body responding working in perfect union with his, rising to meet his, her hips moving to an unknown rhythm. She felt a new sensation spreading through her threatening to totally overwhelm her every fibre of her being. Every inch of her body tingling and trembling with each movement. She longed to take the hardness she felt pressed against her and force it inside her, to feel him fill her.

She tried to plead with him but he only responded by pressing his mouth harder against hers. He moved her wrists so that he now held the both firmly with one hand. His free hand snaked its way down her body, pausing on her breast to once again toy with her nipple before continuing its journey. He shifted his weight slightly to one side allowing room for his hand to slide beneath the supple leather of her legging. Her body convulsed as he found the spot he was searching for, his grinding against her becoming more urgent as he softly moved his finger. Jacantha felt a fire spread through her body, so intense she felt she could not bear it yet desperate for it to continue. Then she felt everything and nothing.

Time and space seemed to stop existing around her. She was separate from her body looking down at herself. She was looking down at herself lying in Trwyn's arms. She studied her hair damp, tangled into the straw, her face and chest flushed and pink. She could see her own chest heaving with each breath so she knew she was not dead. She watched as Trwyn let out a groan his body stiffening before he collapsed onto the straw next to her inert body. He was talking to her; she saw his panic as she failed to respond. Then she felt a tug, as she was pulled down back into the flesh. She blinked her eyes, it took a few second before they could focus again. She looked up at Trwyn, the concern in his eyes seeming to melt away. She lifted her hand to his face pulling him down to her. This time their lips met gently, tenderly the urgency had gone.

Noise in the courtyard broke the spell, voices shouting, sounding the alarm. They heard the sound of boots running across the stone flags. Jacantha jumped to her feet hastily pulling her clothes back into order, she ran her fingers through her hair shaking out the straw caught there. Through the stable door she could not see what had caused the commotion, she saw people running towards the gates and heard her name mentioned as enquiries as to her whereabouts echoed across the courtyard. She instructed Trwyn to wait a few minutes before emerging to join her, then she ran from the stable to discover what had happened.

As she drew nearer the gate she could see two wagons, both appearing empty at first. Then from the back of each a man was brought forth. The first was lifted carefully, obviously gravely injured or sick, the other hauled unceremoniously and thrown to the ground. Boots connected with him as he fell. Jacantha shouted for them to stop. Eyes turned towards her with questions, eyes she noticed that looked moist with tears.

Then everyone was talking at once, gesturing towards back and forth between what would appear to be the victim and the attacker. She struggled to make sense of what was being said and raised her hand for silence. She ordered the sick man be immediately taken Celdwady for treatment. People seemed reluctant to take him, to move away from where they perceived the real action to be. They appeared to be loitered waiting to hear some form of sentence passed. Only when she shouted her orders once more, anger evident in her voice did they obey.

She turned to the two men who had driven the wagons, and instructed they were to be taken to the hall and she would join them in moments to unravel this story. Finally she turned to observe the man on the floor, his face showed only contempt toward those gathered around him. She turned to Trwyn who had just appeared at her side, and requested he take the man, with the assistance of a few others, to the dungeons. She ordered he be held under guard until she could find out what had occurred but charged the man receive no further injury until the truth of the matter was known. Tasks assigned she turned on her heels and strode off to the great hall to try to make sense of the confusion.

The two wagon drivers stood surrounded by a group of her own people by the great fireplace. Disgust was evident in the tone of the voices as she approached, although she could not work out the subject of their discourse. She moved to sit in the throne at the head of the room and gestured for all others to be silent while the men were brought before her to tell their story.

The men described how, while out hunting near the border they had spotted a small party moving through the trees. Three bound men being herded along by six on horseback. After observing them for a short time one of the hunting party had recognised one of those bound as a member of the court guard. They had acted immediately and fired upon the riders a rain of arrows. Three had been killed, two had fled but the one they had brought back and was now under guard, had been thrown from his horse and apprehended. When they had approached to untie the captives they had been horrified to find them in a pitiable condition. Despite their best efforts to save them, two had died on the journey.

The remaining man had rambled deliriously becoming agitated. Although they would have much rather taken him to the first village they came to for assistance he had been so insistent that he must be brought to the castle they did not dare resist his wishes. They had borrowed the carts in an attempt to make the man more comfortable, and to ensure the other could not escape, apologising for the fact this had delayed their arrival. The men fell silent, reluctant to repeat what the assumed to be the man's ravings, only at Jacantha's urging did they repeat the story he told of watching her being raped in Wend Y Mawr's castle.

The silence filling the room at the end of their tale was stifling. Jacantha knew all eyes were upon her, waiting to see how she would react. Inside she felt sick at the thought of what they had told her but outwardly she showed no sign of it. She left orders for the men to be fed and made comfortable and sent messengers out into the castle to gather everyone here in the great hall. She announced she would check on the condition of the sick man and hear his story from his own lips then return here to pronounce her intentions. With that Jacantha swept from the room heading to Celdwady's chambers where the man had been taken.

As she walked down the corridors she slowed her pace. If the story she had just heard was confirmed by the man's own lips action must be taken. She wondered how she could remain impassive hearing the details of the tale but knew she must. She must question him in detail and be sure that nothing was omitted however hard it would be to hear.

When she entered the room the smell of death filled her nostrils. The man was laid on a pallet in front of the fire. Celdwady leaned over him, his lips moving but no sound escaping them. She stood waiting for him to finish, his apprentice Brawd bustled into the room bearing arms full of herbs. Brawd looked at her and dropped his eyes. She had no doubt he had heard the story himself from the man, but she knew at that moment she herself would not as Celdwady leant forward and closed the man's eyes.

After a few moments Celdwady rose to his feet and turned to face her, his eyes showed his concern at the course events had taken. He dismissed Brawd from the room before beginning to speak.

"There was nothing which could be done, even had he arrived sooner I could not have saved him."

The words came slowly from his lips. She could tell he was weighing up how much to tell her, resigned to the fact he must give her the full facts he repeated the dead man's words.

He had repeated the same story to Celdwady that the other men had gathered and relayed from his ramblings except the final message. That he had not told them the man had considered that message had been for her alone, told only when death was too close to risk the message not being passed on. Jacantha swayed momentarily, then regained her composure hoping her lapse had gone unnoticed.

How Wend had misjudged her if he thought she would ever give herself willingly to a man like that, a man capable of committing acts like that. She knew her people would rather die than watch her submit to his demands.

Celdwady watched her, the resolve which now settled across her face told him it would be fruitless to urge caution. He knew that she must act and be seen to act. Without speaking another word he watched as she turned on her heels and strode back towards the great hall. He would do all he could to ensure her safety, the time was not yet right for the next stage of the prophecy but he knew she must stare her enemy in his eyes. All Celdwady could do was prepare himself for the momentum that would begin to gather over the next few days. The thought she may fall could not even be contemplated, he must trust in higher powers to watch over her safety. She would ride out to war but she must return and he would do all in his power to ensure

As Jacantha stood in front of the throne the room fell into silence, everyone awaiting her decision. She took a deep breath then addressed them,

"I know by now you have all heard the tale which has been brought back to us. This insult shall not pass unanswered. Tonight we shall eat and drink, tomorrow at first light we ride. Wend Y Mawr wants my attention, well he has it and by the Goddess he is going to regret he ever sought it."

A chorus of approval filled the room only two faces showed concern. Those of Celdwady who stood impassive in the doorway and Trwyn who stood gazing at her from the corner of the room worry and anger etched across his features.

Chapter Eight

Wend had risen late, last night his men had indulged in their pleasures while he had sat and watched. He had paid close attention to each man in turn, looking for signs of betrayal in each one. On the whole he knew he had little to worry about, his men lived for instant gratification of their vices rather than the accumulation of power. Only one or two of them had given him cause for concern. These were older men maybe they knew their time was limited, their usefulness and ability to fight nearing the end. There was no retirement here, you retired when you were put in your grave.

Wend looked towards to concubine stood in the corner of the room awaiting his pleasure. He called her towards him but then changed his mind. He had a taste for fresh meat this morning, he was at leisure to take his time and savour his amusements. He ordered her to bring the girl they had taken captive the day before.

The girl was led into the room, she looked about her. Her vision was hazy still from the potion that had been administered several times more since her arrival here. The room was large but the huge bed seemed to fill the space imposing its presence on anyone entering the chamber. She noticed several hooks protruding from walls, leather straps and whips lay around the room, the bedposts bore signs of scratch marks gauged deeply in to the wood, likewise the headboard. Instinctively she stepped back away from it.

Wend patted the bed next to him inviting her to take a place beside him, cautiously she sat down, too scared to refuse. The girl stiffened as he slid his arm round her pulling her closer. He smiled maybe the drug hadn't taken all the fight out of her yet. Impulsively he changed his mind about his intentions for her. He had intended a life here at the castle for her but now he wanted to revile in his violation of her no matter what the cost.

He threw the sheet back revealing his naked body to her, despite the experience yesterday his sheer size and bulk added to her fear. His muscles which had been hidden beneath his tunic were now exposed and she realised how easily he could overpower her and force his will upon her. Realising the hopelessness of her situation panic set in. The girl looked round the room frantically looking for an escape route, finding none. She tried to pull away from him, to put distance between them. Wend grabbed her arm dragging her back to him, his fingers digging into her tender flesh and threw her down roughly onto the bed. He fell upon her there was no pretences of gentleness this time. His teeth closed upon her nipples, a trickle of blood escaping his lips and running in a rivulet down her breast. All thoughts of training her as a concubine had gone from Wend's mind.

He wanted to hear her scream, to hurt her. The girl tried to push his head away, the haze from the drugs clearing as pain seared her breast. Wend had forced his hand between her legs, thrusting his fist into her. The girl let out scream after scream as pain flared through her entire body. The sound of her obvious agony only excited him all the more. He moved his hand and thrust into her, forcing his full length deeper and deeper into her while his hand now sought new pleasures. He slid his fingers between her buttocks finding the tight entrance there. The girl clawed at him trying to rip his hands from the grip they hand upon her body, screaming as he forced his fingers into her. Her screams almost silent now from the hoarseness of her throat. She struggled to breathe as her sobs wrenched the air from her lungs. The more she fought the more aroused Wend became, he grabbed her by the hair, hauling her up from the bed.

He dragged her across the room to where a table stood and forced her down so she was bent over it. Blood ran down her thighs as he buggered her. Her screams had ceased but Wend had not noticed his only concern his own gratification. His grip on her hair held her in place stopping her from slipping to the floor. With a primal roar Wend came within her. He collapsed forward pinning her body to the table as he savoured the feeling of the energy coursing through his veins. He straightened releasing his grip on her the girl's lifeless body slid crumpled to the floor. He looked down at her. It was a shame she might have made a good concubine he thought to himself. His own desires satisfied for the time being, he stepped over her and gathered his clothes.

Wend spent the evening wandering round the castle, despite his earlier pleasures he was restless. Every where he looked he saw the signs of decay around him. He looked up wooden beams swollen from where the damp had seeped in through gaps in the roof when it rained crossed the ceilings. It had never bothered him before he had paid no attention to the fabric of the castle in years. He could not explain why it bothered him now it made no difference to any of those residing here. He stopped to examine a tapestry hanging in the corridor, holes had appeared where insects had feasted upon it. The scene had depicted the castle in its prime, he remembered as a small boy watching as his mother and the other ladies of the court had put the finishing touches to it.

Thoughts of his mother raised strange emotions in him. He almost felt regret for the pain he had been forced to cause her to gain power. She had loved his father with all her heart. In Wend's eyes she had been too good for the man who had sired him. As a small boy he had worshipped her, he had felt her pain at her husband's indifference. He thought back to the evenings he had sat as a small child comforting his mother as his father took his pleasure with other women in front of her. He had been convinced once his father was out of the way and once she had grieved his loss she would have been happier. She had clung to him in her grief over her husband's death. He had not anticipated her father's death would upset her so much. She had never seemed to pay any attention to the old man and he had heard her openly condemn him for encouraging her husband in his treatment of her. Wend had thought she would have been happy he had avenged her.

Instead she had turned against him. It had given him no pleasure to shut her away, locking her up in the turret room, but she had left him no choice. She had ranted at him, openly challenging him as a murderer in front of all those who attended at court. The fact it was true was irrelevant, he could not have her running round questioning his authority. Locked in the tower she had given up on life and faded away quickly. Within a month she had passed away the last link with family and the last chance of redemption.

He ripped the tapestry down from the rings it hung from and flung it away into a dark corner. These memories were coming more frequently, he considered them a waste of energy. He could see nothing from the past worth dwelling on. The future should be the only thing on his mind and as far as he was concerned that lay in his control. He would have Jacantha, she would learn, if not to love him, then to at least respect his rule. They would have sons and he would raise his kingdom to riches in his own way. He would have control over both kingdoms and reap the benefits. He would not change his lifestyle she would have to adjust, fit in with his way of life. He has believed his mother had been wronged by her husband's treatment yet her reaction to his attempts to please her had only proved that it was she who had been at fault, incapable of understanding her place.

He smiled at the thought of pleasures he would teach Jacantha. He had no doubt that in his hands he could rouse passions in her she would never otherwise have believed. She would learn that he was master, though he hoped that she would not learn too quickly, the thought of punishing her pleased him. He allowed the image of the lash striking her buttocks to linger in his mind for few moments. She would learn to obey him or her people would face the consequences. He would restore the castle to the grandeur of past court life. He would create a castle worthy of his power his queen would sit at his side. He may even allow her to wear clothes in the great hall something none of the other women presently at court were permitted to do, Wend smirked at his own thoughts.

He thought of his men, they too would have to change. They would have to learn fighting skills from her warriors. They would learn better techniques, better strategies and then they would expand the borders of his kingdom even further. They would still have their pleasures met but he would build great barracks for them instead of them spreading themselves round the castle. Maybe he would let them keep the existing concubines in their new barracks he mused.

He would create new playthings from amongst Jacantha's warriors to keep for court. The thought of their lithe, athletic bodies pleased him, by keeping them separate from the others they would stay appealing for longer. He would once again invite those from other kingdoms to visit with the pretence of friendship he would learn how to defeat them. Anyone who stood between him and his ambition would be disposed of. He would need to tread carefully at first he didn't want Jacantha to rebel before he had tamed her. Not for one moment did it cross his mind that she would not comply, that she would not give herself willingly. Surely she was aware by now of his power, his message must have been delivered by now, and she must know that she could not win. He strode to the great hall eager to consult the orb he wanted to see if he could tell from her demeanour if his message had arrived at her court yet.

The room was dark as its image formed within the orb but he could make out the red of her hair against the white pillow on her bed. It was early still the fact she had retired already surprised him. He grinned as he considered the only early nights she would have in the future would be those where he chose to take his pleasure privately. He sat watching her sleep, her repose restless as she tossed and turned something obviously on her mind. He tried to tune into her mind, trying to read her thoughts but failed.

Unable to access her thoughts, he projected himself into her mind sending to her images of the woman who he had taken in her stead. Mentally he forced her to submit to his touch his hands running over her flesh, to feel his body pressing against hers. Her movements became more pronounced as she struggled to escape his imagined grasp, he made her experience his lust and desire. He took his time, pulling back from her mind when she threatened to wake, torturing her dreams with his presence. Despite her resistance he could feel her body begin to respond to the thoughts he placed in her mind, he smiled taking that as a sign he had succeeded.

Time passed as he sat watching her, he became aware of the first glimmers of light shining into her room. Her eyes opened and she stretched out in the bed. He found himself hardening at the thought of waking up next to her, especially now he believed once the initial victory was earned she would easily be seduced to further depravities. He undid his leggings releasing his manhood from its imprisonment just as she slid naked from beneath her sheets. The sight of her body in the orb caused him to gasp, it did not matter how many times he had seen her she always took his breath away. He closed his eyes imagining it was her hand pleasuring him rather than his own.

When he opened them again there was movement in the room, she was dressing. He watched as she pulled on the soft leather garments, a secret striptease in reverse. He found himself excited by the fact he had seen what no other man had, the soft downy hair between her legs as it disappeared beneath leather leggings designed for spending hours in the saddle. The curve of her breasts as she forced them into a leather bodice, the top of the soft mounds still evident above the supple material.

Then he paused, what he saw dragged him back to reality. She had not stopped at the everyday leather garments. She was now pulling on the thicker heavier leather bodice he had glimpsed beneath her armour. Someone else now entered the room bearing an armful of metal. He watched as her breasts disappeared, strapped under the metal plate across her chest, her arm slid into the long metallic glove that protected her sword arm. At that moment he knew the message had been delivered, he studied her face looking for a sign of her intention, he saw only a grim determination.

He stood for a brief time indecisively he had waited for her response. He had been so sure of her yielding to him now he could not judge her intentions. He would ride out to meet her it was still possible that she intended to surrender to him. He reasoned with his own doubts the armour meant nothing only that she was wearing the full battle dress she could just as easily believe that it was the correct dress for the act of submission. In his fantasies he may have thought about her prostrating herself naked before him but it would be more acceptable to her people this way.

He rushed out into the great hall shouting for his men to hurry to dress, his impatience overruling all logical thought. Saddling his horse, he continued calling out for his men to join him. By the time he was ready only thirty of his men had joined him. In his desire to meet her at the border Wend decided not to wait for the others, he dug his heels into his mount and spurred it to movement.

Chapter Nine

The stables were a hive of activity. The horses were being saddled, their head guards and protective armour strapped into place. The armour, a mix of leather and metal designed to protect the steeds without adding too much excess weight, gleamed in the early light. Those too young or elderly to ride out helped with the saddling, every buckle and strap doubled checked before a rider was hoisted aloft to take their seat. Trwyn had taken it upon himself to personally supervise Jacantha's horse as it was prepared alongside his own. The beast stood a good two hands higher than his own mare and was well known for its unpredictable nature, it glared at him now as if recognising a rival for its mistress's affections. Although Jacantha was a skilled rider Trwyn still felt uncomfortable each time she climbed in the saddle, he knew he had no basis for his feelings but still part of him resolved once they were joined he would make her a present of a new steed, something a little less spirited.

****

Celdwady stood in the courtyard watching the activity he took no part in these aspects of court life, he had no doubt that had he tried he would have hindered rather than helped. By this evening Jacantha would have come face to face with her enemy this was his concern not the battle that would accompany the encounter.

The runes had reassured him that she would return, but so much more depended on this encounter. His worry was how it would affect her emotionally standing face to face with her father's killer so soon after his death. Now this added information regarding Wend's intentions for her only added to his trepidation, it was essential she be able to remain focused on the prophecy everything else was secondary. He motioned to his apprentice Brawd to join him and in silence they slipped away from the activity heading away from the castle towards the woods beyond.

****

Jacantha took a deep breath and strode out into the courtyard. She had met with the Captain of the Guards last night along with the other high-ranking warriors, the plans had been made. Others had wanted to lead with archers but from all she had heard she dismissed this, Wend would easily shield his men from the arrows as they sped through the air. She believed their only hope was in surprise and forcing their way amongst Wend's men making it impossible for him to protect them all at once. Now was the time to show them all her leadership skills.

She walked to her mount trying to exude a confidence she did not feel. She took the reins from the young boy who had been assigned the honour of saddling her horse and threw herself up in the saddle. She could fell Trwyn's gaze as it bore into her back she resisted the urge to look round at him. The expression on the young boy's face had told her that Trwyn had been taking a personal interest in her safety. She was flattered, but it irked her that at a time such as this he allowed his personal feelings to take precedence over protocol. Each person had their own well-rehearsed tasks to perform if one person took it upon themselves to interfere with another's duties it meant they were not fulfilling their own.

Taking their cue from her, as one the rest of the warriors not in the saddle mounted their horses. As she dug in her heels and moved towards the castle gates they fell in rank behind her. She knew without looking that Trwyn had manoeuvred his mount so he was as close as he could be without breaking rank to ride alongside her. She knew others would have noticed and resolved to remind him that whatever her feelings towards him, he must remember, at all times, that in battle, she was nothing more than his Queen, there was no place for emotion on the battlefield.

The first hour they rode in grim silence, each man and woman thinking only of the task ahead. The tension hung heavy in the air, Jacantha felt if she were to reach out she would be able to feel it with her fingertips. Taking a deep breath, she began singing, recalling the battle songs she had heard round the fires on winter evenings. Gradually the men joined their voices to hers and the tension lifted. The thought that the foe they faced used magic dispelled for the time replaced by the pride and self-belief of her own men. They continued in this way for several hours until they drew closer to the border. Then the silence descended again but the tension this time was replaced by confidence.

****

Celdwady and Brawd reached a small clearing in the woods that stood close by the castle, after careful consideration Celdwady decided this place would do. He would rather have made the journey to the sacred grove but time was short. He had calculated from the runes that Jacantha and Wend would clash just as the sunset. It was essential he be prepared by then. Brawd set about laying out the altar that they had brought with them. He chanted as he laid out each object, pouring water from a nearby stream over them to purify and prepare them for the ceremony ahead. Once everything was in place they settled down in meditation to wait for the day to pass.

Tonight, they would seek visions to help them understand the path that must be travelled with greater clarity. In order to achieve what Celdwady hoped both men had fasted since they had retired from the meeting the previous evening. If all went well they would connect with the Guardians who dwelt in the ether, if they were lucky they would commune with the Lady in person, but that was too much to hope for.

****

Jacantha glanced upwards towards the sun. She had deliberated between continuing or setting up camp for the night. They had rested briefly to allow for food and calls of nature. Trwyn had hovered by her side constantly until she had pulled him away from the others and reminded him that their match had not yet been finalised and that his behaviour would place any union in jeopardy if it was seen to interfere with her rule. Sullenly he had resumed his place within the ranks, the fact he knew she was right had given him little comfort. After a long discussion with the Captain and her most respected warriors the agreement was made to ride on and hope the element of surprise remained on their side. If Wend had intelligence of their coming then they would meet him on horseback with sword in hand not lying in their beds.

The borders of her kingdom were now in sight. In the distance the remains of villages scarred the landscape. Villages close to the border had long since been deserted, Wend's raiding parties had not only pillaged but destroyed whole communities. The buildings now shells ravaged by fire, carcasses of animals lay where they had been killed their bones long since picked clean. People had gathered and taken all they could with them as they fled destroying anything that could not be carried rather than leave it for the enemies benefit. She looked at the fields that had once grown crops now gone to seed and the woods growing unchecked spread out into the open land. Many had not left in time and had fallen victim to the Wend's tyranny.

Fathers and husbands had been killed, wives and daughters raped first before being killed or taken as prisoners, a fate to which death would have been preferable. Children had hidden and watched the slaughter only to be left orphans fending for themselves until found and taken to the safety of the castle. Others had not been so lucky, some had been found and their blood had mingled with that of their parents. Many more had starved or frozen during the winter months before they had been discovered, the fact they had died scared and alone only adding to the pain of those who found them too late.

Jacantha found her anger welling up at the thought of two children she herself had found after one raid. When they had first arrived in the village they had not expected to find any survivors, the flames had already long since burnt out and the buildings were reduced to little more than ashes. Only a few blackened stone buildings stood still, as with many small villages most building had been wooden and were destroyed completely. Bodies were strewn all around the dirt turned a deep red brown by the blood which had flowed and soaked in leaving a stain that no one had been left to remove. It was only as they moved the bodies creating a giant pyre for all those who had been slaughtered that she found him.

She had discovered the small boy, he was three or four at most, clinging to the body of his mother unable to comprehend what had happened. In his mother's arms a baby, a few days old at most. The baby cold and stiff, yet the little boy had been determined they should take his little sister with them. She thought of his tears as they had lit the pyres, she had held him physically restraining him from rushing forth into the flames to save his sisters body as they licked at the blanket she had been wrapped in. He could not fully comprehend all that had happened only that his family was gone. It had been too dangerous for them to stay and see the spirits depart on their journey. His eyes had watched the smoke until it was out of sight. She would put an end to it. There would be no more mindless slaughter. She would defeat Wend whatever it took, she never wanted to see that haunted look in another child's eyes as long as she lived.

****

It was a close to sunset when Celdwady lit the candles on the altar. It was time. He withdrew a flask from his pack and tipped the liquid into the bowl on the altar, a sweet smell permeated the air. He walked round the grove selecting herbs from the undergrowth, uttering thanks for each as he plucked them. He deposited them into the liquid then taking a candle set the contents of the bowl alight. A thick acrid smoke filled the air. Brawd now stepped forward to join him and both men knelt before the altar inhaling the smoke drifting from the bowl.

Softly they began to chant and as the sun set, clarity came to Celdwady, and what was to come began to unfurl before him. Visions filled his mind behind his closed eye lids, voices whispered secrets of the past, present and future. At times he was aware that Brawd was there sharing what he saw but at other times he was alone. Then he saw her, the Lady did not speak, she had no need for words to convey her message. A feeling of strength and peace filled both the men as they continued to kneel. The visions drew back leaving them knelt in the woods once more. Aware the evening was not yet finished the once again bowed their heads in supplication and began to pray.

****

Wend heard Jacantha's army before he saw them. The rumble of the approaching hooves reverberated in the ground. He closed his eyes and allowed his vision to go ahead of him it was a magic he used very rarely as he could not travel far from his body. He allowed his sight to glide out over the trees looking down on the landscape before him.

He saw her magnificent at the head of her army but the size of the army caused him to doubt her motives for the journey. His arrogance convinced him that he could not have misjudged the situation but his doubts nagged at him still. She must know no matter how many men she brought she could not win. His defeat of her father should have taught her that. This show of strength must in his honour he reasoned, she was merely demonstrating to her people that she came to the union for the good of all. He called his men to a halt, he would let her cross the border and come to him. He sat and waited.

****

Jacantha saw Wend sat stationary before her as they approached. She wondered how he had anticipated their arrival. It was possible she thought given how few men he had with him that they had simply heard their approach while out hunting but something in his manner persuaded her this was not the case. She motioned to her own troops to stop and fall into rank alongside her. Despite the distance between them she could almost feel Wend's eyes moving over her body. Now was the time to deliver her reply to his message. She slid from the saddle and stepped forward to stand before her troops.

At her gesture the prisoner was hauled down from the horse over which he had been slung and dragged forward. He had been stripped naked and his arms were bound behind his back. His body wore the scars of his treatment, angry black-green bruises spread across his flesh. The man trembled apprehensive of the fate that awaited him knowing it would not be pleasant. Jacantha pulled the hunting knife she had sharpened the previous evening especially for the task.

She stepped behind the man, careful to make sure she still maintained eye contact with Wend. Defiance poured from her gaze as she reached round in front of the prisoner and grasped his genitals in one hand. Then in a fluid sweeping arc her other hand brought the knife up. A scream tore through the air as the blade sliced through the flesh. A jet of liquid scarlet soared through the air before cascading onto the ground. The guards holding the prisoner released his arms and he fell to the floor. His screams replaced by whimpering as his strength slipped away with the blood now soaking into the soil. Jacantha held her hand aloft displaying her prize then hurled the severed genitals to the ground. She spat upon them, then slowly and deliberately ground them into the dirt with her boot. She watched as the look on Wend's face changed from lust and expectancy to fury, and she smiled.

Turning her back on him she remounted her horse, and pulled out her sword. With a squeeze of her heels her horse jumped forward, the signal for all her warriors to do likewise and the battle begun.

****

Celdwady felt a shudder in the air and he knew it had begun. He renewed his chanting with pronounced vigour, a glimpse at the sky told him the sun had set and the moon had joined them. He had lost track of all time while in the trance, the contents of the bowl on the altar had long since burnt away. Brawd reached forward filling the bowl with powdered incensed as he lit it crackled letting off sparks as a sweet aroma began to fill the air. The sight of a faint red rim on the moon made him gaze in consternation.

The voices began whispering through the glade seeking to reassure him, to impress upon him the complexity of the situation. Brawd now joined him once more in the chant to call for the spirits to watch over Jacantha and counter Wend's magick if possible. Nothing was quite as it seemed he must trust to the gods that this was the way things must be to restore balance. In the distance the wolves began to howl.

****

Wend's men had barely time to draw their swords before Jacantha's troops were upon them. Wend still reeling from the sight he had just witnessed cut down the first man to reach him. This was not how it was supposed to happen before any others could close in on him he cast the shield spell around himself and those few of his men close to him. He could see they were badly outnumbered but pride would not let him call a retreat. He was determined he would regain the upper hand, feverishly he formulated a plan.

Then she was there, a few feet in front of him. The twenty or so men not protected by his spell had fallen and lay dead or dying in the dirt. She urged her horse forward, it stepped over the bodies to allow her to confront him. Sword raised aloft in hand, she made to strike at him but her sword bounced against the shield spell. Repeatedly she struck in his direction finding herself unable to make her sword connect. Her frustration grew as time and time again she swung at the man sat before her just as her father had done before his demise. She knew she should pull back but anger pushed her on.

Wend pushed his way into her mind. He felt the hatred towards him burning like the fire in a forge. He pushed past those feelings driving his mind deeper into her soul. He sought to impress the images of them together onto her. Not the images of the rape but of his fantasies where she was a willing participant. For a brief few moments he could feel her body responding, a slight quickening flood through her body then she shut him out. Her face had become pale, yet he could see the briefest glimpse of flesh behind the armour, flesh which was flushed from arousal.

Now it was Wend who smiled, she would be his still but it was not time, yet. Patience was required. He urged his horse forward, the shield spell still holding. He brought his face inches from hers. Then he uttered a few words, and a fog began to form.

Jacantha was reeling, her senses confused by the fog and what had just taken place. She called to her troops and heard them in the distance hail her back. She turned her horse towards the voices. The wolves howled, they seemed to be close by but she could see nothing through the dense fog. She tried to focus on the voices, moving cautiously in the direction they had come from.

Jacantha struggled to gather her thoughts. She called out to her troops to regroup and made to step back away from him to join them. In that instant while her attention was split he acted. He pulled his horse round alongside hers and grabbing her sword arm with one hand, he pulled her to him through the shield his spell had created with the other. He covered her mouth with his tasting her lips. She froze too startled to respond and immediately push him away. His tongue forced its way into her mouth as he pulled her closer. He held her tightly against him feeling her heart racing as she struggled to free herself. Again, he sought his way into the deepest recesses of her mind. He was pleased with what he found. That she would hate him he had never doubted he had killed her father after all. But there deep buried inside her was a lust to match his own and despite her hatred there was a physical attraction for him.

Then with a strength which took him by surprise she forced him out of her mind. As a parting gift she left him with one of her own, the image of her bearing aloft his severed manhood. The shock of the image caused him to loosen his grip and she was gone. She wrenched her arm from his grasp and disappeared through the fog he had created. He heard the wolf chorus close by. Calling his men to follow him, he turned digging in his heels and headed for home.

Another wolf raised its voice, closer to her this time startling her horse. It took all her skill not to lose her seat as she clung to the reins trying to calm the stallion. Then through the fog she saw the eyes, one pair at first but then joined by more. She swore under her breath. She still had the sword in her hand, but to fight off so many would be impossible. Then another howl, through the mist another pair of eyes moved towards her. She could make out the shape of the wolf as it gained ground, it appeared larger than normal. There was something different about its eyes and almost human quality. Then it stopped, she slid the sword back into its sheath.

The connection was there again. She had no doubts that this was the same wolf that had appeared in the castle at her father's funeral pyre. It looked up at her. Somehow it seemed to be linked to her a voice now in her head telling her it was time she left. It let out another cry and as it did so a gap appeared through the mist. Silently she gave thanks and spurred her horse through the gap in the mist. The mist sealed itself behind her again, and she knew that by tomorrow there would be no signs of what had taken place. The wolves would cleanse the woods of the remains. She closed her ears to the sounds of the wounded as they met their end as the feast began.

She re-joined her troops and learned only one of her troops had fallen. There was no way of reclaiming his body now from amongst the dead. She gave the order to ride for home. One last chorus from the mist caused her to look over her shoulder one last time.

The wolves would feed well tonight.

Chapter Ten

Celdwady lay in the grass exhausted, Brawd collapsed alongside him. He turned his gaze to Celdwady, endless questions about what had happened and what was to come raced through his mind. Celdwady looked pale and he decided that this was not the time to ask them. The sun had disappeared from view and the moon was now high in the sky. The red ring remained staining its purity, yet it seemed to burn brighter than ever. Brawd drew himself up to his feet and began packing away all they had brought. Only once he had completed his task did he then go to Celdwady handing him bread and ale they had brought with them from the castle.

Brawd sat beside him. He had been nervous when he had been told he must leave the sanctuary of the sacred Grove. He had travelled for days to arrive at Jacantha's court worried how he would be received upon his arrival. They had told him nothing of the reason he must go, he had assumed that he would arrive to find Celdwady injured or ill. Instead he had been met by a man with remarkable vigour despite his obvious age. Of course, he had been taught the prophecy but like so many of the apprentices he had studied with they had not really believed in it.

After eating Celdwady had regained his strength and was now sitting in the roots of a magnificent oak at the edge of the clearing. He looked at Brawd, searching his face to discover if the younger man had shared the visions. The gaze that met his told him all he needed to know, as he had suspected, the young man had only seen part of it.

"I do not know how much they have taught you of the life of a Guardian, I suspect very little, it is something that you are supposed to gain knowledge of for yourself. But as time is an issue and you have left the Grove earlier than usual I will explain a little. Guardians are immortal, but only in that our spirit carries the skills with each rebirth. There are thousands of Guardians who are in spirit, they watch over the mortals and the forests as the Lady orders. In each age a certain number of us return to the flesh. At most there are a hundred or so who walk the earth at any given time. We return charged with specific tasks, mine was to watch over Jacantha as she fulfils the prophecy. I do not know what yours will be. Only you and the Lady know the purpose for which you have been reborn. If you are not aware of it yet do not fear, you will know when the time is right."

Brawd contemplated this.

"They will never accept me. I lack the way with words you have. I am good with ceremonies and the rituals but when they come for advice I cannot find the words to sooth their fears. This warrior way of life is so different from that which I have lived at the Grove. They have such different ways."

"That will come in time. Listen to them, sit in the great hall on an evening by the fire and listen to their stories. Learn their lives, then you will understand them better. They are good honourable people. They have their faults but on the whole you could not have asked for a better placing. You are younger than many who leave the Grove, many do not venture out until they have passed fifty or more years there by then they are set in their ways. Your youth will work in your favour, you will learn to settle into the ways of castle live quicker. Now we should return I wish to consult the runes before Jacantha returns."

The two men rose to their feet and made a survey of the land to ensure they had taken all they had brought. Celdwady offered a prayer of thanks for the visions they had received and the hospitality of the woods which had sheltered them safely the previous hours. They prepared to head back towards the castle when both men stopped. They both turned their gaze to the moon. They had only till the next full moon to prepare. At the next full moon everything which must come to pass would begin and once in motion nothing could stop the destiny which must unfold.

"We are solitary because we must watch others leave that is true. But the very essence of the Guardian requires we be separate. We must guide those under our jurisdiction, emotional responses cloud our judgement. Take young Jacantha, I was there the day she entered the world, I will be there the day she leaves it. I care for her more than I should, yet, my years have taught me how to hold back those feelings. I would not be able to guide her if I allowed myself to feel more. It is not that you do not care for those you spend time with it is that you care enough to allow them to follow their destinies despite caring."

Brawd was unsure he had found himself caught in the centre of the story, not knowing what his role would be. Looking at Celdwady he had no doubt the older man knew more than he was willing to tell. He had so many questions yet was unsure he was ready for the answers.

Celdwady turned to him now "When you are ready for the answers my son they shall be given. It shows wisdom to acknowledge that you are not prepared but be assured when the time comes for all to be revealed, you will be."

Brawd shuddered, the man's ability to read his thoughts still unnerved him. Though plenty of other Guardian's in the Grove shared the ability to communicate telepathically Brawd had yet to master the art. Celdwady possessed the skill to hear his thoughts with such clarity he had seen matched by few others.

He thought back to their initial meeting Celdwady had been waiting to greet him at the gates upon his arrival. He should not have been surprised given the older man's skills, the runes had foretold his coming. He had been greeted with a warmth he was unused to, the Guardian's tended to be aloof solitary creatures.

He little more than a baby when he was taken to the Grove. He had come to learn that the Guardian's watched the stars and only when they formed the correct alignment was a possible future Guardian born. The Guardian's would send out and gather up all male children born while this took place. There had been thirty of them when he was born all taken from their families and brought up within the Grove. Over the years the numbers had shrunk, boys were sent home when it became clear they failed to attain the skills required. Of the thirty taken with him only three remained he wondered whether it was watching the others leave that had caused him to draw back from forming any further bonds of friendship. He looked at Celdwady again the older man was smiling at him.

"Our powers mean we will outlive many of those we come in contact with, I have walked this earth over a hundred years. In other circumstances I could live a hundred more but my path is already chosen. That is why you were called soon, you shall take my place here and I shall move on. My path is not clear to me at this time, I assume I shall return to the spirit and wait for my next calling but time shall reveal if I am right. You will see children born, watch them as they grow and have children of their own. You will say the rights over their pyres and inside you will feel pain at their loss but to the rest of the world you will appear unfeeling. And they will respect you for your strength."

Part Two; Point of No Return

Paula Acton

Chapter Eleven

Jacantha rolled over in her sleep again. They had arrived back at the castle mid-morning many had questioned the need for her haste on the return trip. Some of the men had urged her to make camp on the return and continue their journey by daylight but she had wanted to put as much distance between herself and Wend as possible. She felt guilty for the pressure she had put on the horses insisting they travel at full speed for most of the ride. While the others had eaten before turning in for a few hours sleep, she had gone straight to her room avoiding Trwyn.

She had seen him approaching as she finished removing the armour from her horse. She had called to one of the boys who were waiting to help any who requested assistance and allowed him to finish seeing to the horses stabling. It was something she would not have done under normal circumstances but she needed time to think before she could face him.

On entering her room, she had stripped and called for hot water to be brought. She had scrubbed at her skin until it was red. But she knew the feelings which had disturbed her could not be washed away. How could her own body betray her? It must have been a spell. She could not accept that a man she hated and despised as much as she did could also inspire such feelings of desire.

The emotions she had felt were different from the ones she had experienced with Trwyn. Those had been based on love and affection. These feelings she felt for Wend were animalistic, primitive, solely about the physical. She tried to think about it logically. If one had only ever seen Wend Y Mawr without knowing what sort of man he was that perhaps it would be an explanation she could not deny his physical attributes. She knew what he was and she knew what he was capable of, so how could she still experience these feelings.

Exhausted both mentally and physically she climbed into bed. Her dreams, however, brought no solace. She found him waiting there for her, the touch of his hand on her arm, his lips seeking out hers over and over again as she struggled to escape. His dark eyes greedily moving over her body, holding her in place unable to pull away. She tried to replace his image with that of Trwyn, and for a while would succeed but as soon as she let her guard down he would be there again. In her dreams it was Trwyn who lowered his mouth to her breast but it was Wend who looked back up from it.

Her eyes flew open, she laid on the bed trying to decide what she should do. Part of her longed to sneak through the corridors and sneak in to Trwyn's chamber. To seek a comfort in his arms that may push the dreams away, let his touch cleanse her skin replacing the sensations Wend had placed in her mind. She knew that that was unacceptable but also she was scared that he would sense somehow what had happened in the mist. Although it had been against her will she knew he would feel he had been betrayed. Finally she decided she needed air, she rose and dressed.

She wandered aimlessly through the corridors. She greeted each person automatically as she passed without really seeing them. Eventually she arrived at a staircase, she paused. The staircase was one of the few that had not been regularly maintained. She ducked under cobwebs as she wound her way up, careful not to lose her footing on the worn steps. The tower was no longer used. Her father had chosen to build up the battlements round the castle during his reign rather than restore the ancient watch tower. The roof had fallen since her last visit up here. As a child she had often snuck up here despite being warned of its dangers.

It was a clear afternoon she could see almost to the borders of the kingdom. The sun illuminated the view with barely a cloud to obscure its rays. Under other circumstances it would have been the perfect day to saddle her horse and ride out but now she could only think of the contrast with the previous evening.

Looking down into the courtyard she saw people moving like toy dolls, going about normal daily business, but she knew nothing could be normal again. She cleared the rubble to one side making space to sit down. She needed to clear her head, to think straight. She needed to talk to someone but could think of no one whom she could confide in. No one would understand her confusion, she didn't understand her reactions herself. She closed her eyes, her back resting against the ancient stones, and tried to think through what had happened.

When she had first seen him she had felt the hate for him, for everything he had done. With each failed attempt of her sword her hatred had grown, she wondered if her father had felt the same way before he died. It had only been when he forced the images into her head that she had felt anything else, it had to be the magick. That would explain it, they were not her feelings, only his. But did it? Not fully, it didn't explain why, when he had grabbed her and kissed her, she had felt her body respond, why though her mind screamed for him to get off her that her body longed to taste more.

She did not hear the footsteps coming up the tower. She heard a stone dislodge and opened her eyes to find Celdwady stood looking down at her. She sprung to her feet startled. Then impulsively she threw herself at him, burying her head against his shoulder and let the tears flow. He held her and stroked her hair soothing her as her father would have done. When at last her tears subsided she stepped back from him, embarrassed by her own show of weakness.

He smiled at her "You should have come straight to me,"

it was then she realised he knew everything.

"Why?"

The question escaped her lips before she had time to think about it. She bit down on her lip scared to hear his reply.

He motioned for her to be seated again, she sank to her former position resting against the wall.

Celdwady settled himself on a lump of fallen masonry, he took a few moments to compose himself before he began.

She had expected him to begin by answering her question but instead his first questions threw her

"Do you love Trwyn? Are you ready to be bound to him?"

"Yes but..." her voice trailed off, and he waited patiently for her to find the words to continue. "How can I be bound to him when I must sacrifice myself, it wouldn't be fair to him. He is a good man he deserves more than that"

"Have you considered that that may be his decision to make? Don't get me wrong he should know your time together will be limited but it may be his fate to love you and he will, no matter whether you are here or not."

"But how can I be joined with him when...when...when I..."

Celdwady raised his hand and interrupted her "When you responded to a man you loathed?"

"Yes"

The admission spoken out loud from her own lips sickened her. Admitting her feelings to herself had been hard enough to accept but to say it to someone else sickened her.

"Your love for Trwyn has nothing to do with the feelings that Wend made you feel. It is hard to explain at the minute but I shall try to sooth you as best I can at this time. Soon we will take a short journey and all will become clear to you, but for now you must trust me. Your attraction to Wend is that of opposites. You are the light and he is the dark, the two of you are day and night, neither of you can exist without the other. Between you, you hold the balance of this whole world in your hands, not just your own kingdoms. Up to now the balance has been heavily on Wends side"

He stood, reached down and drew Jacantha to her feet. "Look around your kingdom, look beyond your own borders what do you see?"

"Nothing"

"Precisely. You should see other castles in the distance, smoke from hamlets, villages and towns but there is nothing, he has destroyed all around you."

He waited, allowing his words to sink in.

Jacantha studied the landscape, she followed the roads along which thriving villages had once stood providing a prosperous trade route between kingdoms. Now dotted along them she saw blackened scars where they had once stood. From this vantage point the full extent of Wend Y Mawr's exploits was evident. Only the few miles within reach of her castle still showed signs of habitation, just beyond the castle walls a makeshift village had sprung up of hastily constructed wooden huts to house the overflow of those who had moved her seeking protection of the solid walls and troops within the castle. The sight before her reminded her of the duty she had sworn, she must put her personal feelings to one side and find a way to defeat him.

Celdwady continued

"Now he seeks to possess you as well, but as he affects you, you affect him. His very desires will be his downfall. I cannot tell you all, I do not know all the turn's fate has in store. But I do know our time is limited, in four weeks at the next full moon you will face Wend Y Mawr again. There is much to do before then. You must be bound to Trwyn before that time, and we must take a journey for a few days that will prepare you and make all clear. But now you must rest. I will seek out Trwyn and act in your father's place in the match. You must return to your chamber and sleep now."

He pulled a vial from within his robes and handed it to her, he stood and watched as silently she turned and slipped out of view down the steps. He turned his eyes towards the desolate waste land that Wend's kingdom had become and muttered a prayer under his breath

"May the Lady give her the strength to endure what must come."

Chapter Twelve

Wend was in a celebratory mood when he arrived back at his castle, the loss of twenty men forgotten in thoughts of her lips. He hadn't gotten quite the response he wanted, he had hoped he would be bringing her back her with him as he returned, but he could wait. He had felt the fire within her as his lips had locked on hers. She may never love him, she would resist him, but he knew he could overcome her, physically at least. When the time was right she would be his. He kept repeating the words to himself as a mantra, she would be his.

The castle was in a state of confusion on his return. The rest of his men had risen and finding a party gone had set out to follow but had taken the wrong direction. Realising their error, they had returned to the castle to discover if there had been any news and had decided it would be best to wait there for their leaders return. Wend cursed himself, realising in his own haste he had not left instructions of where they were headed.

Nadredd stood back watching him, listening to him account to previous evening's proceedings. He had never seen Wend like this. He had never known him to make foolish decisions such as this, riding to meet an army with a handful of men. Nadredd was concerned that the man he considered a friend, almost a brother count act so irrationally. Every bone in his body was telling him this was wrong that Wend should turn away from this path while he still could, but Nadredd feared it was already too late as he observed the look in Wends eyes.

Wend approached him clasping him by the shoulder, his eyes bright as he talked of her response when he had kissed her. Nadredd pretended to be happy for him, to agree with Wend's expectations for the future but inside a chill went through him. He did not believe she would ever give herself willingly and he was apprehensive for their futures if Wend did not succeed. He smiled back at Wend, congratulating him, while inside he stifled the urge to scream at him that this course was folly.

The men called for ale to be brought and set about forgetting the previous evening in drink and the women. Wend stood watching them for a few moments before he made an excuse to Nadredd and disappeared into the small chamber aside from the hall. Nadredd watched him go, he was unable to shake off the feeling that he needed to speak of his concerns to Wend. He was determined he would do so at the first opportunity he got whether he wanted to hear his fears or not.

Wend approached the orb and placed his hands upon it but nothing would appear, he wondered why that should be, he had never failed before. He tried again, focusing his mind on the object of his desire, the orb glowed but no clear image would form. The explanation must be that he had depleted his energies with the shield spell he could think of no other reason why it would not obey his wishes. He would wait until later allowing his power to regain strength and then try again.

Rather than dwell upon his failure he turned his attention to a table at the rear of the room. The concoction was nearly distilled, the dark liquid bubbling to produce the potion he used to control the concubines. He knew he would have to venture out to collect more thistles for the next batch his supplies were growing low. He had been working on improving the potion desiring that while it should still make the women compliant it should not dull their senses as it did at present. He wanted the women to happily perform the depravities he demanded but retain the ability to feel the pain he enjoyed inflicting.

He would need to isolate a few of the concubines for trial or possibly one or two of the breeders who were nearing the end of their bearing days. Yes, that would be better he could be sure that the original potion was not interfering with his results. It was a shame their bodies would have been spoilt by childbirth, but he smiled as he contemplated their soft skin, how easily it would mark beneath his lash.

In another bottle bubbled a separate liquid, if he were successful this potion would only require a single dose to prevent the concubines conceiving allowing him to alter the potency of the other potion as required. He loathed the idea more than ever now that he would have to force the potion upon Jacantha to make her submit to him. He wanted the fire he had felt within her to remain undiminished for their union. If he could resolve the potion strength then he could make her willing without dampening the flames within her.

He rang a bell and the chief concubine appeared after a few minutes. She had gained her position by her ability to survive castle life, she had played along with the role of obedient servant. If Wend had realised the truth, that the concoction no longer had any effect on her, other than to ensure she could no longer carry a child, she knew would have been in danger. He poured a small amount from the fresh batch into a glass and watched her drink it before handing her the flask containing the rest. She took it silently. Once upon a time she had felt guilty about drugging the others, now she accepted that her own desire for survival was stronger. She stood waiting his dismissal, nervous as his eyes seemed to look into her soul.

At nearly forty she had outlived many of the women who had been brought and forced into servitude, but she knew her looks were fading. She also knew she was in danger for a greater reason, she had been a girl when the man before her had brought her here. While she had aged she was one of the few left to testify to the fact that he had not. Had he not been so sure that his potion controlled her still he would have disposed of her, she had no doubts regarding that. She was careful whenever in his presence to give him no reason to question or doubt that she was under his control.

Wend looked at her. He had not noticed how much she had aged until recently. The sight of her repulsed him, yet she had her uses. The thought of finding another who would so willingly obey him in betraying her sisters was something he could not waste energy on at this time. He moved closer and thrust a hand between her legs, his fingers slipped inside her easily. He withdrew his hand and wiped it on his trousers. The woman trembled, as if sensing she had just failed a test.

He turned his back on her, then announced that her services would no longer be required in the great hall. She would retain her position preparing the others, as long as she carried on performing those duties as was expected of her she would be allowed to continue living in the castle. Neither needed to say that there would be no other life other than life in the castle, both knew she would never be allowed to leave other than to go to her grave. She thanked him, as with a motion of the hand she was dismissed. She scurried from the room before he could change his mind, knowing her safety now depended on avoiding his attention. The potion she clutched in her hand gave her a week or two at most to consider her options before she need face Wend to collect the next batch. Her thoughts were a whirl of emotions as she fled back to the concubine's sleeping chambers.

Wend turned his attention back to the table and picked up an old book. As a young man learning from the stranger, he had scribbled books of thoughts and bits of information he had gathered. He had not been the best student, he knew that, he had resented the time it had taken to extract the information, the time spent learning the names of all the plants before they had began with the real magick, and he had thought the stranger a fool.

A fool with knowledge he wanted but the stranger had droned on about responsibility, he had talked about the uses for which the powers should be used. The stranger had not realised the potential these abilities had in the hands of someone with the ambition to truly test them. He tried to recall the strangers name, he must have known it at some point yet it escaped him, it was not important the man was long dead no one had mourned his passing. Had the stranger truly mastered the skills which he taught he would have protected himself. No Wend mused, the man may have had the knowledge but he was lacking in talent and the imagination to appreciate the true extent of the gift he had possessed. He had a feeling that there was something he was missing, something he had not taken into account. Maybe the answer was in here, he moved round the room lighting extra candles. Then pulling his chair into the circle of bloodstones he settled down with the book, searching for the answer that evaded him.

Hours later, as the candles began to splutter out of existence, he put the books down. He had found nothing that could explain his slight feeling of unease. Yet he still felt, there was something he needed to know hidden within the pages. He decided he would return to the books later, for now he needed to get out of the castle, possibly a change of atmosphere would aid his thinking. He grabbed a heavy cloak hanging from a hook on the wall and a small sack. The great hall was full of writhing bodies as he passed through, he paid no attention to them, nor they to him. Only Nadredd noticed him slip away.

Nadredd waited a few moments before he grabbed his sword and followed Wend from the castle. He had expected him to head to the stables, which would have made it more difficult to follow, but instead, he had headed out on foot into the woods at the rear of buildings. Nadredd kept his distance, watching as Wend appeared to move randomly from one clump of bushes to the next.

Nadredd moved stealthily using the undergrowth as coverage, he believed he had followed unobserved, as Wend continued seemingly unaware of his presence. He was startled therefore when Wend called that if he were intent on spying he could make himself useful while doing it. He approached him; looking down at Wend's hands, he saw they contained several different types of fungus. He gave him a questioning look, although he was aware of the potions Wend made use of he had never been privy to the ingredients that were used. Wend chose not to notice and pointed to a bunch of thistles, instructing him to harvest the younger ones. Nadredd went over and picked them, all the time observing Wend, debating how to broach his concerns.

"Wend, we have known each other a long time, I think of you as a brother," he paused waiting for a response. Wend remained silent, Nadredd took this as a sign he may continue. "I am worried about you. You are not yourself, lately I have noticed changes in the way you act. This girl has got under your skin, are you sure she is...."

Wend interrupted "Worth it? Nadredd it has gone beyond that, she is necessary. I do not deny thoughts of her drive me mad. I desire her, more than

I have ever desired any other woman, but there is more to it than that. I must have her, yes that is true, but it is not solely her I wish to possess, I want all she brings with her. Look around you, how much longer can things continue as they are. We raid, we take what we want, but the pickings are getting scarce. Do you think that rabble in there are ambitious enough to want more glory? Do you believe they are skilled or loyal enough, to challenge new borders to satisfy our needs?

Every battle I waste more and more energy protecting those pathetic creatures, they have become too lazy and gluttonous to even defend themselves in a fight. They care only for their pleasures and do not want to work too hard to achieve it. I cannot allow things to continue as they are. Of all of those who dwell within my walls, you are the only one I could trust to willingly lay down your life for me."

"So, that is your plan? You think her warriors will fight for you? You truly believe that they will be commanded by you?"

"I think they will do whatever she tells them, and she will do as I tell her"

He stepped over to Nadredd and clasped him by the shoulders "And you my friend, will be there alongside me, imagine what we can do with not only her army, but the craftsmen, we can build an empire, we can stretch our borders. No one will be able to defeat us,"

"And if she doesn't come?"

Wend looked at him "She will"

Nadredd knew further discussion was pointless, though Wends vision of the future reassured him he was still thinking of a bigger picture, he could not quiet the unease that dwelt within him. Only time would tell if Wends plans would come to fruition, Nadredd could only be sure it would not be as simple as his friend believed.

The two men continued in silence, Wend gathering various mushrooms and herbs and Nadredd gathering the thistles, until the sun began to slip from the sky. In the distance a wolf howled, and the hairs on Wends neck stood up. Something about the wolves, was that what he sought to remember?

He motioned to Nadredd to follow him and they returned to the castle. He left Nadredd in the hall and returned to the chamber, he looked towards the orb but refrained from attempting to use it, one failure he decided, was enough for today. Setting aside the cloak, Wend began to prepare the mushrooms, he had something special in mind, something he had not done for many years. Once he had finished he placed them in a bowl and added a dark liquid from a flask, it would take a few days to brew. He blew out the remaining candles and once again entered the great hall.

He stood for a moment, he had no real desire to join in but Nadredd's questions had struck a chord. Until he had her in his power he must keep his men loyal. He could not be seen to be weakening to them. He spotted Nadredd seated across the hall, a mass of dark hair bobbed up and down in his lap. He strode over, loosening his belt as he did so. He wrapped one end of the belt around his hand and stood behind the girl. With a fluid movement he brought the leather down across her buttocks, a red welt immediately springing up across her pale flesh. The girl yelped and Nadredd grabbed her hair, forcing his manhood further into her open mouth. Once more, Wend yielded the belt, watching the angry red marks appear, and with each blow he delivered Wend watched Nadredd force himself deeper into the girl's throat. He felt himself stirring, her pain the catalyst for his desire.

He reached down and grabbed her hips, pulling her up so she bent at the waist. In a quick movement his trousers fell to the ground and he thrust into her. His hand in the middle of her back, ensuring with each thrust, he forced her head lower. He could feel the energy building as Nadredd came closer to release. He forgot about the girl, his body continuing almost mechanically, as he allowed himself to tune into the energy instead. It hung in the air much like the fog he had created the day before, looking round he could see small blue flashes as the energy built around those engaged in sexual acts.

A blue flash in front of him alerted him to the fact Nadredd had released himself deep into the girl's throat. Through the haze of the energy field Wend watched as she gagged trying hard to swallow down the other man's tribute. Nadredd was watching him now; he thrust harder and saw the energy building again round the girl. Nadredd had slipped his hand between her legs and was teasing her as Wend drove into her. He felt the girl shudder and a blue flash escaped her body.

He withdrew, fascinated by this display of the energies he was observing, he was sure no one else could see this phenomenon. This was a new development, not yet ready to contribute his own share, he moved over to where two girls awaited being called into service. He flung the first to the floor, forcing her on her back with her legs spread, the second he forced on to all fours, above the first, facing the opposite way. Each now had their heads buried between the legs of the other. With fascination, he watched as a blue glow began to form around their entangled limbs, mentally speculating on the reason for its appearance.

The belt, still wound round his hand, found its mark again, this time he was rewarded not only with the sight of the welt rising but the urgency it provoked in girl on top. He brought it down again, this time to the side so the end of the belt curled round to catch the girl underneath. He watched the two women squirm in pain as a welt appeared across the side of the lower woman's breast. He dropped to belt and brought his hand down across the top girl's buttocks, smiling at the hand print that appeared, and the faint blue sparks that came from it. He repeated the blow watching the sparks grow stronger.

Finally, sensing his own growing urgency, he knelt behind the girl on top and entered her, the girl underneath still lapping at her and now him as well. He plunged himself into her, watching the blue sparks coming from her body grow in volume. She came too quickly, before he was ready, he sensed a shift in the energy, it was moving away from her towards the next woman. He pushed the spent woman aside and moved round to enter the girl who had laid beneath them both. This time he was rewarded with a bolt of energy which seemed to fill the whole room as he timed his release to hers.

He rolled over and lay on his back. It felt like the energy had ripped through his body, he felt electrified in a way he had never experienced before. He was no longer aware of what was going on within the room, only that he was connected to the energy in some new manner. A blue haze now filled the entire room, he was vaguely aware of hands on his body, a warm mouth lowering on to him. He allowed the energy to surround him and immerse him enjoying the sensation as it swept through him.

Nadredd sat back watching Wends display; he knew something was happening, although what he could not tell. He could feel a change in the air, then as Wend finished with the last girl and rolled onto the ground, he had seen a faint red glow begin to form round him. Wend had seemed to grow in stature, already a big man, he had seemed a giant towering over the girl in his grasp. He knew from the roar Wend had let out, that he had come deep within the girl, yet he lay there now, his still hard manhood stood erect from his body showing no signs of fading.

Nadredd grabbed another girl, he forced her head down into Wends lap. Wend lay there motionless, yet his body responded to the girl's motions, and when she looked up at Nadredd again, a trickle of semen spilled from her lips. The glow around Wend increased, yet he remained erect. Nadredd did not know the source of Wend's power, but he knew that the sexual energies maintained and strengthened it. That much Wend had confided in him, the question was what was happening now, and what he should do about it. He worried that laying here like this, Wend was vulnerable, a few of the men were unhappy at the previous day's events, they were starting to realise just how they were disposable in Wends eyes.

While Nadredd was lost in thought at what to do for the best, he failed to notice that his fears were being realised. He was not the only one who had noticed Wend lying unresponsive on the floor. By the time Nadredd spotted the potential attacker, he was only a few feet away from Wends prone body, dagger in hand. He lunged towards him as Nadredd flew to his feet; the dagger plunged towards Wend's chest. A few inches above its target, it flew out of the man's hand.

The man appeared to be screaming but no sound came from his throat. Then starting from the hand which had held the offending weapon, smoke began to pour from the man's body. There were shrieks and screams from around him as people backed away from flames that began to appear, devouring his flesh. He began to circle frantically, looking for assistance before throwing himself to the ground and rolling in an attempt the put the flames out. No one moved to assist him, it was evident whatever was happening with Wend, his powers were increasing.

All watched with horror as the man continued to burn, all the time seeming to remain conscious of what was happening to him. Eventually, one of the men could bear to watch it no longer and grabbing up a sword, moved to thrust it into the man's chest to end his suffering. The sword appeared to pass straight through him, failing in its mission; too scared to try again the man retreated.

Eventually the man ceased to move and the flames subsided. Nadredd ordered his charred remains be removed from the hall, the men were reluctant to obey but the fear of the punishment disobedience may bring spurred them to action. The first man to reach out, hesitantly to the body, had expected to be burnt by the heat that such a blaze must have required. Instead he turned to Nadredd with surprise and announced the body was freezing. Nadredd reached out his hand to feel for himself, the remains were ice cold. He motioned for them to remove it and then dismissed all the men from the hall.

The concubines he ordered to remain, though a few had fled in the panic that had accompanied the man's demise. He ordered one to Wend, they all stood frozen on the spot, having seen what had happened to the man, he understood their reluctance to obey him. He grabbed the girl nearest him; she struggled as he dragged her across the room. Tears streamed down her face as he forced her mouth towards Wends still erect manhood. A slight change in the atmosphere told him he was right, that somehow Wend could sense still what was happening around him, and that the man's destruction had been intentional.

Nadredd stood over the concubines as he instructed them one after the other to attend to Wend. The Nadredd watched as the red glow around Wend grew stronger and intensified with each one, his eyes did not see each individual blue spark that left their bodies and held Wend mesmerised. He settled down on the floor near his friend and waited to see what would come next.

Chapter Thirteen

Celdwady stood over her. She had slept thirty-six hours thanks to the nightshade and horse chestnut potion he had given her. He had brewed it stronger than was strictly necessary while being careful that the dose would not be fatal, but she needed her strength for the weeks ahead. He was tempted to leave her and allow her to wake naturally once it wore off but time would not allow that. There was so much to do in the next few weeks, he himself was still unsure of so much that was to come.

Brawd stood behind him, a small vial clasped in his hand. He passed it to Celdwady and made to leave the room but was stopped by a gesture from the older man. It was time that Brawd begin his education in earnest. The scent of lavender drifted into the room as Celdwady removed the stopper from the vial and let a few drops fall onto Jacantha's lips. He watched as it took effect and she began to stir.

Jacantha opened her eyes slowly, it took a few seconds before the room came into focus and she saw her visitors. Celdwady passed the vial to her and ordered she drink the rest of the vial. She obeyed without hesitancy. A minute later the draft had taken its effect and she felt restored and sat up. Celdwady sensed Brawd's discomfort at their situation. They were alone in the room with their queen half dressed, something the young apprentice was not prepared for and his sheltered upbringing had ensured he had not experienced before.

Celdwady doubted that Brawd had ever seen the female form undressed, it was however, something to which he must become accustomed. Here in a place such as this the people only recognised male and female in terms of the pairings they made. The women fought alongside the men, they wore the same armour into battle and after, when it was removed, only a mate looked at the flesh for anything other than to check for injuries. He remembered his own experiences when he had first arrived, even he had felt stirrings at the sight of so much flesh but it had soon passed as it would for the younger man. Celdwady's suggestion that they meet in his chambers in half an hour was met with relief by Brawd, who was having difficulty removing his gaze from Jacantha's bare shoulders.

Once they had left the room Jacantha slipped from beneath the blankets and dressed. She crossed the room to the window and looked out down at the courtyard below. It seemed the castle had continued life without her, people moved back and forth carrying out their daily duties. Horses stood saddled impatiently pawing the ground as they waited for their riders. Groups of people moved in unison heading out to the fields or carrying wood or water for use in the kitchens. In the midst of all the bustle and movement, one lone figure stood still.

Trwyn stood alone in the centre of the courtyard, his eyes turned upwards toward her room. He seemed to be waiting for some sign that she had awakened, she stepped back unsure of whether her presence at the window had registered. She remembered her conversation with Celdwady and wondered if their union had been arranged. Again, she felt doubt about the fairness of the situation, was it right to enter into such a match if destiny held her fate firmly within its grasp.

She grabbed her brush and stood before the mirror brushing her hair then binding it into a long plait with leather thongs. She stared at her image in the mirror, in the last few days something behind her eyes had changed. She couldn't find words to express what it was she saw there, strength, a certain hardness. All Jacantha knew was there was a glint there she had never noticed before, the reflection of her eyes in the glass reminded her of something, but what it was escaped her. She turned and headed to Celdwady's chamber ready to learn more of her fate, as she turned a corner she glanced back just in time to see Trwyn heading towards her chamber.

She knocked and waited to be admitted, a voice within replied and she opened the door. When she entered the room Celdwady and Brawd were bent over a parchment. She hesitated not wanting to disturb them. Without turning around Celdwady motioned she should be seated. She obeyed, and waited, it never entered her head that as queen she should have been treated more deferentially, though she was ruler is was the Guardian, who commanded respect. A few minutes later they had finished with the parchment. Celdwady took a seat opposite her; Brawd hovered for a moment, before taking a seat next to her. She and Brawd sat like children waiting for a lesson to begin, she stifled the urge to giggle at the situation, an action which did not go unnoticed. Celdwady looked from one to the other and laughed.

"Do not look so worried both of you, you look like naughty children waiting to be scolded." The tension in the room lifted slightly

. "First, let us deal with your impending union. I have discussed the situation with both Trwyn and his father at length. I will not lie, his father has concerns as any parent would, but Trwyn wishes the match, whether it last a day or a lifetime. As time is an issue here, and he is eager for the event to take place, it has been agreed the ceremony will take place in two weeks' time, at the rising of the new moon. I take it this is acceptable to you?"

He paused to allow her time to nod her assent.

"Before that time, we, the three of us, will take a short journey. I have discussed the necessity of this with the elders. Although they think it highly unorthodox, they have been made to understand the gravity of the situation. Your brother will stand as ruler in your place during your absence, it will only be for a few days but will help him gain confidence which he will need in the future."

Celdwady stopped to register their reactions. Neither spoke but waited for him to continue.

"I have discussed with Brawd the visions I have had, some of which he has shared. We have four weeks until the next full moon to prepare for all that must come. The day after tomorrow we must leave for our journey. I am tempted to tell you of where we are going and what to expect but the runes have warned against it, so there is no point asking. Jacantha, I told you before you must place your trust in me, and now I repeat that request. For this morning I would like you to display that trust, by relating to us everything that has happened to you since your father's death."

He looked directly at Jacantha as he said this.

"Some of it you may think of no importance, or be reluctant to repeat but it is imperative we know all that has passed. There may be knowledge in there you do not see the importance of, which will prove to be vital to what is to come."

The next few hours passed with Jacantha relating everything, from the arrival of the wolf at her father's pyre to the present. When she described what had passed between herself and Trwyn she blushed but the responses of the others did not escape her. Brawd's blush was almost as deep as her own, his eyes avoided her but Celdwady appeared to be thrown deep into thought as she described the feeling of leaving her body. Her encounter with Wend, she found harder to describe, faltering to find the words to explain her feelings. Celdwady asked a few questions clarifying his mind on certain points, then dismissed her arranging she should meet him that evening on the tower where he had found her before. Brawd remained silent though she could sense his unease with what he had heard.

When she left the chamber, she felt strangely relieved. By recounting her experiences, it seemed she had put them into perspective, in sharing her thoughts it felt like a weight had been lifted from her. She headed to the great hall, hunger guiding her footsteps as she followed the aroma that drifted along the corridors. She had been surprised to learn from

Celdwady how long she had slept. Worry forced its way into her thoughts about how she would be viewed by the other warriors when they saw her. They had lost only one man, yet they had failed to achieve what they had set out to. Then on their return, she had abandoned them to sleep for such a long time. Would they understand?

As she entered the hall her worries were relieved. She was greeted enthusiastically, whatever reason Celdwady had given to the elders to explain her need for rest, had been accepted. Word had been passed amongst the rest of the warriors and she was met with smiles and jovial teasing regarding her repose. She spotted Trywn seated at the far end of the room he saw her at the same moment, and responding to his gesture, moved to join him. He rose as she approached. Jacantha was surprised when he suddenly grabbed her and kissed her.

She stood in shock, not responding to him, until the cheer filling the room permeated her senses. Then she remembered, they were to be bound, obviously the news had spread and met with approval. He released her and stepped back hesitant, fearful he had overstepped the mark; she apologised and kissed him back quickly to allay his fears. As she took her seat, a plate appeared before her, she thanked the woman who had brought it for her. A glance at the top table revealed her brother glaring at her for not taking her proper seat, she smiled at him knowing he would not stay mad at her for long. She ate heartily finding that she was ravenous, she mopped up the last of the rabbit stew with a chunk of bread, then giving

Trwyn a grin finished what remained on his plate also.

Trwyn sat beside her, watching every move, and again Jacantha wondered if he had seen through the fog. After her meal she asked him to accompany her on a walk, there were things she had to hear from his own lips before she could feel secure in the decisions which had been made. He seemed reluctant, Jacantha was confused given that since their first kiss he had used every opportunity to be by her side. After a little coaxing and teasing he finally agreed and they left the hall together, the nudges and winks passing between those present not passing unobserved by Jacantha, she merely smiled at them as they passed out of the room.

They walked in silence Trwyn appeared happy to allow Jacantha to lead the way. A short distance from the castle was a small brook; Jacantha removed her boots and settled on the banking, her feet slipping down into the cool, glistening water. Trwyn settled beside her, a hand strayed to her hair and his lips sought hers.

Jacantha raised her fingers to his lips, holding him back

"Patience, there are matters we must discuss first."

Trwyn tried not to look hurt

"What is there to talk about? My father and Celdwady have arranged the match, everything is set. Unless, you are going to tell me, you have changed your mind already?"

"No! Of course not, but it's not that simple."

"Yes, it is! I love you and you love me and we will be joined, forever." He gazed into her eyes as he said the last word.

"But that's my point, it cannot be forever."

Trwyn tried to interrupt her but she placed her fingertips to his lips once more.

"We do not know how long we will have, it could only be weeks. You cannot claim to be unaware of the prophecy, you know it talks of sacrifice, my sacrifice. Neither of us can be sure what form that sacrifice will take, but we are warriors and that sacrifice usually ends with death. I need to know you understand this. I need to know, that if I have to lay my life down you can accept that. And I guess this is the biggest question, can you say that you can stand back and allow whatever must happen, to happen without interference?"

Trwyn was silent for a minute before replying

"I don't care if we have a day or a lifetime, I just know that my life would be empty without you. I know that I may lose you and I have to be prepared for that, but I believe we will be reunited, so I can live with that. I cannot promise to stand by and watch you fall, how could anyone promise that but I can only give you my word that I will try."

Jacantha looked at him. She knew how hard it would be for him, she would do all she could, spare him as much pain as she could but even if she did not go through with the match he would suffer. She leaned in and kissed him. His hands reached to pull her body to his, his hands moving over her body but she pushed him back.

"Soon, we must wait till after the ceremony, it is important. However much we may both want more we must not get carried away or place temptation in our path."

He tried to protest, after all who would know,

"We will be joined in a couple of weeks, even if you caught on with child now no one would know, I know you want me, nearly as much as I want you." His voice teasing as he tried to persuade her, his fingertips traced circles on her thigh.

She held firm, slapping his hand away.

"Please, it is important to me that when I give myself to you, I do it fully."

In a playful tone she added. "You forget I am Queen I have an example to set. I cannot risk letting you get me into trouble, what if the match were delayed for some reason, just think of the scandal."

He looked at her, then smiled

"Alright my Lady, if that is important to you, then it is important to me." He paused "I may as well have a swim to cool me down instead then."

Jacantha did not notice the mischievous glint in his eyes at his final words.

In one swift movement, he scooped her up and laughing threw her into the water. She surfaced laughing, all other cares forgotten, for this afternoon at least, he was the boy she had grown up with, and she was just the girl he loved.

She swam to the banking, reached up for his out stretched arm

"Boy, are you in trouble now"

and she pulled him down into the water. For the next few hours they splashed in the water before climbing out and laying spread out in the grass, the sun beating down upon them dying their clothes.

It was dusk by the time they returned to the castle. They sat together in the great hall for dinner, again enduring the nudges and winks of those present. Jacantha again found herself devouring the food, Trwyn laughed, watching her fill her plate with piles of wild boar, until the dish in front of them stood empty. Seeing her looking round for more, he rose and walked over the open fireplace, taking up a knife, he carved more meat from the hog turning slowly over the smouldering logs and returned it to her. She graciously accepted, helping herself to more of the warm meat before finally leaning back and declaring herself full.

As everyone finished their meals and the plates were cleared, the tables were moved against the walls and those present gathered round the fire. Jacantha sat next to Trwyn on one of the long benches, her head leaning on his shoulder, as stories were told by others to the assembled crowd. Jacantha felt a contentment she would not have thought possible with so much still unresolved. As she looked around the room at the others gathered, each face told its own story of the hardships they had endured, and the solace they took where they could. Realising the hour was growing late she made her excuses to Trwyn; he rose escorting her from the hall. He pulled her into the shadows of an alcove and kissed her, the kiss was slow and tender, before parted ways for the night.

Trwyn departed for his chambers in the barracks, he was aware that she was meeting Celdwady but did not question why or think to follow her. She had mentioned earlier the journey she must soon leave on, he was unhappy at the thought of her leaving him behind, as he retired to his bed he was intent on finding a way that he could persuade her to allow him to join them. He soon slept, his dreams full of scenarios where he came to her rescue, all the while aware he could not save her from her destiny, and more determined than ever to try to do so.

Jacantha climbed the stairs to the tower once more, her feelings now so different to those of forty-eight hours ago. Celdwady awaited her on the tower. His furs made him seem larger than he was, he looked like a bear silhouetted against the moon Jacantha thought as she approached. He motioned for her to sit by him and they sat upon the fallen masonry where he had held her on their last meeting here. Jacantha's gaze turned to the stars and the waning moon. She felt a sense of peace spread throughout her whole being.

She looked back to Celdwady

"I am ready to begin."

He nodded and handed her a crystal, she looked down at it. A moonstone, pure and unpolished, she turned it over in her palm letting her fingertips trace the rough edges. Celdwady instructed her to close her eyes and began to lead her through meditation exercises. As she concentrated she felt the air around her grow heavy, her senses picked out Celdwady's voice and she focused her mind solely on following his instructions until he commanded her to open her eyes. For a moment the moon brilliance hurt her eyes before the adjusted, she realised she was seeing everything around her with greater clarity. As she had during her encounter with the wolf her hearing too seemed to be picking up sounds far beyond her normal range. Celdwady gave her new instructions and as she focused her gaze on the moonstone as he had told her to do, a faint light began to emanate from it.

Chapter Fourteen

Wend was unaware of the passage of time. Faces of women, sometimes above him, others lowering and raising heads from his groin blurred in his vision. He could not feel their lips or flesh against his although he was aware of the actions they performed. All he saw clearly were the brilliant lights created by the energy as it surrounded him. Gradually the bursts of energy begin to decrease in intensity and frequency; the room seemed too charged to hold anymore. Slowly he began to be more aware of his surroundings and he felt the tension ease within his manhood as his erection began to subside. A concubine was just about to lower herself down onto him, when he raised his hand and said

"Enough".

He could not fail to see the look of relief on Nadredd's face as he sat up and looked around the room.

"How long?"

His voice sounded strange to him, as if something about it had changed.

"A little over a day. How do you feel? Do you remember what happened?" Nadredd's questions flew at him in rapid succession.

Wend paused before answering, how much to share? A part of him longed to tell someone what he had experienced, yet to share his secrets made him vulnerable

"I feel better than I have ever felt before. I remember everything that happened though some I will admit is a little blurry. Who was the man? I could see his energy and saw what happened but could not recognise his face."

Nadredd considered this before answering,

"It was Gethwyn. You say you saw it, does that mean you were in control of it? That what happened was intentional? Do not get me wrong he deserved it." He added hastily.

Wend thought about this, he did not wish to give away how little control he had felt over of what had happened.

"Of course."

He immediately felt a slight pang of something like guilt, he may not have always told Nadredd everything, but this was the first time he had told him an outright lie.

Nadredd knew Wend had lied to him. He had stood by his lord through so much over the last few years and although he knew the difference in their positions, he had thought that Wend trusted him. He looked at Wend once more, he seemed to have recovered so Nadredd asked permission to be excused, and returned to his chamber.

On entering his chamber he went to the window and looked out. In the distance he could still see the ruined remains of his childhood home. He allowed his mind to drift back to the day when Wend had ridden into the village. He had been little more than a boy, fourteen almost fifteen; he had been an orphan for years. The other villagers had barely acknowledged his existence, he knew there was something about his parents that marked him as different, but never knew what it had been.

After Wend had been through the town, there had been no one left to ask, he would never know the reason he had been an outcast. He had survived by begging scraps from the few who would tolerate the sight of him, but mostly he survived on his wits and quick fingers. He had stayed hidden, watching as Wend and his men cut down all they came across, except the younger women, who they had herded together in the village square. He had seen the buildings, engulfed in flames and towers of black smoke which rose high into the sky. He had wanted to flee but something held him in place, part of him longed to see, needed to see, what would happen next. He watched the bodies pile up, until he knew that the men of the village were no more. He had then turned his gaze to the women huddled together. He remembered even now, the fear he saw in their eyes, he had also known several of the village women were missing.

He watched as the women were divided into two groups, the younger, prettier ones bound and thrown into wagons, while the older ones were left stood in the middle of the square. The anticipation of what their fate would be excited him. He had peaked through enough windows in his quest for survival, to believe he had an idea of what was to follow. When it started he was shocked, what he saw bore no resemblance to the lovemaking he had witnessed before in his nocturnal wanderings. The screams at first made him feel sick, but he still could not move away. He could not tear his eyes away from these strange men, who ripped the clothing away revealing bare flesh, before climbing on top of them, grunting and laughing, as they took advantage of the defenceless women.

As he watched longer, he found the screams began to excite him, he felt something stirring in his loins, it had never happened before except occasionally on waking. These new feelings confused him, while watching through windows he had been amused rather than aroused, yet now he felt the urge to touch himself as he watched these women violently assaulted.

A noise behind him made him jump; he turned to see a girl crawling away through the undergrowth. He recognised her immediately. She was one of those who had shunned him the most, considering him as dirt to be trod on, as if he were devoid of feeling. At that moment his fate was sealed, he smiled as he leapt up and grabbed her. He had made his decision. The villagers had not cared for him they had made it clear he was not wanted amongst them. He would take a prize to the conquerors that would show he could be one of them. He remembered the pleading voice, the tears as he dragged her from the undergrowth, pulling her despite her efforts to resist, towards where the men's leader stood watching his men take their pleasure.

As he approached, several men made towards him to strike him down, until the man he now knew as Wend Y Mawr, commanded they stop. He had walked over to where Nadredd stood, Nadredd desperately tried to hide his fear. Wend had laughed, and demanded to know who he was, and what he wanted. Nadredd had stuttered as he gave his name, and offered the prize, in return for a place amongst them. Wend's face had contorted into laughter at the thought of this boy joining his men. He looked down at this scrawny little vagabond, wondering what he thought he could offer.

Wend later admitted he had been on the verge of striking him down for his insolence, but there had been something in Nadredd's eyes that had stopped him. Wend had turned his attention then to the girl, she was young and very pretty, he felt his own passion quicken at the thought of her soft flesh. He looked at the boy again and noticed the boy's obvious excitement at the activities that were taking place. It had dawned on Wend he had the opportunity here, to mould this boy to do his bidding. He could create a loyal servant from this rascal, who would betray his own village folk.

Nadredd felt himself hardening at the remembrance of what had happened after this. He moved across the chamber and rang a bell to summon a concubine. He stripped off while he awaited her arrival, standing before the mirror he looked at himself. No trace of that scrawny boy remained good food and hard fighting had put weight and muscle onto his frame. He had gained another foot in height since that first day they met yet he still felt small stood aside his leader.

The only one who had not changed since that first day was Wend. Wend had not aged one day since that fateful meeting. not one grey hair had appeared or a single line on his face in the thirty years that Nadredd had served him. Nadredd had seen others who noticed this fact dispatched under one pretext or another. He was the only one who knew of Wends secret, the only one Wend had trusted to live knowing it at any rate.

The door opened and a small blonde girl slipped in Nadredd smiled to see the same shade of blonde as the bitch he had handed Wend that first day. He ordered her to her knees, and let his mind drift back to the past again.

Wend had tied the girl's wrists and ankles together and ordered she be slung over his saddle. Nadredd had stood by watching while the rest of the men continued taking their pleasure with the women in the square. He watched as one by one the women ceased moving, broken bodies lay discarded in the dirt. When all the men had satiated their lust, the few women that remained alive were disposed of. Nadredd had been slightly disappointed that he had not been invited to join in but said nothing for fear they turn on him.

The men mounted their horses, Nadredd feared he would be left behind, however, Wend motioned to one of the men to bring the boy, and Nadredd had found himself hoisted up in front of the man. He remembered the ride back to the castle, at first he had been nervous, he had never ridden on a horse before, but he was soon distracted by what was happening on Wend's horse alongside them. The girl had started to wriggle, trying to get down from the horse, she began kicking her feet and beating her bound wrists against the horse's belly. Wend grabbed her dress and yanked it up revealing her soft white thighs and her undergarments. Taking his knife he had cut them away to reveal her pale buttocks. He brought his hand down hard across the while flesh, a red handprint was left where his gloved hand had met its mark. The girl's body convulsed with pain and she lay still again. Nadredd could not take his eyes off the sight of her backside bobbing into the air with the movement of the horse. Occasionally she would try to free herself again, only to receive the same punishment again until it was impossible to distinguish an individual mark.

Upon reaching the castle the rest of the men had dispersed, either taking horses to the stables or unloading the cargo of women and goods from the wagons. Wend slid from his horse then hoisted the girl over his shoulder. He motioned for Nadredd to follow him. They passed through the building, which appeared enormous to Nadredd, through the winding corridors until they reached, what Nadredd now knew to be, Wend's private bedchamber. Nadredd had looked round in amazement, he had never seen a room as big in his whole life the bed was larger as the rooms he had seen through the cottage windows back in the village. Wend was amused by the expression on the boys face, he motioned he should enter the room and stand by the window.

Once they were in there, Wend threw the girl on to the bed, her wrists and ankles still bound, escape impossible. For the first time since Nadredd had handed her over, his eyes met hers and he saw pure hatred glaring back at him.

Wend rang a bell and a woman came running in, he ordered her to fetch water and soap. Nadredd stood looking about him unsure of what was expected of him, waiting to be told what he should do. When he looked round again towards Wend, he noticed the older man was stripping off. The woman appeared again, now carrying a bucket and towels. He motioned to where Nadredd stood and ordered the boy be stripped and scrubbed.

For the first time in many years Nadredd was conscious of his appearance, he glanced round for a mirror and was shocked to see himself. Dirt coated his skin, his clothes little more than rags, if he had realised how he looked he would never have dared approach this great lord. The woman swiftly began peeling away his clothing until he found himself stood naked. He looked down at his own undernourished body and then across at that of the man who stood before him. Although Nadredd was just a boy, he could not help feeling inadequate as he compared their physiques and found his own wanting. Wend motioned that the boy to move to the side of the bed, he wished him to witness what was to come, it would be the beginning of his education.

The girl lay on her back looking up at them, fear and hatred blazing from her eyes. She had only recently turned sixteen, her curves not fully developed. Wend cut the rope binding her wrists, only to tie them again, but each individually this time, to the bed posts. He proceeded to cut away her dress before finally cutting the binding on her ankles, they too were tied to the bedposts but loosely to allow her legs to be lifted and manoeuvred as Wend chose.

The woman with the bucket now began to scrub at Nadredd's skin. She started at the top, forcing his head down towards the bucket while scrubbing the soap into his scalp and face. He did not see the girls exposed flesh until the woman was satisfied that she had removed all the dirt, all he could hear was her sobs and the oaths she aimed at him for giving her away.

As he stood upright, and the woman began cleaning the rest of his body, he watched as Wend lowered his head to the bud like breasts of the girl tied to the bed. He watched in fascination as the nipple came to life, hardening with a few flicks of Wends tongue. Nadredd became aware of his own manhood hardening; this time he felt embarrassment that he was unable to control his body in the presence of the others. The woman washing him seemed not to notice and the smile from Wend when he saw it, suggested he was pleased rather than angry.

Wend pushed the girl's legs further apart, spreading them wide. Slowly he inserted his fingers inside her, making sure that the boy had a good view. The girl writhed on the bed but to no avail, her protests and curses earned her a swipe across her face with the back of Wends hand. Wend was already hard but he now stroked himself to show the boy how to prepare his body to take a woman, it was obvious from his reactions he was still a virgin, much to Wends satisfaction. He noticed with amusement the boys own hand, move of its own will towards his own member. He motioned to the woman she should wash that area, and the boys hand was pushed away and replaced by the woman's soapy fingers. Nadredd had felt like his whole body would explode as soft fingers caressed him, he leant back against the wall as his knees buckled at the sensation.

He watched as Wend now entered the girl, a hand clasped firmly over her mouth to silence her screams. As Wend increased the speed and power of his thrusts, the woman altered the pressure she applied to match until the Nadredd could control himself no longer and for the first time released himself over the concubine. Embarrassment and pleasure combined for Nadredd, he looked down at the woman kneeling before him then across to Wend thrusting into the girl on the bed trying to judge from their expressions whether he had failed by not controlling himself. Wend roared with pleasure at the sight of the boy looking sheepish and flustered, the woman went back to scrubbing the rest of the boy as if nothing had happened.

Wend withdrew from the girl, and seemed to wait for something; he sat on the end of the bed watching Nadredd as the woman continue to scrub him. Nadredd had been confused, he hadn't realised that Wend's intentions for that evening were not based on the girl, but on his education. It seemed the girls crying and screaming were irritating Wend, he looked round then, laughing grabbed one of the filthy rags Nadredd had worn and forced it into her mouth. She gagged at the filthy fabric being thrust between her lips and tried to spit it out, Wend grabbed another piece and used this to tie round her head ensuring she could not.

Once Nadredd was cleaned, the woman and Wend both seemed to examine him, he remembered feeling like he had failed some sort of test. He only found out later that Wend had been pleasantly surprised to find such a pretty boy hidden under all the dirt. He had looked in the mirror again and seen a different boy looking back at himself, his hair not brown as they had thought but blonde curls that framed his face. On Wends command the woman had dropped to her knees before him, taking him into her mouth.

He instinctively reached down and grabbed the hair of the concubine now performing the same task upon him, forcing her to take him deeper into her throat as he relived the sensations of that first occasion. He dragged her to her feet, spinning her round and throwing her to the bed. He thrust into her but in his mind, for Nadredd it was not the concubine beneath him, it was the village girl he now drove himself into, just as he had all those years ago.

Wend had watched as the woman brought Nadredd's virgin flesh to life again, Nadredd had marvelled to find himself hard again so quickly, and protested when Wend had ordered the woman to stop. His disappointment had not lasted long Wend had taken him by the shoulders and brought him to the end of the bed.

It was Wend who grabbed the girl's knees and pulled them further apart to allow Nadredd access to her pleasures. He had followed Wend's instructions, first allowing his fingers to explore her, at first he had thrust them into her, until it was explained that he should take his time. Wend had then instructed him to allow his tongue to taste her. At first the taste of her juices disgusted him, he tried hard to hide his distaste, but the way she squirmed, attempting to move her body out of his grasp, only excited him and he found that the taste was bearable. His fingers dug into her hips as he now nipped at her with his teeth beginning to enjoy the sensation of inflicting pain on her. Finally Wend indicated he should enter her he climbed up above her body trying to position himself as Wend had earlier. After a couple of failed attempts he did so, clumsily, the girl's pain at this second violation evident despite the fact her second attacker was not as well-endowed as the first had been. He began to thrust, his body taking over, driving into her, unaware of Wend's movement behind him.

He lowered his head to her breast as he had watched Wend do, and was concentrating on attempting to thrust into her while licking at her nipples, when the pain shot through him. He felt like he was being torn apart, hands grasped his hips as something was forced deep inside him, tearing at his insides. It took him a few seconds to gather his senses and realise what was happening, he tried to voice his protests but a hand clamped over his mouth and a whisper at his ear ordered him be still. Trust me, those were the words he had heard at that moment, and he had placed his trust there and then.

He lay still, his own manhood buried deep inside the girl, as Wend thrust into him. Gradually the pain subsided then he was shocked to discover, his own member seemed to be growing harder and the sensation now flooding his body was one of pleasure. As Wends pace quickened, he found himself beginning to move again to thrust deeper into the girl. He noticed the blood on her breast where he had bitten at her nipple in the shock of Wend's assault upon him, he bent his head, the metallic taste on his lips excited him all the more and he drove harder into her. It seemed Wend was pleased with this and he now found his hips grasped tighter he drove himself between the two. Each thrust back of his was met by Wend, and then the weight of both men was driven down again, into the girl below. Eventually Nadredd could handle no more and released himself deep into the girl, his whole body shaking as the orgasm overwhelmed his senses, only to feel the power of Wend's orgasm deep within himself.

Nadredd came with hoarse cry; he could almost feel Wend inside him again. He understood now it had not been about sex but power but for the boy he had been it had been so much more.

He had stayed in that room for days; they had taken it in turns with the girl violating every orifice numerous times before she was thrown to the men and replaced with a new girl. Sometimes Wend mounted him as Nadredd took his pleasure, sometimes they would lay the girl on her side and both mount her together.

Eventually Wend allowed him to leave the room, he took him to the great hall at meal times allowing him to sit at his side. He had been in awe of everything he saw, the first meal in the great hall, he had watched as others helped themselves, waiting to be given permission to eat. Then he had gorged, still scared he may be thrown back out to fend for himself. Wend had dressed him in his own clothes though they dwarfed him reinforcing the difference in size between them in Nadredd's mind. If he thought about it now he had almost been treated as a pet.

The good food had meant he rapidly began putting on weight. Muscles began to develop for the first time, as he learnt to wield a sword, until he started to look like a man rather than a boy. When this happened Wend had stopped entering him, he installed Nadredd in his own chamber alongside his, he still summoned Nadredd to take part in his private games, but now both men saved their attentions for the chosen subject of their sport. They had never spoken of what had taken place, but there was a bond between them. He had seen Wend bugger other boys when they were young and pretty but no other had been taken under his wing as he had.

This was why, he now felt so betrayed that Wend had lied to him that after all they had been through, all they had shared, he finally realised Wend still did not trust him.

Wend had returned to his own chambers, he felt bad he had not been honest with Nadredd but he could not admit that he had not been in control. Rather it had been the energy that had taken on a life force of its own, channelling its self through him. He needed to learn how to channel it. He had gone into the chamber off the great hall as soon as Nadredd had left him and searched through everything he could find looking for the answer but it had eluded him.

For the first time Wend cursed his own impulsiveness, he had been arrogant, convinced he could learn everything he needed from the strangers books. It only now occurred to him that maybe, the stranger had taken some knowledge to his grave with him. Possibly the potion would reveal the missing information he needed, another twenty-four hours it would useable, but for its full effect, it would require another day after that. He had no choice but to wait.

Chapter Fifteen

Jacantha woke early, ready to set as soon as she had eaten, she had spent the previous day packing what she would need for the journey ahead. She had avoided Trwyn the previous evening, retreating to the tower to concentrate on her focus and meditation as Celdwady had instructed her. She knew Trwyn was unhappy about her leaving the safety of the castle without his protection but she had refused to listen to his protests. She had arranged for her breakfast to be brought to her room to avoid meeting with him this morning, she needed her mind clear for what was to come.

She ate the bread and cold meat that had been left just outside her door quickly, and then pulled on her clothes quickly and grabbed her pack from the floor. There was an unusual stillness within the castle. Normally the hustle and bustle of daily life began with the first rays of the sun yet today it was as silent as it had been after her father's funeral. She saw no one as she headed for the stables; all the stalls were occupied as she opened the gate to her horse, which stood patiently eating from his manger. She saddled the stallion and led him out to the courtyard. Celdwady and Brawd were there already waiting for her and they were not alone. It seemed the entire population had appeared from the shadows and come to see her off.

Trwyn moved forward from the crowd and took the bridle, holding the horse as she mounted. His face showed his displeasure at what was occurring, she turned away from him aware everyone was watching, she had no doubt while she had concentrated on preparing for this Trwyn had voiced his disapproval to all who would listen.

She could feel the tension emanating from all of those gathered around her. Every person aware of the importance of the unfolding events, they had all heard the story of the prophecy from childhood. Yet they, like Trwyn, were wary of the idea of their Queen having only a priest and his novice to protect her on the journey. It had been suggested, by Trwyn Jacantha suspected, they take a guard with them but Celdwady had refused. It was important that this pilgrimage be undertaken with secrecy, a guard would draw unwanted attention to the travellers.

The elders had been unwilling to agree initially, Trwyn's father had argued vocally on his sons behalf but Celdwady had held firm, intimating that they would place the whole prophecy in jeopardy. The Elders had been unwilling to risk any action that may affect the destiny of their Queen and Trwyn's father had delivered the news to his son, to say he had responded badly had been an understatement. Jacantha had heard his oaths and curses from the top of the tower where she had been sat at the time. Jacantha adjusted her position in the saddle. She looked down at Trwyn and smiled, she could see the concern in his eyes; she had taken the precaution of ensuring his companions would halt any attempt he made to follow her.

She pulled the cloak in to position and placed the hood over her head obscuring her from view. She could still smell the faint scent of smoke despite the numerous attempts she had made to wash it out since her father's death. Celdwady motioned to her that he was ready and the three horses moved off slowly. The people gathered moved back to allow them to pass. Everyone was quiet, Jacantha made out the odd prayer of blessing been whispered as she passed. She could feel Trwyn's eyes on her as she passed him, she regretted that they were parting with him feeling as he did but she knew it had to be. The castle gates were opened for them, they passed through and Jacantha heard them close behind her with a resounding thud.

The first few hours passed in silence, each rider deep in their own thoughts. They rode west passing a few small hamlets which had not yet been disturbed by Wend's raiding parties. Even here the shadow that hung over her kingdom loomed as people lived in a state of perpetual preparation for flight should the need arise. Where once she would have travelled with care for the risk of a careless child running before the horse she saw only glimpses as they peeked from windows. At the sight of stranger approaching the people assumed the worst and hid in fear.

Around midday they halted for a quick meal of bread, cheese and cold meat. Celdwady had taken care that the kitchens should provide food which would sustain them, yet require little in the way of preparation or cooking. They ate still in silence, all reluctant to speak of the reasons for this journey, only when the meal was finished did Brawd finally speak. Questions fell from his lips in quick succession, only to be dismissed by Celdwady with the assurance all would become clear in time. Brawd's dissatisfaction at this answer was evident however he did not challenge Celdwady. The three remounted and continued their journey in silence once more.

As dusk approached Celdwady announced they would make camp for the night. Jacantha busied herself gathering firewood, it felt good to have something to do and soon she stood back and watched as the flames flickered into life. Celdwady placed a pot into the flames containing broth that he had brought from the castle. As soon as it was warm they devoured it, the days riding and fresh air had increased their appetites. For an hour after dinner Celdwady regaled them with tales of old avoiding the subject of their travels once again. Long forgotten names from childhood brought back memories for Jacantha of sitting on her father's knee being told the same stories. In the distance a wolf howled. Celdwady stopped, and listened. Brawd looked round nervously, he had been so far from the castle since his arrival, the land was unknown to him and the thought that no assistance could reach them suddenly hit home.

Jacantha stood, as the warrior amongst them she knew it would be down to her to protect them should they come under attack she surveyed the place where they had stopped. She had not thought to question Celdwady when he chose where they would pitch camp. Now she realised that while it was well hidden from the road, the trees that surrounded them made them vulnerable. Celdwady smiled. He chided her for her concerns, did she not consider that he had put protective spells around them. They had nothing to fear here. He instructed Jacantha to take out the moonstone. As she pulled it from her pack it began to glow faintly where her fingers touched it.

She sat down by the fire and concentrated her gaze on it, as she did so the glow increased. Celdwady seemed pleased with her progress. After a while concentrating on the stone, the intensity of the light coming from it increased. Jacantha found she no longer had to force her thoughts towards the stone. A change had taken place and it seemed she were tuned in to it in perfect harmony. The light increased and diminished as she willed, and she felt a sense of peace descend over her.

Jacantha closed her eyes. She heard the wolf once again in the distance. This time she knew it was calling to her, calling her to join it. Her mind left her body as it had before in the stables, this time she felt in control willing her mind to follow the call. She felt the sensations of flying through the air, the wind tousling her hair and the breeze on her face, as she moved towards the wolf. Then it was there, stood in a clearing before her. A second wolf stood a few paces behind the first, waiting patiently. The wolf smiled at her and settled down on the ground wait.

Jacantha returned to her body, Celdwady was studying her. She told him what she had seen, explaining about leaving her body and answering the call. Brawd questioned its meaning he gift of leaving the body was rare, something that took hours of practise but was seldom mastered by the most talented Guardians, that Jacantha could achieve this with no training astounded him, Celdwady shook his head. Although he had his own thoughts about the meaning, he would not share them, they would find out soon enough. The three lay down to sleep, each with the same thoughts running through their heads. Jacantha slept deeply, visions of the wolf running through her dreams, the moonstone still in her hand glowed with an intensity matching that of the waning moon overhead.

They all awoke refreshed the next morning. Brawd started to gather berries but Celdwady stopped him, they must fast until after tonight's ceremonies. They cleared away all traces of their inhabitancy then set off on the final leg of their journey. Brawd was now starting to struggle in the saddle. Unused to travelling he found the ride hard going but bore it patiently. They slowed their pace for a while allowing him to slip from the horse and walk for a while. As morning passed into afternoon they had made good time still. Celdwady announced they were less than an hour's journey from the grove which was their final destination. Relief passed visibly over Brawd's face at the thought their journey was nearing its conclusion.

They reached the edge of the woods. The trees here were ancient, boughs bent and twisted with age. They dismounted and led the horses deeper into the trees. Ferns and bracken snapped and cracked under foot, occasionally tendrils of Ivy wound themselves round their ankles threatening to trip them if they were not vigilante. As the moved further into the trees sunlight became scarcer losing the battle to break through the dense canopy.

They reached a point where it became impractical to try to lead the horses any further the gaps between the trees narrowed, until it became a squeeze for them to get through. As loath as Jacantha was to leave them tethered here, she could see no option they could not lead them further and to leave them at the edge of the woods left them as vulnerable. Celdwady reassured her they would be safe and she stood and watched as he muttered strange words round the horses casting protection around them. The horses themselves seemed to go into a trance, they stood motionless, and as Jacantha reached out a hand towards them, she found she could not touch them. Her hand should have been passing over the horses flanks but there was nothing within touching distance, her hand seemed to pass straight through them.

Celdwady took a few steps deeper into the forest and stopped to look round. A great oak stood before them, he called Jacantha forward. He instructed Jacantha to place her hands upon the bark. As she did so she felt a tingle in her fingertips, the tree was so old her fingertips slid into the cracks in the bark, as she allowed them to trail across the trunk almost as if caressing a lover. It seemed the tree took a deep breath and, as it exhaled the sensation passed through Jacantha's body, she was overwhelmed by a feeling she could not put words to. For a moment she felt faint, she stumbled falling forward, her body pressed forward against the bark. The rough wood scratched her face at her face where it pushed against the bark. Brawd moved to assist her but Celdwady held him back.

Jacantha took a deep breath she could feel a pulse deep within the tree. It now seemed to breathe in time with her own breath. As she inhaled it seemed strength filled her body, she was connected to everything around her. She pushed herself upright, and turned her gaze to the direction they wished to go in. She reached a hand out in a sweeping arc and a path appeared granting them passage through the trees. Celdwady exhaled unaware he had been holding his breath. He could have easily performed the task of clearing the path himself but he had needed to see how receptive she was ready for this evenings ceremony. Brawd looked at her, awe in his eyes at the task she had performed, a realisation dawning that he would witness something this evening that no other Guardian had ever seen.

They moved along the newly revealed path, until they reached the grove. Here the trees had seemed to stop at an invisible boundary, leaving a circle in the centre where the sun shone down onto the grass. The circle was no more than a few metres in diameter yet, after the density of the trees it seemed much larger. Jacantha was disappointed to find the circle empty. After her vision the night before, she had been certain the wolf would be waiting for her. She lay down on the grass in the centre of the circle and watched as Celdwady and Brawd busied themselves around her, preparing for what was to come.

As dusk approached Jacantha changed from her dusty travelling clothes into a plain white robe Celdwady had handed her. Its coarse fabric scratched at her skin as she pulled it over her head, she tied a thin leather thong round her waist, the ends hanging almost to the floor. When she emerged from behind the tree where she had changed, she found the others had also changed their clothing. Celdwady wore a green robe, Brawd an identical one in brown.

Brawd moved around the clearing waving purifying sage, the smell filled her nostrils overpowering all other scents as it smouldered, releasing its scented smoke. Celdwady had set out an altar on a fallen tree at the edge of the clearing. He placed the candles, the statue that represented the mother that Jacantha recognised from his private altar within his chambers, next he placed the symbolic elements signifying the elements of earth, air, water, and spirit, as she approached he lit the final candle completing the elements with fire. Jacantha and Celdwady both glanced at the sky, the sun was just slipping down to meet the horizon. It was time to begin.

Celdwady led Jacantha to the centre of the glade and instructed her to knee. He moved round the grove collecting herbs, placing them in a crucible from a bag hanging from his robe he took a vial of oil pouring it over the contents Jacantha expected him to light the contents but instead he placed the crucible onto the altar as it was. Celdwady and Brawd took up positions on either side of her and began to chant. She knelt staring at the altar nothing seemed to be happening, but then what had she expected? Despite her earlier experience she had not yet developed a belief in her own powers. She remembered Celdwady's recent lessons on focusing her mind and fixing on the altar, willing for a sign to appear that something was happening.

Celdwady moved to the altar and picked up the moonstone, it was dull and showed no sign of the previous evening's luminance. Jacantha stretched out her hands to receive the stone, immediately on her touch, a light started to emanate from it. Jacantha felt the air around her change. It was like being underwater everything around her seemed blurred and muted. She could see Celdwady's lips move and knew words were issuing from his mouth but she could no longer distinguish them. He was handing her a drink, she reached out and took it still clutching the moonstone in her other hand. she placed the cup to her lips and felt the sweet liquid trickle down her throat. Everything seemed to swing into focus again, yet far sharper than before. Then at the edge of the grove she saw it.

The wolf walked slowly towards her. From the corner of her eyes she could see Celdwady standings still, Brawd was backing up away from the wolf. It flickered through her mind maybe this was her destiny, to be a sacrifice to the wolves in order to ensure victory. The wolf moved closer, its muzzle now inches from her face. Their eyes locked with each other gaze. Jacantha realised she felt no fear, almost of its own will her hand dropped the cup and reached out to stroke the soft fur of the wolf's face.

Everything started to blur again, the very earth she knelt upon seemed to fall away beneath her. The wolf stepped closer she could feel its breath on her face and its fur brush against her skin. Everything was now became a whirl of lights and fog. Jacantha still clutching the moonstone in one hand, she reached out with the other trying to hold on to the wolf to anchor herself, for what she believed was coming next. She felt herself being lifted and turned in the air, yet she felt no hands or claws or teeth upon her body. As she spun, she only felt a breeze, gentle as a breath upon her body. Faces seemed to be appearing through the swirl.

One minute it was the wolf's face she could see, the next a woman's face. The spinning slowed and she now felt arms around her pulling her as if into an embrace. She was filled with a sense of love but also deep sadness. Her vision cleared and she found herself gazing into the eyes of the most beautiful woman she had ever seen. The woman's eyes were a deep green; looking into them was like staring into eternity. The shaggy wolf's mane had been replaced by flowing white locks. An aura shone from the woman, white light radiated from her, enveloping Jacantha in its warmth. She felt herself being placed gently back onto the ground again.

The woman stepped away from her, a sense of loss filled Jacantha, even though the woman moved no more than a few feet away. She watched as the woman stepped towards the others. Brawd had dropped to his knees, his eyes lowered to the ground in worship. Celdwady had bowed his head at the woman's approach. Jacantha watched as the woman lifted a slender hand to his face and lifted his gaze to meet hers. No words were spoken but Jacantha sensed something of great importance had passed between the two of them.

It was then she noticed the second wolf, this was the wolf from her dreams that had called her to this clearing the previous evening. Stood at the edge of the clearing it was larger and darker than the first had been. The wolf that had turned into the woman had been large yet still slender and graceful with a pure white coat, Jacantha realised now, that the wolf form from which the woman had emerged, was the wolf that she had seen several times over the last few weeks, beginning with the encounter at her father's pyre.

The new comer moved forward uncertainly, looking at the woman as if requesting permission for something. The woman smiled and gave an almost imperceptible nod of her head. As the second wolf stepped forward he too transformed. In his place a huge man stood, dark eyes penetrated Jacantha as he moved towards her. Where the woman was light this man was darkness, for a brief moment she thought of Wend before forcing him from her mind. Long dark hair framed his face; red sensual lips appeared from within the long dark beard as he spoke. It was only one word but it seemed to fill the air, its importance stopping time itself

"Daughter."

The woman had moved to his side, now Jacantha saw their arms outstretched towards her. Jacantha stepped forward into their embrace.

The moon was high in the sky when Jacantha slipped reluctantly from their arms. She now knew everything; she understood the past and knew what was now expected of her. They had shown her what must happen, the act which she must perform to save her people, the sacrifice she must make for the future of them all. She looked towards Celdwady and Brawd, it was obvious from the looks on their faces, they had also been party to the story she had been told. Jacantha felt dampness on her cheek and realised she had been crying. She could not determine whether the tears fell for what the past had revealed or what her future would force her to do. She looked again at this strange couple who had shaped her destiny. They were gazing at her their eyes full of love.

A wind blew through the glade a whirlwind of leaves obscured Jacantha's vision. When it passed two wolves stood before her again. The smaller white wolf raised her head and let out a long low howl, the larger darker one responded, before the two turned and trotted away into the night.

Jacantha slumped to the ground, suddenly overwhelmed and exhausted. Celdwady rushed to her side and gently lifted her; he motioned to Brawd to get a fire started. Celdwady cradled her in his arms, watching her shallow breathing until it deepened into a natural sleep. He looked down at her; he had suspected only part of what she must face. He looked up as Brawd spoke

"Will she do it?"

Celdwady slowly nodded his head,

"She must. Now rest, we will discuss things when she awakes."

Jacantha stirred in her sleep, Celdwady stroked her face to sooth her, he allowed himself to penetrate her thoughts. He would never have normally violated her privacy this way, but he must on this occasion. He felt her turmoil, her emotions in such conflict. He interjected his own image into her thoughts to ease her mind, he counselled her fears and reassured her of the outcome, and then as soon as he sensed she was calming, he withdrew. Overcome with weariness the two men now fell into a deep sleep, a short distance away in the trees, the two wolves settled down also to watch over them.

It was early when Jacantha awoke; the moon still hovering above despite the fact the sun had begun its journey across the sky. She poked at the embers of the fire stirring the embers back to life. She shivered and looked round for her travelling clothes. Her companions still slept as she pulled on her clothes beneath her cloak. She was aware now of her hunger, she rummaged in the bags they had brought with them and found some cheese and salted meat. She huddled close to the fire and ate letting the previous evenings revelations replay in her mind. How could she go through with her binding to Trwyn? She could not betray him the way she must, he was a good man he deserved better.

She added more wood to the fire, a chill had set in the sun was obscured behind clouds which loomed, heavy and dark. As she sat waiting for the others to awake, doubt clawed at her insides. She knew what she had to do but uncertainty gnawed away at her, but she knew now the consequences of failure. That was unthinkable, she had been shown a vision of the desolate wasted landscape that would be all that remained of her people if she failed.

It was only a little time before Celdwady awoke. One look at Jacantha told him she was resolved to do what was needed; now he need only convince her she must allow Trwyn to play his part. He felt her pain at this course of action, to betray anyone went against her nature but it must be done. They roused Brawd and set about packing away all they had brought, Brawd went to collect the things from the makeshift altar but Celdwady stopped him. He removed the candles and the athame but left the crucible in place. From his bag he took a mixture of herbs which he placed in the bowl along with those he had placed in it the night before, he muttered an incantation as he set them down.

The journey back to the site where they had spent the first night was quiet. Rain had begun to fall dampening their clothes and spirits, Brawd struggled to remain in his saddle slipping as the leather became wet and slick. Only once they had reached their campsite and coaxed a fired into existence did they begin to discuss the previous evening's events. Huddled under a makeshift tent Jacantha constructed from a blanket they began to speak, Brawd was full of questions eager to learn all he could.

"Who were the man and woman who appeared? Are they who I think they are?" He asked eagerly.

Jacantha sat back, allowing Celdwady to instruct his apprentice,

"Yes they are, they go by many names but here in this place, she goes by the name Amante Celeste. Her companion is known by the name Cydymaith Arglwydd. They are the Lady and Lord who govern all living things on earth. It would also seem she is the beautiful stranger of legend, whose prophecy we are trusted to see to fruition."

He paused to look at Jacantha, she avoided meeting his eyes.

Brawd took the opportunity to interject

"But they never said how she was to fulfil the prophecy? How is it to be done?"

It was Jacantha who answered now.

"They told me what I must do. That is all I can say I cannot discuss it with anyone, only ask that all trust me, even those who I must betray."

Her voice faltered as the last few words left her lips.

Celdwady continued,

"You will not be betraying anyone. You are doing what must be done to protect them, all of them. I too was given a vision of what must happen or at least part of it. I was shown the part I must play. We all have our parts to play in this matter. Each vision was for each of us individually, to show us our own parts and to show us what we must know and no more. We must each perform our own tasks to the best of our abilities and trust to the greater powers that all will go as it should. It is a question of faith and belief.

Look about you, each plant and tree is concerned only with its own growth and survival, yet none can survive without the others. It is the Lady herself, along with her companion who ensures the balance. Every living thing is connected, part of a force far greater than we can ever imagine but for life to continue all must remain in balance. There must be an equal mix of light and dark, day and night, good and evil, when one has too much power then all living things are in peril. When one living being, be it plant, animal or man takes more than their share then balance is threatened Wend Y Mawr has taken more than his share already and still lusts for more. This is the situation now and all we love hangs in the balance, and if he is not stopped then all will be lost."

His words hung heavy in the air. Jacantha reached into the pack and retrieved the moonstone. It glowed brightly but now she saw something else as she gazed into it. From deep within the stone two deep green eyes gazed back at her. The eyes of the wolf gave her courage. She would find the strength to follow this through.

The three settled down and passed the night in deep sleep, Jacantha dreamt of what she must do, in her sleep she played out different scenarios, looking for a way to ensure success. Next morning they set off on the homewards leg of their journey. A tension accompanied them as each thought about the weeks to come. Conversation between them was brief and purely of necessity. Celdwady kept a constant watch on Jacantha looking for signs she would falter, that her resolve had weakened. He was relieved that he saw nothing to give him cause for concern. Jacantha seemed to have accepted her fate though knowing her as he did it would not ease her pain at the act she must perform. He was curious about the parts of the prophecy which his own personal vision had omitted, wondering how much more had been revealed to the young woman riding alongside him. The scholar in him longing to know all, yet his faith kept it in check knowing that he would know all in time.

It was nearing dusk as they arrived back to the castle. Trwyn was waiting for them as they reached the stables, relief evident as he greeted them removing any last traces of resentment at their absence. Celdwady and Brawd dismounted the latter glad his journey was over and swearing he would only ever travel by foot in the future. Celdwady instructed Brawd to go rest they would make an early start tomorrow. Brawd bade them good night then hoisting the bags containing the robes and other items they had taken, left for his chambers. Celdwady then moved a distance away, where he could observe what passed between the two who remained.

Trwyn helped Jacantha down from the saddle, and helped her remove it and rub the horse down. Jacantha stood waiting as Trwyn led her horse to his stall and filled the manger with fresh hay. The horse was hesitant at being led away by anyone else but she reached up giving him once last pat on the neck before he allowed himself to be stabled. Jacantha smiled, she knew Trwyn disliked the horse and suspected the feeling was mutual, in some ways the man and beast were too similar. Trwyn had remained silent, despite the many questions he harboured, he longed to ask her what had happened but feared her answers more.

It was Jacantha who spoke first

"Trwyn do you love me? Love me enough to trust me no matter what I ask of you?"

"Of course I do, what happened? What makes you ask that?"

Fear in his voice that he could not disguise.

"I need you to listen to me. I cannot tell you anything about what happened or what must happen. I just need you to believe in me, believe anything I do I have to do. There will come a time where I will ask more of you, when that time comes, you must do as I say without question. I need you to understand, there is so much more at stake here than just my life. I will be with you as long as I can be, I will love you forever. My heart will always be yours."

"I cannot say I understand. I do not see why, whatever you have to do, you must do alone. Why can I not help you? Why can I not fight by your side?"

Anger now replacing the fear as he grabbed hold of her turning her to face him.

Jacantha let out a laugh

"My darling, if only it was so simple. I must play my part the part I was born for. Your part in some ways is just as important and you must play it whether you wish to or not, we cannot change fate nor should we try to. You must trust me."

She raised her hand to his lips as he made as if to speak

"Enough" she leaned in towards him and pressed her lips to his.

He pulled her tightly into the embrace. She could feel his urgency, his need for reassurance. A new sensation swept through her, she could not explain exactly what it was. There was love there, and sadness but overriding all was a desire to protect this man who placed his faith in her. She knew if he were to ever discover the truth of what the prophecy involved, it would destroy him. She felt more than ever the need to see it through, to protect not only this person she loved, but all of them. She pulled back from him smiling; only a week and she could give herself to him fully. Taking him by the hand, she led him towards the great hall.

Celdwady stepped back into the shadows. He was relieved she had shown no signs of wavering. He felt a wave of pride wash over him; she was the nearest thing he would ever have to a daughter. He had watched her grow from the day she had been born, every passing hour leading her closer to her destiny. Many times he had thought she would not be able to face it, but now he knew, there was strength deep inside her he had not given her credit for. Under different circumstances she could have achieved so much, he shook his head, what was he thinking, she would achieve more in the next few weeks than anyone could ever imagine. As for the future, well that was not as certain, only so much could be known, that was enough, for now at least.

Chapter Sixteen

The men had all gathered in the great hall, they stood patiently awaiting Wend's appearance. Since the events a few days ago he had remained shut away in the chamber off the great hall, they knew better than to disturb him in there. The men had discussed the events between themselves, careful not to say anything which could be reported back as traitorous. They all sensed a change in the atmosphere around the castle, the air seemed heavier and a sense of foreboding crept over them all. So far it had not affected their lifestyle, but they now gave serious thought to their futures. Several had already contemplated taking the wealth they had accumulated and fleeing but fear held them back. Wend's new powers had given them extra reason to be cautious; no one could be sure how far these new powers could extend. The unspoken decision between them all was to wait for the opportune moment to flee.

Wend strode into the hall, he was aware of the men's thoughts. Over the past few days shut away, y he had studied the scrolls of parchment, which had remained untouched, ever since he had slain the stranger so many years ago. He had not found the information he sought but had found other knowledge which had helped him to control these new powers. He knew the men were ready to abandon him but he no longer cared, they would be surplus to requirements soon, but for tonight they would have a purpose.

He raised a hand and with a flourish he caused ignited every candle in the room, to the men gasped as they flickered into life illuminating the room. He stood back as a large bowl of ale was placed on the table before him. He took the potion which had been brewing in his private chamber and uncorked the bottle. He could feel all eyes upon him as he poured it into the bowl and stirred the contents. It bubbled as it mixed with the liquid ale already in there, frothing until it threatened to overflow, before subsiding again. He knew each man there was wary of the potion, at the moment, though not one of them would have spoken openly, he knew they remained nervous of him; he dipped in glass flagon and withdrew a portion. Lifting it to his lips as all those present watched he swallowed it down in one, the ale barely disguising the bitter taste of the herbs and fungi. Now in turn each man stepped forward and took their turn. Once all had drunk he ordered the bowl removed, he did not wish to risk that in the delirium to follow any mistakenly drink a second draught.

The concubines now filed into the room, they lined the walls at one side of the room waiting for Wends instruction. Wend sat back in his throne and waited for the potion to take effect. Two of the concubines took their place at either side of Wend; he had selected them earlier while issuing instruction to the rest for tonight's proceedings. As he felt the first effects of the potion, he motioned for the women to take their places. He watched now as each girl knelt in front of one of the men, he motioned to the girl at the left of him to assume her place on her knees. The men stood in a circle, only Wend remained seated, though still part of it. All waited motionless, nervous but anticipating the pleasure which must surely follow such an elaborate beginning. Wend felt the start of the tingling sensation and gave to signal for the concubines to begin their work.

The thongs of leather securing the men's leggings were quickly untied, releasing the men ready for action; lips wrapped themselves round the newly exposed manhood's. Wend rose to his feet and kicked the chair away to complete the circle properly, it was important this be done correctly or it would all be in vain. His vision blurred as the energy began to build; the blue haze starting to form. He fought against the sensation overwhelming him; he must keep focus, not drift within the energy this time. He forced his eyes to regain focus clarity on the events on in the room around him. He grasped the hair of the girl in front of him, controlling her movements, slowing her pace to maximise the effects.

Each girl had been instructed to make it this first part last as long as possible this holding the men back from release the first time. Later, with the potion in full effect it would not matter, a pleasant side effect being the increased ability for sustaining erections. Already explosions of energy burst around the room, from men unable to hold back. The girls carried on with hands and mouths, ordered to only stop and allow other activities once their assigned man had achieved his second longer lasting erection. Wend closed his eyes he could feel the potion taking effect, he shuddered as he came in the girl's mouth, he barely softened before he was ready to begin his plan in earnest.

He opened his eyes. the energy bursts in the room now told him all the men had achieved their first climax. He gave another signal and the girls moved positions, the spare concubines, who had been stood round the edge of the room waiting, now joined them. This was the important part now. Bodies joined forming a perfect circle; he had stressed the importance that the circle not be broken at any point. Flesh melted into flesh, fingers and lips reached out to bridge the gaps between couples. Wend laid on his back, one girl straddling him, while the other leant over him fondling her breasts as Nadredd entered her from behind. Wend looked past them all. He gaze was focused on the circle now forming above them.

The energy now rather than appearing in individual bursts, formed a steadily increasing ring above them. He watched as the ring spread inwards towards the centre of the room, forming a dome of light above them. As the activity around him increased, he felt the power surging through his veins, he closed his eyes again. Images flashed through his mind, Jacantha beckoning him, he heard wolves howling and the moon, full and bright, hanging heavy in the night sky. As he looked at it, blood drifted across its white surface and he smiled. The next full moon! that That was when she would be his! His eyes flew open he was exhilarated by what he had seen.

It did not matter now if the circle broke, had he had seen what he needed. she Jacantha would come to him in the woods at the next full moon. He now sat up, throwing the girl in his lap onto her back and plunged himself deep inside her. It was now Jacantha's face he saw below him as he penetrated her the woman deeper with each thrust. Her nails dug into his flesh as he drove into her, exciting him more. He did not notice as her moans changed to anguished groans, with every thrust draining more of the girl's life force, until her hands dropped limply from his body. He looked down it was not Jacantha beneath him, just a dead concubine. He lifted his head and looked round the room in search of her.

In the drug induced haze, he now saw her everywhere. At first, he thought he saw her across the room, her head in the lap of one man, then in another place, head buried in another girl's lap while she was buggered from behind. His anger rose as her vision appeared around the room, engaged in acts with other men that she should be saving for him. Wend could no longer distinguish reality to him it was Jacantha he saw each time. It was then he spotted her in the worst betrayal, she lay on her back Nadredd driving into her, her arms wrapped round his neck while her legs wrapped round his back pulling him closer into her.

Her head thrown back in wild abandon and Nadredd laughing as he drove into her, over and over again.

Wend jumped to his feet, he would could not stand by and watch their betrayal, she was his Nadredd knew she belonged to him. He looked round for a weapon then realised he did not need one. He slowly and deliberately he raised his hand towards Nadredd. Nadredd, unaware of what was happening felt the heat begin to grow within his body. He staggered to his feet looking round and looked round he saw Wends raised hand, but could not believe what he was seeing. Incomprehension and confusion filled his face as he looked towards his friend, Wends face glaring back at him with hatred and contempt.

Everyone was now aware of what was happening, all everyone stopped what they were doing, trying to make sense of what they were seeing. Voices, shouting, barely penetrated Wend's consciousness, he was focused on concentrating his powers on Nadredd. he would not let him die quickly. No Nadredd he must suffer for his betrayal. He stepped forward, grabbing the concubine who now had appeared to him as Jacantha by the hair, his other hand still outstretched in Nadredd's direction. He pulled the girl to her feet, then the slap he delivered across her face sent her flying back to the floor. Nadredd tried desperately to move but felt himself rooted to the spot, the heat spreading through him becoming unbearable. Wend reached down and dragged the girl to her feet again by her hair; she would also be punished for her betrayal. He spun her round so she faced away from him, his fingers twisted in her hair, holding her head tightly next to his.

He growled in her ear. "Watch what I can do to your new favourite!" The girl tried to protest innocence, yet confused by as to what crime she was supposed to have committed the words came out incoherently, she pleaded with Wend, her voice only anger him, his grip on her hair tightening each time she spoke. Nadredd now was in agony, he struggled trying to make sense of what was happening, he tried to hold back the pain and fear in his voice as he begged Wend to explain what he had done. He professed his loyalty, friendship even his love for Wend, yet all went unheard.

Wend now forced the girl forward, bending her over the table that had earlier held the potion. Not dropping the hand aimed at Nadredd, he released her hair and forced himself between her buttocks. Glaring at Nadredd, he forced himself into the girl brutally, tearing her flesh as he entered her. In his mind it was still Jacantha beneath him, he sought to dominate her, prove his mastery over her, show Nadredd that his betrayal changed nothing, that Jacantha was his property.

His lowered hand grasped her hip, fingers digging into the soft flesh. With each thrust into the girl the heat engulfing Nadredd increased. He was screaming out loud now. Smoke began to seep from his Nadredd's skin, not the flames which had covered the man previously but a smouldering heat emanated from him that slowly burnt from deep within.

Everyone else in the room was still in stunned, silence silently they stepped back away from both wend and Nadredd. Furtive glances were swapped between them as the potions effects began to wear off at the sight they were witnessing. The girl was screaming now as well, she too was beginning to smoulder as Wend continued violating her. Wend did not notice this new development, his focus remained firmly fixed on Nadredd.

Nadredd fell to his knees, his screams changing to agonised, guttural groans still he looked pleadingly at Wend, still desperately trying to work out the reason his lord had turned on him. Wend felt his climax approach he dropped the hand aimed at Nadredd, to grasp the girl's backside as, he pushed the flesh apart, allowing himself deeper penetration, as he drove his full length into her. Over and over, he thrust, driving himself further and further into her torn flesh. Then with a bloodcurdling roar he came. As he did a flash of light engulfed the girl's body and she lay dead slumped over the table. He looked down, seeing not Jacantha but a concubine lying before him.

Wend looked round the room unable to comprehend what had happened at first and then the realisation slowly dawned on him. The potion slowly released its grip on his mind, he looked first at the girl lifeless in front of him then to Nadredd lying on the floor writhing still in pain. Wend pushed the girl's body aside and rushed to Nadredd's side. He dropped to his knees, cradling Nadredd's head in his lap. He Wend looked down at him, what had he done? Wend raised his hand surely his power would allow him to repair the damage he had wrought. As his hand passed over Nadredd he saw him flinch. The smoke once again began to appear from Nadredd's skin. Wend looked round in frustration, he began bellowing at everyone to leave. Slowly everyone began to back away out of the room until the two men were left alone.

"Why?" The single word from Nadredd contained more pain than any other could ever have held.

"What have I done? Nadredd, I am sorry. I thought it was her, I saw her with you. I thought you had betrayed me I thought she had betrayed me." Tears now formed in both men's eyes.

Nadredd reached up despite the pain and clutched Wend's arm "please, please, finish it. I forgive you but please I cannot stand the pain, end it now."

Wend looked round and saw a dagger discarded on the floor. He picked it up "I am so sorry" with a swift movement he sank the dagger into Nadredd's heart. He sat holding the body as Nadredd's blood pooled around them. For the first time in Wend's life he shed a single tear for someone else.

From her hiding place behind the wall hangings, the head concubine had witnessed everything. Her mind was made up, it was time to get out of here. Silently she slipped along the wall and out of the doorway. Careful to avoid meeting anyone she slipped back to her chamber, she had packed a few meagre belongings when she first began to worry about her position. She had been around long enough to know a boundary had been crossed.

With Nadredd's death, Wend had proved no one was safe, he would strike at anyone he suspected of betraying him. She took one last look round then made her way towards the corridors at the rear of the castle. No one took any notice of her, she hoped she would be far away before anyone realised she was gone and that as she was no longer considered useful that Wend would not bother searching far for her.

Chapter Seventeen

The days passed quickly for Jacantha. Preparations for her joining to Trwyn seemed to have taken on a life of their own. It seemed she herself had little to do as everyone else rushed around her. Delicious smells floated from the kitchens constantly as more and more food was produced for the feast that was to follow the celebration. Every corner of the castle had been swept and scrubbed. Several times she had heard warriors returning from the hunt scolded for crossing floors with dirty boots. Everywhere she looked in the courtyard she saw ceremonial robes hanging from windows being aired.

Jacantha stood looking around her room. Tonight would be the last night she spent here. She had decided that this, her childhood chamber should be left as it was and she would begin her new life with Trwyn in a new shared chamber. Most of her personal possessions and clothes had been moved already. The room now stood bare only the bed, the mirror and a single chair remained in this room. The dress she would wear tomorrow was laid carefully over a chair. Her only other possessions remaining were her hairbrush and the clothes she would wear to bed tonight. She wondered what Trwyn was feeling now, did he share her nerves at what was to come or only feel excitement at the thought of their union.

She had avoided spending much time with Trwyn since her return from the journey with Celdwady. Celdwady had questioned her about this only yesterday, concerned that it was as a result of the vision she had received. She had soothed his fears explaining with a blush rising in her cheeks that it was not, that the reason was she was finding it hard keep her emotions and urges in check, and they had agreed between them to avoid the temptation. She blushed now to herself, as she thought about the way her body responded now at the slightest touch from Trwyn. The heat that flooded her entire body as their lips met, the desire she had to pull him too her. Her need for him scared her.

She had tried discussing the subject with a couple of the other women, having no mother to talk it over with. They told her the urge was natural but that it would fade once the act itself had taken place. She could not imagine these feelings ever fading, the description of the act its self the women gave her sounded nothing like she had expected. They made it all sound more of a chore, a duty to be endured, they said nothing of desire after that first night. Jacantha shook her head, no it would not be like that for her. She knew she would not have long with Trwyn, she would make the most of it. She would make sure once she was gone, he would have good memories to carry him through.

She had been giving more thought to the future this last few days, or rather the lack of it. Her brother must be groomed for rule and he must be bound to a woman strong enough and wise enough to support him. She had raised this with Celdwady yesterday.

Jacantha had someone in mind but she knew that although no objections would be made while she was here but once she was gone that would be different.

The girl had fought by her side since they were both girls; she was only a year or two younger than her. The fact she was a few years older than her brother would not be an issue, her family's status however would be. The family had been blighted the last few generations, in that the men had died young. The women, though good warriors, had never reached the elevated ranks the men did, due to the fact that during child bearing they had been absent from the battlefield. Despite this Jacantha saw her as the perfect partner for her brother. Jacantha had urged Celdwady to begin placing the idea out into court. She knew Fleura was not only a skilled warrior, she was also wise beyond her years and she had patience which Jacantha knew would be needed in a match with her brother. As much as she loved Arth he could at times still manage to infuriate her with his inability to believe in his own decisions.

Jacantha had engineered that the Fleura would be seated by her brother during the feast despite the looks of disapproval from the elders when she suggested it. For the first time ever, Jacantha had used her position to get her own way. She smiled at the remembrance, she had not actually lied to them just merely hinted that it was part of the prophecy which had been revealed to her and demanded they trust her. Jacantha felt the need to get out, to spend a few last hours of single life out in the open alone; she was under no illusion that once joined Trwyn would only leave her side when it was absolutely necessary.

She slipped swiftly along the corridors ducking behind tapestries to avoid detection when she heard approaching footsteps. She exited the castle by a small door at the end of the corridor that ran alongside the kitchens normally it was reserved for taking the slops out. She knew she could not be gone long, as much as she longed for one last burst of freedom, she knew that the ceremonial obligations must take precedence. There was roughly two hours until sunset, by the time the sun sank below the horizon she must be in the great hall for a feast with all the women of the castle. Trwyn would already be out of the castle, tradition demanded the men spend the evening in the woods outside the castle walls and then arrive at the castle soon after first light for her capture and the binding ceremony.

She laughed out loud at some of the traditions of the ceremonies. Not the actual binding itself, that she had always thought beautiful, but those that came before it. The men would ride into the castle an hour after first light, Trwyn would charge to her room and capture her. The idea amused her, in reality he would stand no chance. The idea that she could ever be the helpless damsel waiting there to be conquered, made her laugh. In the olden days the man had had to fight the woman properly, he had to prove his worth to her and show himself at least her equal on the battlefield. That had changed when the beautiful stranger had arrived and made the prophecy which changed everything.

Since that time things had altered, her daughter while beautiful had not been a great warrior, it was not her fault she had not been borne of warriors, so it had not been held against her. She had been wise and kind but in order to hide her deficiency with a sword, her ancestor had decreed that the idea of risking limb in a fight the morning of the wedding was ridiculous. He had created a ceremonial version of the conquest so that his wife to be had been spared the blushes of public humiliation. Jacantha wondered why he had bothered she need only have stood holding the sword to allow herself to be conquered and wondered if her own ancestor's abilities had also been in doubt.

She remembered her mother telling her tales of the times before the change. Stories of bonds made for advantage, where one of the parties was less than keen on the match. The fight would either end in bloodshed if it was the woman who objected or if it was the man unhappy with the choice swords would be dropped so defeat was ensured. She wondered now, if she had to fight Trwyn for him to win her hand, could she let him win? Would she be able to let him defeat her in front of everyone?

She was not sure her vanity would allow her to and would Trwyn accept victory knowing it had been given not earned. Maybe the new way was better, if she lived in olden times no match would be taking place.

She stood undecided what to do. She needed to do something, something to mark this momentous moment in her life. The feast was the beginning of her official transformation from a girl to a woman. Again, she found laughter issuing from her lips at the thought some might still consider her a girl. She had led them into battle already, she could hold her own against any man in combat. Yet because she was not bonded she was a girl. What if she was not getting married, would she always remain a girl even when the wrinkles creased her face. She thought of the few unbound women in the court, they had been classed as women, but she realised now that the only ones older than her, were ones whose partner had died usually on the battlefield, before they had chance to be officially bound to each other.

She looked round again. She needed to do something symbolic to mark this change in her life. The tree. It stood in the corner of the walled garden belonging to the castle. As a child she had climbed it many times. It had been years since she had last done it, she had left childhood games far behind her as the battles with Wend Y Mawr had intensified claiming more victims. She reached up grasping the lowest branch and hoisted herself up into the lower boughs. Winding between the branches she made her way upwards until she reached the slimmer branches that could not bear her weight.

She gazed slowly around surveying what lay in her line of visions. The castle loomed large to one side, on the others she could just see over the top of the walls. She remembered as a young child it was like looking out into a different land, a wilderness waiting to be explored, in her mind she had made up stories about what waited out there amongst the trees and fields. She remembered other children being free to wander from the castle whenever they wanted, yet she had always had a nurse or a guard following her. Only when she had slipped away from everyone, had she been able to disappear out the castle walls with the other children. She lay back against the rough bark. The last rays of the sun, barely penetrating the leaves to warm her.

Now the landscape bore signs of the hardships they were enduring, though she could not see far from her vantage point the fact she knew what lay beyond her vision could not be ignored. She watched as the sunset, sinking slowly towards the horizon, setting the sky alight in a blaze of orange and red. She could avoid it no longer and slid back down through the branches and headed back into the castle.

Jacantha entered the great hall slightly out of breath from her exertions. All the other ladies sat waiting for her were dressed in their finest gowns. She looked down at her normal everyday clothing and felt immediately self-conscious, she knew she should have changed before coming down but in her fear of being late had decided against it. The older women motioned to her to join them by the fireplace. For the next few hours Jacantha barely paid any attention to what went on, they talked around her; she nodded picking out the comments to which a response was excepted. They all talked about the secrets for a long happy bonding. But what was the point in telling her? Fate did not have a long life together planned for her and Trwyn.

As the night drew on the pain of the reality must have shown in her face and mortified one of the women realised their mistake. Their pity was as unbearable to Jacantha as their advice had been, they apologised for their insensitivity, protested that it had been inadvertent. She had known this evening was a mistake, to pretend everything was normal but traditions had to be upheld. The after the apologies the realisation had silenced the other women and Jacantha took the chance to talk more with Fleura, the one she had singled out as a match for her brother. She also took the opportunity to push the match with the women. She spoke to them individually, moving around the circle of women, making no secret of the reasons she believed this match was necessary. The women agreed for the most part, one or two with daughters of their own were more reluctant to agree to her choice.

With these women Jacantha played the politics game to perfection, of course had looks been the main consideration this daughter would have been her first choice, or had this trait been more important that daughter would have been perfect, she told them. She overplayed her brother's weaknesses, reminding them that in many ways, this was not such a desirable match, unless the woman was of a certain character. She looked across worried in case her words put Fleura off as well, but it appeared that she had been correct in her assessment of her and that Fleura was aware of the need to play this the right way. By the end of the evening Jacantha had gained a public show of support for the match, they would influence their husbands, how many would follow through in private Jacantha was less certain of.

It was getting late and Jacantha knew she would have to be awake in a few hours to prepare for the ceremony. She made her excuses to the women and slipped back to her own room. She slid beneath her sheets, her final night as a single woman and fell into a deep sleep dreaming of what tomorrow would bring.

Chapter Eighteen

Wend had remained in the hall with Nadredd's body until the next day. He had held him in his arms as the body grew cold and still he had been unable to let go. He could still not believe what he had done. He had destroyed the nearest thing he had to family. Even thoughts of Jacantha and the family he would create with her brought him no solace.

Activity outside in the halls had made him rise to his feet. People were furtively scurrying about the corridors he could hear the whispers as they tried to creep past unheard. Wend strode over and flung the doors open, the people in the halls froze. Wend looked at the startled expressions and demanded everyone come to the great hall immediately. He turned on his heel and returned to Nadredd's body. He stood the table back upright and lifted Nadredd's body and placed it outstretched on the table. He lifted Nadredd's hands and placed them on his chest and then turned to watch the others arrival in the room.

He stood waiting as the hall slowly filled. A few minutes later as he began the head count, instinctively he knew some had fled. Three were missing one man, the head concubine and one of the younger girls. Wend was furious, how dare they abandon him. He ordered the women back to the main dormitory where the lowest ranked girls slept. He locked the door from the outside, no more would wander while he tracked down the others.

He returned to the hall, the men stood around nervously, each aware the slightest sign of betrayal would be a death sentence. He ordered all the men to saddle up and release the hounds; they would track down the traitors. The men rushed out desperate to show their loyalty and eagerness to obey his orders.

The dogs sniffed round the gates, they seemed to be torn between two different paths. For a moment Wend hesitated, he had almost called for Nadredd to take one path while he took the other he barely stopped himself in time. He paused looking at the men. Did he trust them enough to send them one way while he went the other?

He decided he picked half a dozen men he felt he could rely on the most. He ordered them to take two of the hounds to follow one trail. Whoever they found should be brought back to the castle, he and the rest would follow the other trail. He made a show of chanting incantations, putting fear into the men of what the consequences should they decide to betrayal would be. He gave the signal and the two groups parted both following baying hounds in search of fugitives.

Wend did not have far to go before he found his quarry. The head concubine had fallen in her attempt to flee and damaged her ankle. Her flight had been severely hampered and despite the urgency she knew was required she had not made much distance in her attempt to escape. Upon hearing the baying hounds and the thunder of flying hooves she had desperately looked for somewhere to hide. She crawled deep into the undergrowth, thorns ripping at her skin as she sought to obscure herself from view. The hounds however could not be fooled, following her scent they stood at the edge of the thicket giving her location away.

Wend withdrew his sword and hacked away at the dense bushes allowing the dog's further access until their teeth closed upon the woman and they dragged her from her hiding place. Wend stood over the woman contemplating how to deal with her, he knew there was little pleasure left to be taken from her body. Her piteous cries and begging for forgiveness annoyed him. How dare she betray him when he had allowed her to live past her usefulness then ask for mercy? This was the reward he received for allowing her to continue to live under his roof, she would suffer now, and no one would ever dare betray him again.

He spotted a fallen tree stump and ordered she be dragged over to it. The men threw her over the stump ripping her torn remaining clothes from her as they did so leaving her naked and exposed. The sight of her sagging flesh enraged Wend further it only served to remind him that he had spared her, he felt disgusted with himself that he had allowed her to live. Wend ordered that she be restrained and her legs pulled wide apart. A few of the men began to get excited at the prospect of what was to come; surely they would all get a turn in punishing the whore.

Wend weighed his sword heavily in his hand then turned it round so that he grasped it by the blade. He thrust the hilt deep into the woman's body, the bloodstone set into the handle tearing the woman's flesh as he forced it into her. Rivulets of blood trickled down the inside of her thigh as he thrust it in again and again. The dogs were now dancing around expectantly. Wend noticed the male dog's evident excitement at the spectacle and let out a low laugh. He had trained the alpha male to mount on command, not that the dog needed much encouragement he shared his owner capacity for lust, Wend had lost track of the litters he had drowned from the dog mating with any bitch that came into heat.

He removed the sword and moved so he was at the other side of the stump the woman's head inches away from his feet. He let out a whistle and the dog mounted the woman. She tried desperately to break free as the dog entered her, his teeth closing in on her neck as he did so. She clawed desperately trying to break free from the hands that held her as the dog thrust into her. After Wends sword she did not feel the dog inside but she felt the warm trickle of the blood running down from where his teeth held her and the humiliation of her position. She had expected to be abused if caught but not this, she wished the ground would open up and swallow her and this nightmare be over. She knew Wend would not let her live, at that moment as she wished for death it came with the dogs approaching release his jaws tightened around her neck. The last feelings she ever felt was of total humiliation as Wend snarled "Not fit for human consumption". The alpha male released his gripped and the men allowed her body to fall into the dirt.

The other hounds that had stood back now received the signal and fell upon the body ripping flesh from bone, devouring her as quickly as they could aware they would be called away at any time. Wend motioned to the men to return the way they had come. They would catch up with the other party unless they passed them as they back towards the castle. Reluctantly the dogs obeyed Wend's call as he and the other men remounted and they followed at heel leaving the remains to the forest scavengers to finish off.

They caught up with the other group within the hour. It became evident that their quarry this time had made their flight on horseback. Some of the men nervously questioned whether it was really necessary to chase them down given the head start they already had but Wend would not listen. They would be caught and punished whether it took a day or a week to ride them down. Wend felt the power rise up inside him as his anger rose. He tried to direct his anger ahead of them, as he did with his sight, in the direction they were travelling in. His first attempt failed as one of the hounds leading them exploded into a ball of flames. His second attempt met with more success and in the distance, they heard screams. Wend dug his heels into the horses' underbelly and pressed onwards. Twenty minutes later the fugitives were in sight.

The horse lay in the middle of the track, having torn the hounds away from their earlier meal he allowed them to feed from the dead beast while he turned his attention towards the runaways. It appeared to Wend that the larger creature had taken the brunt of his blast. This was information he would store for the future, now he knew he could reach out and strike at distance, he would have to hone his skills for a more accurate aim. The horses' rider was struggling to stay on his feet, he had moved so his back was against a tree for support. His sword hung by his side, his strength failing as he attempted to lift it.

"Find the woman, bring her back here" Wend barked out the order towards a group of his men, as he slid from the saddle and walked towards the man.

"It's not how it looks" the man began. "I fell for her I did not mean for it to happen, it just happened. I know I should have come to you but, well, Wend you have to understand she was scared, we both know that you would not have been happy for one of your men to pair with a concubine."

"She is my property. That makes you a thief." Wend glared at him. "You knew I would not be happy yet you did it anyway, you ungrateful..." His words were cut off by the man.

"No Wend please it wasn't like that. I thought you would understand if I came and spoke to you but she was too scared. The way you feel about Jacantha that's how I feel about her, I cannot live without her it was killing me watching when she had to be with others."

Wend leapt at him one hand grasping the man's throat the other ripping the sword from his grasp and discarding it on the floor.

"Do not compare what I feel for Jacantha for what you feel for that whore. Do you honestly believe if I did not drug them, a young girl like that would give a fat old man like you a second glance? Of course not, she is a whore it is her job to do your biding, the potion I give them makes sure they do it willingly. Do you really believe that she feels more for you than any of the others here? You are a fool."

A noise behind him in the undergrowth gave away the fact the girl had been discovered. The men, dragging her along, were taking full opportunity to grope her as they did so, her flesh was mottled with red marks where hands had grabbed and pinched her. Red hand marks across her buttocks, revealed by her lack of clothing. Anything she had been wearing had been removed in the short time between her discovery and her delivery to Wend.

Wend reached out and grabbed the girl by the hair and pulled her to him. He looked across at the man. He would show him what a fool he was before he relieved him of his pathetic existence. He ordered the man be bound to the tree and his trousers removed. Next, he ordered one of the eye masks be taken from his saddlebags and fitted on him. He wanted to make sure the man saw everything. Wend watched as the men held the man's head as the eye mask was fitted. His screams, as the hooks were attached to his eyelids, filled the air around them.

The girl stood meekly by his side showing no emotion at all. Wend pulled her forward so they stood inches from the bound man. He slipped a vial from his belt and tipped its contents into the girl's mouth, she swallowed without hesitation. He could not rely on the fact that the head concubine had done her duty over the last few days after her betrayal. He twisted her hair tilting her head slightly and pressed his mouth over hers.

At first, she did not respond, proving to Wend he was right in his assumptions that the potion had not been administered the last few days. Quickly the potion took effect and the girl pushed her body towards his as her tongue darted into his mouth responding to his kiss. He took his time, savouring the mortification of the man bound to the tree. His hands sought her breasts, teasing the hardening nipples while her hand travelled down his body.

He allowed her to undo the thongs and release his erection. He turned her body slightly, so he could ensure the man saw the eagerness in her face, as he moved his hand down between her legs and slid his fingers into her. The man tried to turn his head away to avoid the sight before him, Wend now ordered that his gaze be directed towards the action. The strength had deserted man and he slumped to his knees only his bindings held him up. One of the other men stepped to the side of him and grabbed the man's hair turning his head so he had no choice but to watch.

Wend now forced the girl down on to her knees. He knelt down behind her, holding her head upright, as he whispered into her ear. The girl looked at the man before her, tears streaming down his face mingled with blood from where the hooks had ripped at his eyelids as he struggled to block out the sight before him. She smiled at him, and then lowered her mouth to his groin. Despite the man's humiliation and heartbreak his body responded to her mouth upon him. Wend entered her from behind, each thrust forcing her forward to take the prisoner deeper into her throat. His climax came quickly, so quickly it caught him off guard, he normally could control himself but the events of the last few days seemed to have affected him.

He stepped back and ordered the men to line up and take their turns. The girl following orders Wend's orders, remained on her knees, as a succession of men entered her one after the other. She continued to suck upon the prisoner, stopping when he threatened to find release, only starting again once she was sure the moment had passed.

Once all the men had taken a turn, Wend stepped forward again. He entered her once more, then withdrew dissatisfied. The men had stretched too her much for Wend to take any pleasure from the process. He adjusted his position and thrust forward again. This time he met resistance as he forced his way between her buttocks. His hand slid round between her legs teasing the secret place that he knew would produce results. The girl gasped then thrust herself backwards impaling herself upon Wend's erection. He pushed her forward slightly so that with each thrust she took the prisoners full length into her throat.

He smiled at the man. He would make sure he showed them all he would not tolerate betrayal of any type by anyone. He grasped the girl's hips as she took both erections deep into opposite ends of her body. He allowed his mind to connect with the man's, he sensed the confusion but also something else. The man still had hope. He actually believed he would be allowed to live, having learnt his lesson. Wend laughed out loud and increased the movement of his hand between the girl's legs. He could feel the girl's climax approaching, he slowed his hand slightly he wanted everything to happen in the right order.

The prisoner now was breathing heavily as his own climax approached, surely the fact Wend was allowing him to finally get relief was a good sign. He came with a shudder, the orgasm draining him almost to the point of losing consciousness. He watched still unable to turn his head from the grasp of the hand holding it as Wend brought the girl to orgasm in front of him. Somewhere in his thoughts, his own stupidity now obvious to him.

Wend pulled out and stood up. He grabbed the girl's hair and turned her face towards him. He came over her face, her tongue flicking out trying to devour his tribute from her skin. He pushed her to one side. She lay flushed from her orgasm waiting for whatever he had in store next for her. He stepped back and surveyed the two traitors. He was satisfied that the man had been humiliated, well almost, now it only remained to decide how to dispose of them. As for the whore we maybe she should die but maybe not just yet, there was more fun to have there.

He walked over and stood over her. He looked down at her eager face and relieved himself on her, the steaming urine splashing over her face and body. The men watching laughed. They had been so caught up in taking their turns with her, they had forgotten that the man tied to the tree had been their friend and that they had harboured thoughts of doing exactly what he had done. Wend gave a signal the girl should be taken back with them. One of the men stepped forward and hoisted her to her feet. He climbed up on a horse and one of the other men passed her up to him. He threw a questioning glance towards Wend.

Wend laughed as he nodded his head, the men were so predictable give them what they wanted and they would forget thoughts of leaving. He watched as the man fumbled to loosen his leggings and adjusted the girls position he pushed her forward over the horses neck as he took advantage of the orifice Wend had recently vacated. Wend saw the look on the other men's faces it would be a long ride back for the concubine as they all turns to share their saddles with her.

Wend turned his attention back to the man, he was barely aware of anything now, slipping in and out of consciousness as he gave up hope of reprieve. Wend took a flask of water from his saddlebag and poured it over the man's face letting it trickle between his lips. The man revived slightly and looked up at Wend in gratitude. He did not notice the knife in Wend's other hand until it was too late.

"You betrayed me! You stole from me! And then you insult the woman I intend to be bound to by comparing her to a whore!" Wend spat the words at him.

With a swift movement Wend sliced through the flesh of the man's groin severing his penis. Blood spurted out covering Wend's legs in a ruby sheen. He grabbed the man's face forcing his lips apart and thrust the severed penis into his mouth. His hand clamped down over the man's face. He could not breathe, as he writhed desperately fighting for breath, he swallowed, choking on his own severed manhood. It was over in a minute and the man slumped lifeless against his bonds. Wend spat on him.

He took one last look before mounting his horse and giving the signal for the men to move off. He searched their faces looking for any signs that he had anything to fear from any of them. He smiled as he realised their attention was focused on who take the get the next turn with the concubine. He watched as the rhythm of the horse's movement forced the rider further into her. Maybe he would take the next turn before she was too badly damaged. Perhaps he would take Jacantha for a ride once he had her he smiled again at the thought. Wend was pleased with the outcome of the day he felt things were falling into place, thoughts of Nadredd's body lying in the hall forced from his mid for the present time.

Chapter Nineteen

It was still dark when Jacantha awoke the next morning. At first light the women had joined her in her room to prepare her. She had stood patiently as they washed her and dressed her despite her protests she could manage it herself. The thin fabric of the dress clung to her slender frame accentuating her curves. The thin straps tied at her shoulders seemed so flimsy compared to her normal dress Jacantha worried about its ability to hold up to the long day ahead. She felt vulnerable without her normal clothing. Tradition insisted she be naked beneath the thin dress and she felt resentment that she should be forced to dress in this manner...

The women had brushed her hair and worked it into an intricate pile of plaits and curls atop her head. Flowers gathered at first light had been threaded into her hair and the few tendrils which escaped and trailed down her neck tickled her as they brushed gently against her skin. She sat now looking out the window waiting. The women had left to get themselves ready as soon as they had felt she was prepared. She knew it had been less than an hour since sunrise but it seemed much longer. Her thoughts drifted to her parents, she wondered what they would say if they were here now, what advice they would give her.

Sadness tinged her thoughts as she thought about the advice the women had given her the night before, recommendations to ensure a long and happy match which could never be hers. She shook her head, trying to shake off the melancholy which waiting had brought on.

Trwyn would be here soon. She could see people leaving the castle already, heading to a small grove just outside the castle walls where the ceremony would take place. There had been so much excitement the last few weeks, at times it seemed that everyone else had been more caught up in the preparations than she had been. Maybe that was true, her own thoughts had been torn in so many directions. She spotted activity a distance away, dust rose from a road obscured by trees. Jacantha felt her nerves growing what if it was not Trwyn? What if Wend was taking advantage of their plans to attack while they were otherwise engaged? She pushed him from her thoughts she would not allow Wend Y Mawr to spoil this day. He had no way of knowing what was happening today.

She sat nervously as the dust plume grew closer. Then through the trees came Trwyn and the company which had joined him on his enforced camp out the previous evening. Jacantha went to the mirror and looked at herself. She hardly recognised the face looking back at her. Vanity was something she had never experienced before but now she saw a beauty to rival even her ancestor. She knew Trwyn would love her and think her beautiful no matter what she wore but given the circumstances, it had been important she create as many special memories for him as she could. She returned to the window and sat waiting for his arrival watching his progress as he drew nearer to the castle.

She watched as if seeing him for the first time as he slid from his horse in the courtyard and strode towards the castle. There was an air of confidence about him which was new and if she was honest she found it attractive. She waited mentally following his journey along the corridors as he drew nearer to her chamber. The door flew open and he entered. He stopped in front of her letting his eyes feast upon her. He reached out and grasped her round the waist pulling her towards him. His lips locked over hers and she pressed her body towards his. Abruptly he stopped and pulled his lips away from hers. His hands gripped her arms holding her firmly at arm's length and looked her up and down greedily before he looked into her eyes and smiled. Jacantha shuddered there was something there she had not seen before, no that was not true. It was familiar, she could not think where; she only knew it was not something she associated with Trwyn.

She did not have time to think on it further as Trwyn leant towards her and slid an arm behind her legs, sweeping her up into the air. Whatever had been there was gone; it was her Trwyn that carried her now from the room and out of the castle into the sunshine.

Jacantha relaxed against Trwyn's chest as he carried her towards the grove. Her skin burnt from the heat they both felt where she made contact against him. Only a few more hours and she would be his in both body and soul. The thin film of sweat on his skin told her he was struggling with the proximity of her body as much as she was his. She moved the arm which was wrapped round his neck slightly tightening her grip. Instinctively she let her lips close upon the exposed flesh of his collarbone, just the slightest of kisses yet the tremble she felt pass through his body was undeniable. Finally, they reached where the others stood before them waiting. Trwyn carried her through the throng and set her down in front of Celdwady.

Jacantha waited expectantly while everyone settled into their places. She had faced the enemy in battle but never had she had this feeling, her heart raced and her stomach twisted. For a moment she felt as if she were separate from them all, as if she were viewing the proceedings through a wall of water. She saw Celdwady's lips begin to move and forced herself to focus on the proceedings.

"We are gathered here to witness the union of these two people" Celdwady began "Trwyn you have claimed Jacantha as your prize, do you do so of your own free will?"

Trwyn nodded his ascent, his chest swelled with pride as he looked towards her.

"Jacantha you have been claimed do you accept this man as you victor?" Jacantha now took her turn to nod her head in acceptance.

They stood as Celdwady discoursed on the sanctity of the bond they were about to enter into. Jacantha allowed her eyes to sweep round taking in her surroundings for the first time, candles had been lit and placed all around the grove, even in the bright sunlight she could see their flames dancing. Garlands of flowers had been strung round the lower branches of the trees, brightly coloured ribbons threaded amongst them. Everyone present had dressed in their finest robes the women had flowers threaded in their own hair as they had threaded them through hers.

Brawd stood forward and spoke in nervous tones. Jacantha turned her attention back to him as he stood reciting an ancient poem about the history of the ceremony. Then Celdwady stepped forward again.

"Before I bind your hands, turn to each other and affirm your love of each other by making you pledges."

Jacantha and Trwyn turned to face each other, again there for the briefest moment Jacantha saw something behind his eyes it gone as quickly as it appeared. Trwyn took her hands in his and began.

"I have loved you as long as I can remember, I have worked hard to be worthy of you. For a long time, I never thought this day would come. I will love you for the rest of my life and worship you through eternity."

He looked at her with such love that Jacantha dismissed her earlier thoughts; it must have been the light playing tricks.

"I love you will all my being. I will cherish the time we are granted together and do all in my power to make you happy. I give you my body, my heart and my soul knowing I can trust you to honour them. Whatever fate may have in store for me it cannot change the love I have for you"

She held Trwyn's gaze for a few moments before they both turned back to face Celdwady.

"Are you ready?" he asked. They both nodded.

Celdwady held out his hand and both Jacantha and Trwyn placed their hands in his. He pulled from his robe a length of ivy. He laid it across their hands and began the wind it around them binding the hands together.

"With the act of binding the two become one. Love should grow like the ivy, encompassing all within its reach. It may be torn at, damaged but with strong roots it will survive and grow stronger. Let no one destroy what you have in each other." He looked at Trwyn as he said this.

"In the eyes of the Goddess you are now as one. May you take her blessings forth with you from this place." With his last words he curled the end of the ivy in between Jacantha's fingers and clasped his hands over theirs.

Trwyn turned to look at his wife; his unbound hand reached up and gently cupped her cheek. He pulled her in towards him, they twisted to face each other their bound hands trapped between their chests. His lips met hers in a tender embrace, the urgency contained for the moment, yet still there traceable in the pounding of his chest. They parted and turned to face the crowd. Several women had tears running down their faces, their wistful looks suggesting they were remembering their own special days. They stepped forward now embracing the couple, the men letting the women offer their blessings first before they moved in to offer their own.

After a few minutes the crowd parted allowing the couple to lead the procession back to the castle. As they walked through the throng the children threw flower petals over them. A pastel shower covered them catching in their hair Jacantha laughed as she reached up to brush a stray petal from Trwyn's eyelash.

As they entered the great hall Jacantha caught her breath. She had witnessed many occasions through the years but never had she seen the hall look so beautiful. Trails of ivy were twisted round beams, reaching across the high ceiling. Garlands of flowers were coiled round pillars. Huge urns stood in the corners, foliage cascading from them. Everywhere she looked flowers and leaves greeted her. At the far end of the hall the head table had been set up, the plants forming a grotto around them. As they took their seats she could smell the heavy perfume from the flowers, the sensation made her feel weak and she sank thankfully into her seat.

They waited as the others filed their way into the hall and took their places. She looked across at her brother, Fleura sitting by his side, she smiled as she noticed how attentive he was being towards her. Soon it would be their turn, the thought pleased her, more than just for the kingdoms sake; she wanted him to be happy. The age gap between them meant they had never been especially close but he was her flesh and she wanted to make sure he would be loved once she was gone. Only a few empty places remained at the tables now. The women now began to file in carrying the huge platters from the kitchens, only once every table was filled did they take their seats.

Everyone now waited expectantly as Celdwady approached the head table carrying two goblets. He handed one each to Jacantha and Trwyn and looked round for Brawd, beckoning him to bring something.

Brawd looked sheepish as he brought forward a flagon and handed it to Celdwady.

Celdwady looked at him puzzled, "You did not try this did you?"

Brawd blushed as he answered

"Only a little, I wanted to be sure I knew how it should taste for when it was my turn to brew it."

Celdwady let out a laugh "Oh dear boy, this is only intended for the couple at their feast and a glass each for the other couples. Maybe you should go take a seat, and possibly a swim in the lake once the feasting is finished."

Jacantha suppressed a giggle as Brawd hurried back to his seat a red flush spreading across his face. Celdwady turned his attention back the goblets, removing the stopper from the flagon he poured the golden liquid into the glasses.

He winked at the couple "Drink and be merry put all other thoughts out of your mind for today but each other. But drink plenty the minute everyone starts wandering I guarantee the bottle will disappear." He walked back to his seat chuckling to himself. Jacantha could not remember ever seeing him so amused.

Jacantha raised her glass, she could feel every pair of eyes in the room upon her. Trwyn picked up his, and hooked his arm round hers linking them as they both put the goblets to their lips. The liquid was sweet, mead Jacantha guessed but something extra there as well. They drank deeply finishing most of the contents in one go. Trwyn reached over refilling their glasses and a cheer went up around the room. As one the room came to life, glasses clinked and knives clattered against plates as the food was devoured. Reluctantly Jacantha unwound the ivy that still bound her to Trwyn she was loath to do it, but if either of them wished it eat, it was necessary. Trwyn picked up the ivy and tied it round his bride's head adding an extra decoration to her crown.

Jacantha picked at the food before her, her appetite barely existent and the fluttering in her stomach continued. She looked at Trwyn attacking a joint with relish. He looked at her, noticing she was not eating he picked up a piece of meat and fed it to her. She felt her heart rate quicken as his fingertips touched her lips as he placed the meat between them. She chewed quickly, forcing the food down with a smile. He picked up another piece this time holding it between his teeth and leant over. Jacantha felt the fire spreading through her body as their lips met and she took the offering. She pulled away swallowing the meat without chewing, nearly choking in her desire to feel his lips against hers again.

She longed for the feast to be over so she could be alone with her husband. She sensed he felt the same as he shifted uncomfortably in his seat. She drew back, she knew that it would be a few hours before they could slip away unmissed.

The feasting carried on for over an hour before people could finally eat no more. The remaining food was gathered and placed on tables pushed up against the walls. Benches were moved and a circle formed to make space for dancing. Instruments appeared as if from thin air, and music now filled the hall. Trwyn took a long drink from his glass remembering

Celdwady's warning before reaching for Jacantha's hand to lead her to the middle of the hall.

They moved slowly in perfect unison. Each step carefully placed as they graceful wound between the other dancers. Jacantha could never remember actually learning the dance it was just there something she had always known. Every person connected, moving almost as one, knowing exactly his or her place in the crowd. Jacantha passed by Brawd, he was now looking even more uncomfortable if that were possible. He stood looking down at his feet trying not to meet anyone's gaze. It was evident she was not the only one wishing for the chance to slip away and she smiled at the unfortunate young man's predicament.

The dance finished and the next began, she found herself stood before Celdwady

"May I have the pleasure before your husband reclaims you?"

She nodded and gave him her hand. She marvelled at the grace and elegance with which he moved with as they weaved round the other couples. After a few minutes they found themselves opposite Trwyn and Celdwady delivered her back into her husband's arms. They danced for a little time until neither could bear the proximity of their bodies any longer. They resumed their seats to watch as others continued the dance, moving in and out of each other with practised grace. As Celdwady had predicted the flagon was gone.

Jacantha sat watching as the drink began to have an effect on the revellers, soon they would be able to leave. She giggled as she noticed the empty flagon beneath Fleura's chair, judging from her brothers seeming confidence she guessed he had been its recipient. A number of other couples now seemed to be struggling to contain their passions as well. Knowing looks passed across the hall. Couples who had been bound many years ago seemed to have found long lost urges for their loved ones.

Several of the men now approached Trwyn whispering into his ear, she noticed the good natured digs they delivered to his ribs and could guess their topic of conversation. Jacantha strained to hear them but could make out very little of what was being said. Abruptly he stood and turned to face her, his face flushed from the other men's words. He offered her his hand, believing he was leading her back to the dance floor she accepted it. Suddenly she was hoisted up into the air. A cheer echoed round the room as Trwyn carried her through the dancers and out of the hall.

As they passed through the corridors Jacantha glanced out the windows. The sun was still high on the horizon and she realised she had lost all track of the passage of time. In the courtyard she spotted Brawd at a horse trough leaning over it. By the next window she passed he had climbed into it and was sat submerged to the chest looking slightly more comfortable than he had all day. Trwyn paused briefly to see what had amused his wife so much, joining in her mirth before continuing towards their bed chamber. They arrived at the door to the chamber she would now share with Trwyn. He struggled to balance her while he undid the latch, she reached to undo it for him but stopped, now was not the time to take the lead.

The door swung open and he strode through it, kicking it shut behind them. She had waited for this moment for so long but now nerves took over. The room had been decorated to match the hall, flowers and foliage filled the room. Flower petals lay strewn across the bed. Trwyn gently placed Jacantha down on the edge of the bed and stepped back. His gaze locked on her he removed his boots and tunic. Jacantha had seen him with his shirt off many times but only now she realised how perfectly contoured his body was.

She rose to her feet reaching out to him, her fingers brushing across his skin. He reached up and took her hands and kissing her fingertips before he placed them down by her side. He knelt before her taking her foot in his hand he removed the soft sandals she had worn for the ceremony then repeated the process with the other foot. He placed his hands onto her ankles then slowly moved them upwards lifting the dress as he did so. She could feel his eyes devouring her body as he slowly uncovered it. As his hands reached her thighs a shudder of anticipation shot through her body. She yearned to grab him, to rip the dress off but Trwyn had no intention of being rushed.

His hands slid round behind her caressing the curve of her buttocks, he pulled her towards him, his lips brushing the soft flesh of her taut stomach. Clumsily he raised himself to standing, desperate not to lose contact with her body. He slid the dress the rest of the way up and over her head discarding it on the floor. Suddenly something inside him could hold back no longer he pulled her to him his mouth closing over hers. His lips pressed hard against hers as his tongue slid between her lips.

His hands took possession of her body, one sliding down to grasp a buttock while the other sought a breast. Jacantha now allowed her own hands to resume their explorations. One reached round feeling the muscles tensed in Trwyn's back, the other slid down reaching for him through the leggings that still encased him. She struggled, tugging at the leather thongs that held them in place, unable to undo them. Trwyn lifted her, moving her back towards the bed he placed her down upon it, gently pushing her down onto her back.

He stood at the end of the bed his eyes drinking in her body as he removed his leggings. Jacantha laid back her legs hanging over the edge of the bed, she gasped at the sight of him naked. For the first time a twinge of fear passed through her, would it hurt to take him inside her? Yet she wanted him so badly she would happily bear whatever it took to be joined with him. She willed him to come to her but he resisted.

He dropped to his knees and reaching out for her he grasped her behind her knees pulling her legs apart. His lips brushed against the inside of her thighs as they moved upwards towards the soft downy hair between her legs. His hands now reached between her legs, fingers prising her wider as his tongue darted out and made contact with her. Jacantha felt her body start to tingle at his touch. Each time his tongue connected with her most intimate place was exquisite torture, the thought briefly passed through her mind wondering where he had learnt these skills but it was lost as the sensations rendered thought impossible. He slid a finger into her, then a second, stretching her as he closed his mouth over the little button that was driving her crazy. He increased the tempo sliding his fingers deep into her as he sucked at her. Jacantha's hips now bucked beneath his lips, he could feel her getting wetter with each stroke.

His lips now moved up her body, his hands moving to her breasts as he shifted his position until he was above her. Then he kissed her, his tongue forcing its way into her mouth. She could taste herself on his lips. Then with a single thrust he was deep inside her. His kiss muffled the yelp from her lips, as a brief sharp pain passed through her body. For a moment he remained still, enjoying the tightness of her. Then unable to hold back he began the thrust into her. Jacantha dug her nails into his back as he slid his full length into her. Her hips moved to meet each thrust as he increased his speed.

Jacantha felt herself starting to drift as she had in the stable as her orgasm approached. She was torn between letting the sensations overwhelm her and focussing to remain in her body, to feel each sensation as it tore through her body. She focused and found it required very little conscious thought to remain rooted in the physical. She felt Trwyn's urgency down as he strove to get deeper inside her. She wrapped her legs round his back pulling him in closer. He pulled back almost slipping out of her before plunging his full being into her. She felt her orgasm explode throughout her being; her body communicating with Trwyn's bring him to crisis with a roar that echoed around the room. He collapsed on top of her, the sweat from both their bodies mingling as they embraced.

Jacantha's skin flushed from her first experience, yet she was eager for more. Her tongue licked at Trwyn's neck tasting the saltiness of his skin. Cat like she flipped over, rolling Trwyn onto his back. Now it was her time to explore, she traced the contours of the muscles as she moved down his body. Momentarily she regretted the necessity to let him slip from within her. She glanced up at him as her head moved lower. He laid back eyes half closed waiting to see what she had in store for him. As she reached her destination, she was pleased to watch the smile spread across his face as her tongue made contact.

She ran her tongue along the full length of his manhood, feeling him tremble as she tasted the juices coating him from both of them. Despite having so recently climaxed Celdwady's drink had taken effect and his erection was still hard, as she took it tentatively into her mouth. She allowed her teeth to gently rake against his skin, as she sought to take more into her mouth. She felt Trwyn's hand on the back of her head, fingers entwined in her hair as he gently encouraged her to take more. Teasing him now as he had her earlier, she moved her head taunting his sac with her tongue before again turning her attention to his length.

He reached down and pulled her gently back up to him. He lifted her hips and slid back into her, she slowly began to move her hips taking him further into her.

Trwyn looked up at her and smiled "I love you."

She smiled back at him as she leant forward "I love you too."

Her mouth closed over his, silencing him. Slowly this time, they made love again, taking time to explore each other's bodies.

As the sun rose the next morning, they lay in each other's arm spent, their passion finally exhausted. Jacantha curled up in Trwyn's arms, his breath against her cheek as he slept. They might not have long but she was determined that for as long as she could stay she would make sure he did not regret his choice.

Chapter Twenty

Wend sat staring at the orb. It had been days since he had last seen Jacantha in it. His mind ran wild with thoughts of where she was and what she was doing. He had stayed awake the last two nights in the hope of seeing her return to her chamber to sleep but she had not. He had sensed a change in the atmosphere a few days prior, what he had brought it about he could not tell. He had searched the scrolls again but flung them aside when they failed to yield answers. Now the candles spluttered, burnt down to their wicks they struggled, the flames faltering before, one at a time, they went out.

Sat in the dark, with only the faint glow coming from the orb, Wend's eyelids grew heavy. He slipped into a deep fitful sleep. Images spun through his mind but he could not decipher their meanings. The stranger was there laughing at him, taunting him with his inadequacy and his own impatience, which had taken the final pieces of knowledge out of his grasp. He sat upright determined to shake the images from his thoughts. Now Nadredd's voice came to him out of the darkness.

No longer certain if he was still sleeping or awake Wend lunged towards where he thought the voice had come from. The candle holders crashed to the ground in his wake, hot wax splashing against his flesh scolding where it made contact. Again the voice came behind him this time. He swung round again this time colliding with his chair. The pain in his leg as he landed on the chair told him he was awake but the voice kept on taunting.

"Who are you?" Wend demanded, "What manner of demon are you?"

"Demon? You dare to call me a demon. I who was your friend. I, who guarded your secrets, never breathed a word of your not aging. I who you betrayed, who you killed. You call me demon?"

"Nadredd is dead. I am sorry for that but he is dead. You are not him! Nadredd would not come back to haunt me he understood, he forgave me. I demand to know who you are."

"I am he you betrayed. He whose body you burnt in your jealously. Even now you cannot see your guilt. I loved you I would have laid down my life for you and to you it meant nothing. Even if it had been Jacantha, we have shared everything in, time you would have thrown her aside to us anyway."

"No, never! She will be my queen she is not just another plaything." Fear invaded Wends voice as he frantically searched for the source of the voice.

Nadredd laughed "Of course that is all she is. For the present you value her all the more because you have not got her but once you do you will ruin her as you do everyone you come in contact with. Then you will despise her for her weakness for allowing you to break her. You will corrupt her as you corrupt all around you. I came willingly to that corruption but she will not and in the end, you will destroy the very thing you seek to possess."

"You know nothing" Wend snarled "Do not speak of her. You understand nothing of my feelings for her. You are not Nadredd, he understood, he knew why I must have her. He shared my vision for the future."

Wend spun as the voice seemed to come at him from everywhere but nowhere. He drew his sword slashing it through the empty air hoping its blade would find its mark and silence the voice. He finally found the door in the darkness and exited the room the bright glare of the great hall confusing him momentarily. The men stopped to watch, here was their leader seemingly arguing with himself. They shifted uneasily in their seats.

Wend spun round and as his eyes adjusted to the light and he saw the eyes of the others upon him. He laughed a little too loudly,

"Damn spirits seek to put an end to our fun, we will show them who is in command here." He motioned for more drink to be brought, as it was served to the men he filled his glass and drank it down, immediately refilling it and downing the second.

The men joined in his laughter, though the looks which passed between them, did not go unnoticed by Wend. In the centre of the room, the runaway concubine was suspended by her wrists. Her body was bruised from misuse at his hands and those of his men. He walked over to her and grabbed her chin lifting her face so that he looked into her eyes.

"Hmmm what new sport can we have with you?"

Now the men laughed again, more convincingly this time. His comments a reminder of the fate that awaited those who betrayed him. Even as he grasped her breast, the voice that named itself as Nadredd, continued taunting him, he tried to block it out. He would focus on the girl and the voice would stop, he could not show the men this weakness. He inspected the girl, inserting his hand between her legs told him that there was not much fun left to be had there, she was badly torn already.

His eyes surveyed the room looking for inspiration. He felt strangely pressurised to come up with something for the men's amusement. He needed to distract them from dwelling on his strange entrance. He had never had trouble thinking these things up before but with the voice goading him, he was struggling to keep his outward composure.

He called some of the other women to him and ordered they cut the runaway down. As they did so, she collapsed straight to the floor. He ordered they clean her up as best they could they hesitated, looking at him, fearing they had misunderstood him. At first, they made to lead her away until Wend made it clear that they should perform their task in front of them all. The men stood watching puzzled by their leaders orders, what pleasure could there be in watching a girl cleaned, however as soon as the women began the process they understood. Wend watched as the girl writhed in agony as soap and water were rubbed against her damaged genitals.

The men seeing her obvious pain began to laugh, more than one already becoming aroused just by the sight of her flailing under the grasp of those scouring her body.

"Spread her further make sure she is well and truly scrubbed"

Wend laughed as he issued the order. Two women grabbed her legs pulling them wide apart. A third knelt between her legs taking a bar of soap she inserted it into the girl. Sensing that the situation was now perilous for them all, she made certain she appeared to be relishing her task. The runaway screamed as the soap stung her damaged flesh.

Sensing the men starting to get aroused now, Wend knew he must push them a little further, he must let lust push what they had witnessed from their minds. He took his dagger and grabbed the bar of soap as it slid from the girl's body. Embedding the blade into the soap he handed it back to the woman. Then with his hand guiding hers Wend forced it inside the runaway. He manipulated it so it plunged in and out as a phallus would. The girl on the floor screamed and finding a last reserve of strength struggled trying to crawl away.

The men rushed forward eager to pin her to the floor and get a closer look at proceedings. Now Wend stood and moved behind the woman holding the weapon. He considered his options then removed his belt. He flexed the leather between his hands a few times before bringing it down across the woman's back. A red line appeared snaking its way from the middle of her back down to her buttocks. She in response thrust the dagger harder into the girl.

Wend stepped back slightly his next blow connected across the woman's buttocks, this pleased him more as he watched her body jolt into the air with the contact. He repeated this a few times more watching the welts rise across her flesh. With each blow she doubled her efforts as she worked the dagger in and out of the struggling girl. The girl's screams now came in hoarse spurts as she fought trying to free herself.

Wend sensed the men waiting for the signal that they may join the fun. He undid his leggings and knelt behind the woman yielding the dagger. Spreading her buttocks, he thrust into her. As he did so the other men fell about them to find a way to join in, Wend reached round retrieving his dagger his memory of lying prone and the man attacking him forcing its way to the surface. One man knelt now across the runaway's neck forcing himself into her mouth as she opened it to scream once again. Another bit at a breast, biting with such force he almost removed the nipple, he threw his head back exhilarated, the blood dripping down is chin.

Each man now grabbed at the concubines, pulling them down into this mass of writhing bodies in the centre of the room. Despite the distraction Wend could still hear the voice taunting him. He now realised he could not silence the voice, only control the way he allowed it to affect him outwardly. As he thrust into the woman, something happened.

For the first time in Wend's life he began to soften. He quickly faked his climax determined his men should see nothing of this. Hurriedly he pulled out and replaced his leggings glad the men were too occupied to think anything of his actions. He watched in panic as another replaced him terrified they would realise his lie. Then relieved as they carried on oblivious wrapped up in their own lust. The voice grew louder again now adding this to the list of taunts.

Unnoticed by the others Wend crept away, back into to the secret chamber. Inside he barred the door and crawled into the corner. Hands placed over his ears he sought to block out the voice. His efforts only seemed to goad it more as it repeated the accusations and insults. Finally, he could take no more he curled into a ball and wept.

Chapter Twenty-One

It was nearing dusk the day after their wedding before Jacantha and Trwyn appeared in the great hall. Only hunger had finally driven them from their bed. They had eaten with the others, yet had seen only each other until Celdwady had come to join them. Time was growing short only two weeks remained until Jacantha must face Wend. There was still much to do, plans to be made and finalised. Reality had crashed down around them, bringing them both back to the earth with a resounding bump. Jacantha now spent her days closeted away with Celdwady, while Trwyn passed his with the others training and preparing for the fight to come.

Jacantha sat curled on the fire by the fire in Celdwady's chamber she was reading an ancient parchment retelling the legend of her ancestor. She had never read the parchment before having been told the tale by Celdwady. She marvelled at being the only person in the castle, who had not known the story. Others had learnt it from their infancy, a bedtime story of the woman who guarded their future prosperity. In her father's determination to protect her from the prophecy he had forbidden she be told it by anyone.

She looked up from the parchment now and looked towards Celdwady, "Is this mirror they refer to the same one in my chamber which my mother had?"

Celdwady raised his head at her question he had only half heard what she had said as he had been deeply immersed in the scrolls he was examining.

"Mirror? Which mirror?" he asked puzzled by her question.

"The one in my room, the one my mother kept in her chamber? I was thinking of moving it to my new chamber but it is so heavy."

Celdwady stood up abruptly. Scrolls fell to the floor in his wake as he seemed to search for one specific scroll amongst them. He trailed his finger across scroll after scroll discarding first then the next. Jacantha's eyes grew wide she had never seen Celdwady treat his precious scrolls with so little consideration. He moved round the room, whatever he seemed to be searching for eluding him. Jacantha now left her own reading to watch as he flew about the room. Brawd entered and seeing the disarray immediately set to work picking up the scrolls.

"Stop!" Celdwady ordered him. "Think where did I mention seeing the reference to a seeing orb?" Although the question was asked of Brawd whether it was meant for him remained unclear.

Standing in the centre of the room he seemed to consider for a moment, then muttering under his breath he went across and took down a crumbling, dusty book from the shelf. Carefully he turned its fragile pages, until he seemed happy he had found something of relevance. He turned face the others

"Go now, I need to be alone to study this. Brawd, you will return in one hour. Jacantha, you may take the rest of the day off from your studies, go swing a sword at your husband or something but whatever you do stay away from that mirror."

Jacantha looked at him puzzled she opened her mouth to speak but had no time to question him as Brawd pushed her towards the door.

Once the others had left Celdwady turned his attention to the page. Could it be? He must be sure. He took down another volume from the shelf, he had not examined this one in years. He scolded himself that he had not thought of it sooner. The council of elders was due to meet in a few hours he must be sure before then. He took the book and laid it open on the table and began studying the ancient text.

Jacantha stood in the courtyard for a few minutes before heading off to the stables. She intended saddling up her horse and escaping the castle for a short while but as she approached a cluster of people stood round the entrance made it impossible to sneak away unnoticed. Their voices were raised in laughter but she could not make out what was being said from this distance.

As she grew closer one of the men spotted her and they fell silent. They parted to reveal an embarrassed Trwyn stood in the centre. Jacantha guessed that he had been the target of the banter. She had witnessed the treatment newlywed men had received before, the others demanding full details of the wedding night. She smiled knowing how hard Trwyn would have found the ordeal torn between his loyalty to her and not wanting to be seen as a prude for not sharing the details. Jacantha herself had been guilty of joining in the jibes on previous occasions so was well aware what he must have said.

She walked over ignoring the others and stood before Trwyn. She leant forward and whispered in his ear careful the others did not overhear. Taking instruction from her he grabbed her roughly round the waist and pulled her tight to him. She pretended to resist a little but allowed his arms to engulf her.

Trwyn now took the initiative one hand slipping down her back giving her backside a playful squeeze. The onlookers chorused their approval. Jacantha may be their Queen but she understood the need for Trwyn to appear to be her equal in the match. He himself had thought himself unworthy and knew how important it was he be confident in the days ahead. It was also imperative the men respect him and be willing to follow him into battle for her plans to work. Spurred on by the reaction of the others Trwyn grabbed Jacantha and hoisted her over his shoulder. She struggled protesting, yet she could not suppress laughing at the same time. He slapped her on the backside and set off back towards the castle carrying her to cheers of approval.

Brawd had waited patiently in the hallway for an hour to have passed. Tentatively he knocked on Celdwady's door and waited. A summons was issued from within and he entered to find Celdwady comparing two documents.

Celdwady turned to look towards him "Look here and tell me what you understand it to mean?"

Brawd hesitated then moved over to look at the texts the older man had been studying. He read them then looked up "Some sort of portal? The mirror is a portal?"

Celdwady nodded. he was pleased his young apprentice had grasped his meaning without the need for explanation. For the next hour the two men pulled down ancient manuscripts comparing texts, Celdwady's countenance grave as he weighed up all the ramifications of the knowledge they had found. Finally, he closed the great volume before him and looked at Brawd

"Bring her to me, I shall be waiting outside the chamber."

Brawd flew from the room he raced through the corridors until he reached Jacantha's new bed chamber which she now shared with Trwyn. Brawd banged on the door but did not wait for an answer it being the middle of the reason he did not consider what the occupants may be engaged in. He swung the door open and froze. Before him Jacantha sat naked astride her husband her head thrown back in the heat of passion. She turned her head and looked at him as he mumbled apologies and backed out of the room.

He stood mortified in the hallway. He was unsure how to proceed, he dared not return to Celdwady without her but he could not disturb her again now to deliver the message. He could hear two distinct noises now in the room Jacantha was laughing and the angry voice of a man, Trwyn was obviously furious at the interruption.

The door opened and Jacantha slipped into the hallway, a sheet wound round her, her skin flushed from her recent exertions "Yes Brawd?" she asked.

He looked nervously towards the door behind which he could hear Trwyn banging about, ranting still at the disruption.

"Celdwady instructed me to bring you immediately. It is of the upmost importance, otherwise I would never, never have..."

He began to stumble over his words, not daring to look her in the eye.

"Peace Brawd, it is of no matter, wait here a moment while I put on something more suitable."

She turned and went back into the room, he could hear their voices rose in argument and then the door opened again.

This time it was Trwyn and it was obvious he was not happy. He glared at Brawd before storming off through the castle cursing both of the Guardians. Jacantha re-emerged clad now in a simple dress, Brawd turned quickly hurrying along the corridors, leading her not to Celdwady's chamber as she expected but towards her childhood room.

Celdwady was pacing impatiently in front of the door by the time they arrived. Brawn explained in flustered tones the reason for the delay.

"When I told you to go swing a sword at your husband that was not what I had in mind." He snapped at her after hearing Brawd's explanation.

Jacantha was startled by Celdwady's response, she looked at him questioningly.

Sensing her anger at his remark, Celdwady mentally scolded himself he should not have upset her now considering what he was about to ask her to do.

"I am sorry my lady I did not mean to offend you. Time is at a premium and I was merely frustrated by my own error in not having made this connection sooner, I have made a discovery which may fool Wend Y Mawr into playing straight into our hands."

Jacantha's eyes widened

"What do you mean? What discovery is this you have made is it about the mirror I spoke of?"

"It is important you listen and listen carefully we will only have the one chance to do this and even that depends on the Goddess being good to us."

"What must be done?" The resolve in her voice surprising even herself.

Jacantha leaned closer as Celdwady explained what she must do, when he had finished she took a deep breath and nodded. She stood facing the door her hand upon the handle composing her thoughts before she opened the door and stepped through into the chamber she had considered a safe haven for all of her life.

Jacantha entered the room alone. It felt strange even though it was only days since she had last slept here. So much depended on what happened now, she knew there was no room for error. Celdwady had explained to her that Wend had been using the mirror to watch her but as it was only activated at his end that he had been unable to hear her. She shuddered, thinking of what he might have seen. How many times he may have watched her undress? At the same time part of her was a little excited by the thought of it much to her own disgust. She forced that thought from her head and positioned herself in front of the mirror.

She reached out and placed on hand upon its surface and focused her thoughts. A ripple emanated out across the glass from where her hand rested on the surface and she carefully repeated the words that Celdwady had instructed her to say.

"By the light of the Goddess show me the path. Open this portal that I might commune with its twin. Show me that which I desire to see, and let my voice travel to the place beyond. Let the elements do my bidding and let it harm none."

She took a deep breath as shadows moved within the mirror and shapes formed indistinct and blurred at first but it slowly cleared and the objects came into focus.

She could now see a room lighted candles seemed to provide the only light. At first she could not see him; only as she searched the shadows did she spot him. He was slumped against the wall and appeared to be asleep. She cleared her throat and prepared herself to speak to him. She had to get this right, if he did not agree to what she said it would complicate her plans.

"Wend Y Mawr I would speak with you."

She heard her voice echo in the room on the other side of the mirror, she sounded far more confident than she felt.

She watched as he started looking around him for the source of the words summoning his attention. For a minute she could have sworn she saw fear cross his face. He seemed to take a few minutes to realise where the voice had come from. Then he approached the other side of the portal.

Jacantha faltered she had forgotten how attractive he was despite herself she smiled and self-consciously smoothed down her still tousled hair. Then she thought of Trwyn and guilt tore at her heart. She dragged her thoughts back to the task at hand she could not let the sight of the man before her distract her.

"My lady, your appearance startled me." Wend smiled as he gazed at her it felt like his eyes were boring into her soul.

"I hope that does not mean unwelcome." Jacantha attempted to return his stare but lowered her eyes worried she would betray her feelings.

"I am sure nothing you could do would be unpleasant. You do not realise how I have desired to speak with you. Especially since our last meeting. You have no idea how much I long to taste those lips again."

His tongue slipped from between his lips for a fraction of a second the message reaffirmed by his actions.

Jacantha knew this was the moment; she must play this the right way and drew him into line with her plans...

"I will not lie to you, I to have thought back to that night. You know I came with the intention of destroying you and avenging my father?"

"I expected nothing less of you my little warrior Queen I should have been hurt had you not tried. But as you learned that is beyond your means."

"Yes my lord, that is in part, why I have sought out a way to contact you. I want peace for my people and it would appear that the only way this can be achieved is for you and I to reach an understanding. No one else here knows I am doing this."

"Ah I see and what sort of understanding, do you propose? I have made my desires clear. I want you. You shall be my bride, my queen. Only then shall your people know peace."

"It is the full moon in eight days I propose that we meet; just you and I at the place where we last met to resolve this matter privately."

She flashed him what she hoped was a seductive smile.

Wend could barely believe what he was hearing. He could hear his heart pumping the blood through his veins,

"And for what purpose should we meet? You could simply come to me and deliver your hand into mine."

He smiled; he had to hear her say the words. To hear her finally submit to him, he felt himself hardening at the thought that in eight days, he would finally have his way with her. It took all his self-control to stop his hand moving to his groin.

"We each have our own customs and I must request that you allow me to impose mine on the situation. We must meet in combat one on one, only when you overpower me can I be yours. I am sure the feat will be a simple one for you, you must merely disarm me and pin me to the ground to show your mastery over me. You will then return me to my castle as your prisoner, you shall enter as the victor and therefore worthy in the eyes of my people to take my hand."

Wend burst out laughing. Jacantha froze; scared she had ruined her chances.

"You wish me to walk into a trap? You think that I shall walk alone into the lion's den?"

"No, my lord! I would not be so foolish. My people shall be informed once I have left the castle that I have gone to face you. They are honest honourable people. They will follow the traditions even if they do not find the results pleasant."

"And you my lady? Will you find the results pleasant? Will you come willingly to be my bride? Will you give yourself to me in every respect?"

His tone left no doubting the meaning of the final words.

"I will not lie to you I come willingly only in that I must do what is best for my people. Could I have killed you I would. But I cannot deny I find myself drawn to you, you do not need me to tell you of your attractions I am sure you have had enough experience to know of them. When you forced your lips against mine, you stirred feelings in me I have never experienced before."

"Prove it!"

His words sounded harsher than he had intended as he struggled to keep his feelings under control.

Jacantha hesitated, unsure of what he would demand of her

"How my lord? How can I prove my word to you now?"

A grin spread across Wend's face. "Remove your dress. Stand before me now naked and offer yourself to me."

"No! I will not! I shall give myself to you only after we meet and you make me submit. I shall not base myself by giving myself away so easily. If you want me you must win me."

Instantly she regretted her outburst what if he refused now, she felt the panic rising up inside as she waited for his response.

"I shall enjoy breaking that rebellious streak my lady. But I really must insist that I have some sort of proof that you intend to give yourself to me. But I can be patient. We shall compromise you shall slip the dress down and show me your breasts. I shall be content with that until we meet. But know this, if you refuse or you try to plot against me in any way, I shall destroy every living being in your land. No one will be safe and once I have slaughtered every man, woman and child and made you witness it, I shall still have you and I promise you that if I have to take you that way the experience will only be pleasurable for one of us." Wend had stopped smiling, his eyes had darkened and Jacantha felt his presence as heavily as if he were stood before her.

Silently she slipped the dress down over her shoulders her arms across her chest shielding her breasts from his sight.

"Drop your arms! Show yourself to me. You will soon learn there is no need to be bashful about your body where I am concerned."

She did as he ordered, clutching the material to prevent it falling further, revealing her breasts.

"Are you satisfied now, that I mean what I say?"

"Satisfied by your words? Yes. Satisfied? No! Not until my mouth closes on those little rosebud nipples and I have you naked beneath me but that will come soon enough."

Jacantha looked towards the door as if she had heard a noise outside. She pulled her dress back up

"I must go someone approaches."

"Until we meet then my Lady."

He blew a kiss towards her before she saw his hand move towards his groin, his intention evident.

She made a show of nervously glancing towards the door, as if fearful of discovery, as she closed the portal. Then turning, she fled from the room aware of Wend's eyes still upon her knowing she had only closed her side of the portal.

In the hallway she shut the door behind her and fell against it. She looked at Celdwady and then to Brawd. Brawd opened his mouth to speak but at a look from Celdwady he closed it again. Celdwady stepped forward placing an arm on her shoulder but she shrugged him off. Clasping her hand over her mouth, she turned from them both and fled.

Celdwady watched her flight. Then, turning to Brawd, he spoke his voice grave and pained

"It is done. The wheels have been set in motion and nothing can stop that which must come next."

Chapter Twenty-Two

Wend sat staring at the orb. His hand reaching out to touch the space her face had so recently occupied. The voice had fallen silent for now but Wend knew it would return. The next week would test his patience but now at least he knew at the end of his wait he would claim his prize. He blew out the candles and returned to his chamber and for the first time in days he slept soundly.

He slept a full forty-eight hours, his dreams alternating between images of Jacantha and Nadredd. He awoke feeling much less refreshed than his slumber should have provided for. He was restless knowing that days were still to pass before their meeting. He must find a way to make the time pass quicker. He looked around the room as he dressed. He had seen her chamber; could he really bring her back to such squalor? He knew his men lacked the capabilities to be of much use in renovating the building itself but he felt something must be done.

Nadredd's voice whispered to him he was fooling himself, that nothing he could do would make her enjoy her time as his spouse. He tried to block it out but it feed on his fears, pointing out the deficiencies of his surroundings and of his own failings that he allowed it to become so.

He questioned himself as to why he should care so much about what she would think. She would be his, end of story, her opinion really didn't matter. He realised he wanted to impress her, not that it would affect how she felt about him, but to show her his power. He needed to prove to himself, that his reign had been every bit as successful as that of her ancestors.

He was aware there were piles of goods and gold, taken from those he had defeated, sat untouched since their capture. He could not even be sure what was there he had paid little attention to the individual items only taking anything he believed to have been of value. There was no excuse for this squalor, he was a king, and he could have been living as such but had allowed himself to get so distracted by pleasure. He had allowed the building around him to fall into disrepair the stone walls were as solid as the day they were built but everything else showed signs of age. He grabbed some clothes and headed to the great hall. As he passed through the halls he called out summoning everyone to the hall.

Everyone stood before him he could sense their unease as he issued his orders he noticed the glances which passed amongst them but was undeterred. On his orders the breeders had been brought from their chambers to participate in his plans, he watched their unease at being in such close proximity to the concubines fearful by standing to close they would somehow share their fate. Wend smiled they may be correct once Jacantha's warrior women were here they would make far better breeding stock to produce his future armies. For three days he announced there would be no pleasure taking, they would all work to restore his castle to its former glory.

The concubines would scrub floors, walls and windows. His men would remove any broken furniture into the courtyard and dispose of it on a bonfire. He picked a number of those he felt remained most loyal and began the task of retrieving the treasures stashed away in dusty chambers and bringing them out to be put on display and into use. The breeders would take the lengths of cloth that had been taken and use them to make new draperies for the beds and walls. New clothes for them all could wait and would be made once the union had taken, part after all Jacantha's subjects had more skill.

Protests were muttered amongst his men, he raised his hand to silence them. Yes, there would be changes but he assured them these changes would not be to their disadvantage. They would still have their feasts and concubines but they would be better fed after the union, he had no intention of running two castles her people would be brought here to wait on them all initially until he was sure he had her in his power, then they would adapt her castle to suit their needs.

It would be easier in the long run for them to take over her castle, he knew it was larger and would hold them all in much more comfort. First, he wanted to show her the way in which they lived in the manner and to which she would have to become adjusted, he felt she would put up greater resistance under the shelter of her own roof. Her subjects would be their slaves, that they have to accept, if they did not resist they would be treated well, in the beginning at least.

His men would be the nobles they would be rewarded for their loyalty with positions in his new court, they would be allowed to take wives if they chose, they would no longer fight in the front line they would command others. If he was honest he had little intention of letting most of them continue their pathetic lives but now was not the time to let this be known, for the time being he needed them to do as he commanded believing they were working for their own benefit. As such they needed to start getting used to the new life style. Why should they continue eating from wooden plates when golden ones lay unused?

The men considered his words carefully, their egos, inflated by years of feeding their own lusts, embraced them. Why should they not enjoy the finer things as well as their baser instincts?

For days they worked, until the castle was restored to a pale imitation of its former glory. The breeders had been assigned kitchen duties before being closeted back in their secluded chambers. The tables in the great hall were laden with a feast that would have rivalled his grandfather's banquets. Wend sat back in his throne and admired his domain. The food was held on golden platters; goblets had been filled with mead found deep in the cellars. The tables had been rearranged formally to form a square with Wend's table at the head.

The centre of the room allowed space for the concubines to provide entertainment as they ate, he remembered in the old days, dances would be performed there or they would be amused by troops of travelling acrobats that would perform in return for food and lodgings. He wondered what his men would make of such tame entertainment; he doubted it would hold their attention for long.

There was only another forty-eight hours until he left to bring back his prize. They would feast and celebrate and he would replenish his energy until that time, he had noticed a slight weakening the last few days while his men had observed their enforced abstinence. The men filed into the room, nervously unsure how to act, many had never seen such luxury as faced the now. Each man watching Wend to take their cues for how to behave. Few had ever experienced court life as it had been lived in the old days, manners were a concept they were unacquainted with, he would watch and see which of them were able and willing to adapt.

Wend motioned they should be seated as he stood toasting their hard work. They raised their glasses, several spluttered at tasting the sweet mead for the first time an acquired taste in comparison to the ale they were accustomed to. Wend laughed and called for the concubines to fill second goblets with ale and top up the mead. He declared the feast open and sat, reaching for a fowl and he ripped apart its flesh to devour it. The men followed his example and soon the room was filled with laughter and boisterous tales of deeds committed.

Two young women were led to the centre of the room. They had been captured on a raid several months ago and been assigned as breeders but had failed to conceive. Wend had decided tonight they would provide part of the floor show as this initial feast to celebrate the castles rebirth. He had decided against drugging them; their fear would feed the frenzy he intended to provoke far more. All eyes were fixed upon them as they stood naked and vulnerable clinging to each other. He clapped his hands the concubines gathered around them forming a circle. They dropped to their knees so as to not block the view of the men while still forming a physical barrier to prevent the two women attempting to flee.

Wend stood and looked at the two girls, their gaze fixed upon him as he rose to his feet, they were obviously terrified at the thought of what their fate may be. He motioned to one of the other women to move forward, in her hands she held a long leather strap. She grabbed the hair of one girl, holding her in place while another woman stepped forward slipping the strap round the girl's neck, knotting it tightly; she turned to the other girl and repeated the process. Joined by the strap like an umbilical cord, the girls still clung to each other, as if each could shield the other from what was to come.

"You will fight each other for your freedom the one who pins her opponent for the count of twenty shall be allowed to return to the breeder's chamber. The other shall entertain us here this evening."

He laughed as he saw the look of realisation cross their faces and they backed away from each other. He had no intention of allowing either girl to leave this hall tonight if ever but he knew they needed a reason to fight. Now they would fight for survival. They slowly began to circle each other, the strap extended to its full length as they weighed up their options. With a swift movement the taller girl, snapped the strap trying to jerk her opponent off her feet. The smaller girl dove towards her former friend's waist driving into her pushing her backwards. They fell towards the concubines who knelt behind them. They were firmly shoved back to the centre of the circle by the other women who were aware of the consequences of Wends anger far more than the two in the centre.

The women now fell upon each other desperately, pulling hair and gouging at eyes trying to gain an advantage over the other. The men laughed at their efforts, the performance more amusing than erotic, with neither woman possessing the fighting skills to put on a real show. Wend was unsatisfied, he needed the men to become aroused to produce the energy he craved, as it was they were drinking too much to last the length of time which Wend desired. He got to his feet and pulled two concubines to one side. He whispered instructions into their ears and they ran from the room.

As he awaited their return, Wend observed the two women engaged in a feeble wrestling match and compared them to the warrior women of Jacantha's people. The soft flesh before him did have the advantage of providing the more satisfactory welts when lashed, but there was no challenge in them. He had no doubt, had it been two of the warriors fighting for existence before him they would be putting on a far better show. The two women returned bearing a variety of whips and straps between them. They moved round the circle passing them to the kneeling concubines along with instructions.

The women in the centre now sensed a change in the room they had each been to engrossed watching every move the other made to notice the arrival of the weapons. As they stumbled backwards instead of being pushed back into the centre, half a dozen whips lashed at their bodies. Red angry welts immediately sprung up across their pale flesh where the leather had made contact. A cheer went up around the room at the new turn in events, this was more to the men's tastes. The two women now fell upon each other with increased ferocity realising the stakes had been raised, Wend smiled as he notice the men moving uncomfortably in their seats eager to get up and take a more active role in proceedings.

It was now time to build the energy he stepped forward and took a place in the circle. He took the whips from the woman on her knees before him and ordered her to turn and take him in her mouth. The other men quickly followed suit and now a double circle surrounded the combatant's one of standing men yielding whips if they moved to close, the other of kneeling women greedily servicing the nearest man. The faint glow of energy started to cast its unnatural light in the room. The smaller of the two women fighting slipped and the other took no time in grabbing her advantage, looping the leather strap round the other woman's throat and cutting off her air supply.

The smaller woman clutched at her throat trying to loosen the tightening strap, fighting get the precious oxygen back into her lungs, but to no avail as she slipped from consciousness. The larger woman threw herself down on top of her, claiming her victory as she pinned her inert opponent to the floor. The men counted out her victory and watched as she staggered back to her feet. Wend motioned for her to come to him, hesitantly she obeyed. As he clasped her hand and drew her close to him she saw the smile on his face and the realisation that there would be no escape dawned on her.

His hand reached behind her head, fingers twisting into her hair as he pulled her face to his. As his tongue forced its way into her mouth, his other hand slid between her legs probing her intimately he was pleased to find her tight knowing she had only been used a few times. He spun her round so she could watch, as he instructed the men to take their pleasure with the woman still lying unconscious on the floor. He could feel her heart race, as she watched in horror as the men fell upon her, like a pack of dogs, pawing at her defenceless flesh.

He felt her body convulse, as the woman on the floor was lifted and displayed, her legs spread wide as the men jostled for position to be the first to take her. Others were taking turns to bite at her nipples, hands moved over her body exploring every inch of flesh, and then she was lowered to the ground again. The strap was still tied round both their necks, connecting her to the victor, as she was revived by the pain of one of the men entering her from behind, as they turned her to lie on her side. Another had forced the head of a concubine between her legs and was busy mounting the concubine as she feasted on the fallen breeder.

The blue energy leaked from the bodies as more and more found ways to join in with hands and mouths. Concubines were servicing any flesh that they could reach, male and female, all aware that if they failed to perform their lives were in jeopardy.

Wend stood back watching as the frenzied orgy developed as the loser of the contest disappeared beneath a sea of flesh.

He reached up and grabbed the leather strap round the victor's neck and pulled it down so she had no choice but the bend at the waist. As he entered her, he heard her start to weep, her tightness combining with her tears to excite, him even further as he thrust harder into her. With one hand holding the strap, the other dug into her hip he drove himself deeper into her. She stumbled forward at his force and he pushed her to her knees. He used the full weight of his body now to bear down on her. As her body stretched to try to accommodate him he pulled out and altered position now driving, in one hard thrust, into her backside. He laughed as he felt her flesh rip and she let out a scream.

In forty-eight hours it would be Jacantha he would drive into, but until then he would do all he could to ensure his powers were at their fullest when they met.

Chapter Twenty-Three

Jacantha sat alone at the top of the tower, she had been reflecting on the events of the past few days. Tomorrow she would face Wend Y Mawr. Tonight she would sit alone and wait.

She had fled from the room after showing herself to Wend in the portal and vomited. She had been sickened by both the act and the feelings it stirred in her, she hated the fact past of her had been aroused watching his eyes light up at the sight of her flesh. For the first time since her marriage she had turned from Trwyn in their bed that night. She knew he had been hurt but she was terrified if he looked into her eyes too closely he would see the deceit that lurked there.

The next day she had risen early and spent most of the day closeted away with Celdwady and Brawd. They had delayed the meeting with the elders that had been scheduled for the previous night to allow time to work out how they could benefit best from the new knowledge they had gained with the portal. Decisions had to be made as to how they were going to arrange for her to face Wend alone, they were aware that Trwyn would not be the only one to protest at this idea. That night after leaving the Guardians she had clung to Trwyn knowing what she must suggest in front of the council the following evening. She knew he would not be happy with what was to come but there was no other way.

Jacantha looked up at the moon and silently offered up her prayers for the strength to carry her through. Her mind drifted back to the meeting. They had all been there, each of the elders as well as a few other high-ranking warriors invited along due to the importance of the matter at hand. Celdwady had stood to her right as she rose to her feet ready to face them. Trwyn had jumped to his feet in protest as the words left her mouth laying before them the course of actions which must be taken for them to achieve success. For the first time in their short marriage Jacantha had to pull rank and remind him that, in that room and in this matter, she was not his wife, she was his Queen and that the prophecy overruled all other matters.

Silence had filled the room; the others had moved uncomfortably in their seats as they looked everywhere except at either of them. "Yes, my Queen!" He had sneered at her as he resumed his seat. She had felt tears welling up in her eyes but Celdwady had been the one to step forward and explain the reasons more fully, as she sought to control her emotions. He had patiently reminded them of the words of the prophecy, explained without giving details that he had been granted visions by the Lord and Lady showing him the path which must be taken. Celdwady had then gently reminded Trwyn that he had entered into their union fully knowing that this was something that could not be changed.

Jacantha had then taken over again, Trwyn as her husband, would lead the main attack. They would leave forty-eight hours before the show down between herself and Wend was expected to occur. They would journey into Wend's kingdom and storm his castle, as she prepared to face him alone. They discussed the practicalities of what must be done. Every bloodstone, they could find must be destroyed before she could destroy him, there must be nowhere left that harboured his powers, she would take care of the final one set into his sword.

Questions were asked about what they should do with the people they encountered there. They knew he had taken people back to the castle captive against their will. People that had sought shelter here in the sanctuary of the walled city had told of loved ones taken by force by Wends men.

Jacantha looked at Trwyn "My husband shall judge what must be done, based on what is discovered. I trust in his judgement; the innocent shall not have their blood spilt by our hands."

Trwyn barely acknowledged her comments, a sullen expression fixed upon his face. Next came the harder questions, how did she mean to defeat Wend when all others had failed? Why must she face him alone? Did it not make more sense for a small group to accompany her remaining concealed in case of any problems?

It was Celdwady who stepped forward and reiterated the words of the prophecy. He talked of magic, things beyond their contemplation, which the presence of others would distract from. He challenged them to go against the prophecy and bring the wrath of the Lady upon them all. No one was willing to speak against the Lady, meekly accepting that if this was the way it must be they could not interfere. Any hopes Trwyn had of finding an ally in his protests died now.

Celdwady summed up his own feelings as he finished. "If I could, I would take her place, failing that, I would stand by her side myself. But the Lady has told me that cannot be, only the chosen one can end his reign and even I do not know how. Only the chosen one knows and, for the sakes of all your futures, she is bound not to reveal how it is to be done. I know it is hard, to put your faith in something that is so far out of your own hands, but our Queen can only do this with our full support and trust."

As he spoke the last words he looked again at Trwyn, who looked away from him, refusing to face up to what he knew in his heart could not be avoided.

That night as Jacantha lay in bed beside him, it had been Trwyn who turned from her and the tears had rolled down both their faces as they fell asleep.

For the next two days they had avoided each other, both hurt unable to express their pain to each other, unable to change what must happen. In the end she had sought him out and confronted him on the training field. The others had left for the evening when Jacantha found him alone and threw a sword over to him. He caught it but stood looking towards her "

"I will not fight you." He spoke softly.

She looked at him. "It seems to me you already are. I will not continue like this, I warned you before we were bound, what was to come. You promised me you would accept it."

She had not realised how angry she was with him over his behaviour. He had known all along she must face this alone. Did he really believe she would have chosen it to be that way if she had any choice?

She lifted the sword and swung it towards him. He instinctively lifted his sword and blocked her swing. She launched at him again, with more ferocity this time, the frustration of the last few days fuelling her strength, as she forced him on the defensive. He allowed her to force him backwards, waiting for the onslaught to weaken, before he went on the offensive. Her anger caused her to overreach and slip then Trwyn was upon her, swinging back at her with real venom.

It was Jacantha's turn now the parry the blows raining down upon her. To her surprise, she felt herself growing more invigorated, as the contest continued. Again, she took the offensive, gaining back the ground that Trwyn had gained during his assault. She could sense him tiring and waited to pick her moment. She saw his arm drop slightly, as he pulled back to launch another counter, she seized the moment, dropped her shoulder and charged into his stomach, knocking him off his feet. He lay on his back winded but had no time to regain his breath before she was upon him. She threw his sword into the distance, out of his reach and held her own across his throat.

She smiled down at him triumphantly, a cheeky grin spreading across her face. She leaned forward pressing herself against him, still holding the blade steadily across his throat. She slid one hand down between their bodies, seeking her prize between his legs. He tried to struggle, to push her off but she applied more pressure to the blade as her hand found its target and she wormed her fingers down between the supple leather of his leggings and his warm flesh.

She pressed her lips to his now, loosening his rigid lips, with gentle nips of her teeth. She could tell the effect she was having on him as he hardened in her hand. Her grip on the sword loosened slightly and Trwyn took advantage, he grasped the blade as he flipped her over and reversed their positions.

He grabbed her hand, pulling it from inside his leggings and pinned it above her head. He now moved her sword out of her reach and grasped her other wrist, pulling it to join the other. Holding both her wrists firmly in position with one hand, he now smiled, as his hand repeated the same journey hers had taken a few minutes earlier. She squirmed as he slid his fingers into her, teasing her, knowing the exact amount of pressure to drive her into a frenzy. She struggled trying to pull her hands free, finally she pulled one from his grasp and entangled her fingers into his hair, pulling his mouth to hers.

Now both pulled apart, realising that they were in public, they agreed they should move inside, where they could continue unobserved. The journey back to the bedroom seemed to have taken forever. She smiled as she remembered the feverish lovemaking that had symbolised their reconciliation.

The following days had been spent divided between the training field and the council chamber. Each evening they had clung to each, as if every moment, may be their last. She knew Trwyn feared that she would not return from the meeting with

Wend and if she was honest, she shared his fear. She tried as best she could to reassure him and he in turn ceased questioning her.

She looked up at the stars again. wondering if he were looking up at them, at that same moment. The thought he was gazing with her gave her comfort. She had stood by the gates last night watching until he disappeared from sight. He had led her army out as they began their journey to Wend's castle. Timing was crucial and they had departed early enough to allow them to take a longer route, meaning it was less likely to lead to detection, in order to arrive at the exact time.

She had stood in her official role as Queen to watch them pass by, her brother at her side, as they moved out but, it was as a wife, she had stood watching the dust rise from the thousands of hooves as they moved into the distance. Her heart longed to go grab her horse to ride after him, ride with him until the time she herself must leave, but her head told her it was folly. They must both focus on the parts they had been assigned by fate.

She heard a noise below her on the steps. She smiled knowing that it would be Celdwady. He emerged through the doorway and she gestured for him to sit beside her. He sat beside her, waiting for her to speak. She turned her gaze back to the sky and quietly the words slipped from her lips. She poured out her fears, the dreams she had had as a girl, that she knew now would never be fulfilled.

She longed to tell him all. Tell him what she must do tomorrow and her fears she would not be able to go through with it. On this matter she remained silent, her thoughts bottled up as she knew they must be.

Celdwady reassured her as best he could in the circumstances. He reached out to her and took her in his arms, stroking her hair, soothing her as one would a child. Jacantha buried her face into his chest and closed her eyes as he began to sing to her. He sang the songs of her childhood, for the next hour it was not Celdwady who held her. She imagined she was back in her father's arms, safe and protected. Gradually sleep overtook her and she fell into a dreamless slumber.

Celdwady leaned back against the wall and began to chant, quietly so as to not wake her. His words spinning through the air forming a shimmering haze around them. His protection charm would not help her tomorrow; he had prepared her as best he could but for the first time in his long existence Celdwady felt helpless. This girl in his arms was as dear to him, as any child he might have fathered, had that been allowed. He had spent a lifetime learning his craft yet now, when she needed him most, he could not help her, only guide her. The power she needed was there within her. He could sense it beneath her skin waiting to be unleashed. He also knew that his part was not finished yet that would come later after her victory.

He had already begun making the final preparations for what would come once she returned victorious. He could not bear to even think she might fail, that was not an option. He offered a prayer to the Lady to give him the strength to await his part in what was to come and to resist the temptation to interfere in what Jacantha must do.

Chapter Twenty-Four

Trwyn gave the order to halt a mile from Wend Y Mawr's stronghold. Sunset was an hour away, in a few hours they would storm the building and destroy all they found there. His thoughts wandered to his wife. Somewhere out there she was alone, heading for the show down with this tyrant. His heart longed to leave here and search her out, despite the warnings of the consequences, only the thought of letting her down stopped him. He would willingly take her place be struck down, if that was what was needed. The words of the prophecy whirled around his brain.

They were so vague, she had assured him that he would see her again, if she won but the words... the words talked of her sacrifice. Surely if she must be the sacrifice then she could not return to him. His heart broke at the thought she would not be awaiting his return. No, he must trust her. She understood the nature of the prophecy, she would not make him false promises, he knew her well enough to know that, she had been as honest as she could from the start. He stood and took stock of his situation. There were at least four hours before they could make a move. He addressed the troops, they should take a little rest now, he and a few others would stand guard until it was time.

****

Jacantha approached the meeting place, she had deliberately arrived early. On her journey she had caught sight of the now familiar wolves several times. They had skirted the forest edge keeping pace with her. The seemed to sense her doubts, their presence reassured her that all would be well. She thought of Trwyn and the task he was about to undertake.

He would lead the army for the first time and knew the importance of his mission. Should he fail, her part would be so much harder, though not impossible, or so she hoped. She thought of Celdwady alone with Brawd to protect the children, sick and elderly. If they failed, no that should be if she failed, he would have no chance to protect them from Wend's fury when he learnt of her deceit. She had seen the potion brewing in Celdwady's chamber. He did not need to tell her the draft that would ensure none of those remaining at the castle would suffer at Wend's hand, now she prayed it would not be needed.

She thought of her brother also forced to remain back at the castle, he had protested that he should lead the army but as her father had forced her to stay behind she in turn had done the same. The bloodline must continue, she knew her brother was worried for Fleura, marching with Trwyn, the bond between the two of them had grown stronger since her own union, her brother's happiness like everything else depended on her success.

She dismounted and surveyed the clearing. It was here she had faced Wend before. She felt a flush rise in her cheeks, as she thought of that last encounter, and the kiss he had forced upon her. Tonight, she must go further, she must use his own powers to defeat him. She only hoped that he would be unable to resist her charms, that he desired her badly enough not to question her actions. She led her horse to the side and tethered him to a tree. As she stroked his neck, she thought of her parents. Would they have understood what she was destined to do to save them all? Would they have forgiven her? She returned to the centre of the clearing, the sun was just sinking to the horizon. In a couple more hours, she would decide the destiny of them all.

****

The sun had set a few hours after Wend had started his journey. In less than an hour she would be his. He had ordered his men to tidy up the mess left from the orgy that had taken place over the last few days, they had adjusted well to the idea of an improved court life, and his energies had been revitalised by their activities. Tomorrow the breeders would cook a banquet for him to welcome his bride to her new home. He thought about what he would do to that sweet supple flesh once he had her in his grasp. Would he be able to resist taking her there at the banquet in front of them all? Would he be able to control himself until he got her back to the castle?

He longed to take her there and then, to make her submit to him fully but he knew if she was to be accepted by his men, the proper traditions must be upheld. He had tried to discover what the traditions of her people were, but the information he found was very vague. All he was certain of was what she had told him, that he must defeat her in a duel. A smile crossed his face when he thought how easy that would be, even without magic, he doubted she could have defeated him, but it was a chance he was not willing to take. She would crumble first beneath his sword then beneath his body until he possessed her totally. He knew she was surrendering to him to save her people, but he only hoped that did not mean she would not still put up a fight, the thought of defeating her excited him.

****

Trwyn roused his men. It was time to move on their target. They would begin moving towards the castle on foot, hoping to gain the element of surprise. A few remained behind with the horses, ready to bring them down as soon as the fray began. Several groups of others on horseback had made their way around to the far side of the castle, ready to distract Wend's men if needed, if not they would cut down any who attempted to flee.

They crept along keeping low to the ground. As they neared the castle they stopped and listened. They could hear, what sounded like a feast in progress.

Drunken voices were raised in song and they could hear squeals from women's voices. Trwyn raised his hand, ordering the rest to stay concealed, he and a small band of men crept closer. The windows of the castle were too high to allow them to look in to ascertain numbers they knew that, even if all the men were present, they had them outnumbered. The only thing they could be sure of was it sounded like the majority of men were in the great hall enjoying their leader's absence. He gave the signal and the men moved in on their target.

****

Jacantha saw Wend in the distance before he saw her. She rose to her feet, uttering a final prayer that she could do this, and that Trwyn had reached his destination and was safe. She walked to her horse and drew out her sword. She felt reassured by its weight in her hand, regardless of the fact this would not be the weapon to bring her victory this night. She moved back again to the centre of the clearing and waited, watching as he drew nearer.

****

Wend saw her standing alone in the clearing. It had crossed his mind several times that this was a trap but he felt that she was not stupid enough to try that. He remembered the last time they had met here. He remembered the feeling as his lips had closed over hers. He had felt her hunger for him and the turmoil that caused within her. She hated him for killing her father, yes, she despised that she could not defeat him, but still her body had yearned for his and very soon he would fill that yearning.

It would be interesting to see how the wedding night affected her. He was certain he could unlock the whore within her, she would be a willing participant in his games, well some of them, others she may not enjoy quite so much at first, once he broke through her wilfulness. He would enjoy teaching her place. Her first lesson would come with her defeat in combat, the second, well just because he was determined not to take her before the wedding night, that did not mean that he could not still have a little pleasure on the way home.

****

Trwyn led the attack into the great hall. He came to an abrupt halt as he saw the spectacle before his eyes. An orgy was in full swing, naked couples copulated openly over tables and on the floor. A naked woman saw him and began staggering towards him obviously under the influence of ale or something stronger. She seemed totally oblivious to the sword he held in his hand, as she lurched towards him smiling.

He looked at her in disgust and watched the realisation cross her face that he was not of this castle before his sword cut her down. Another woman screamed as she witnessed the execution. Suddenly the men were struggling to their feet, naked they looked round searching for a weapon. Trwyn headed for the centre of the room, cutting down everyone who crossed his path man or woman. The rest of his army followed his lead, a few of Wend's men found weapons and attempted to defend themselves but to no avail.

Soon the floor was slippery with the thick red liquid spilt from those who had been so intent on their pleasure such a short time ago. Trwyn looked round the room. Blood stones had been set round the perimeter, he ordered his men to destroy them all, before spreading out to search the rest of the building.

****

Wend slid from his horse, leaving it at the edge of the clearing and walked towards Jacantha. He stopped a few feet away from her and smiled.

"So, at last you recognise that this is your only solution. But do not fear it may not all be unpleasant." He offered his hand to her, half hoping she would take it and yield to him.

Jacantha shook her head "I cannot give myself to you, I told you that. The traditions of my people must be upheld, if you want me, you must take me." She raised her sword to make her intentions obvious.

Wend let out a laugh. "So be it my warrior queen, I shall be gentle with you...in this at least."

He pulled his sword from its scabbard. Jacantha's eyes rested on the bloodstone set in the hilt. That would be the last stone remaining once Trwyn had completed his task in the castle.

They circled each other now, both had their eyes firmly fixed on the other. Jacantha launched towards him with a ferocious swing which he blocked. He tempted her to swing again by dropping his sword slightly drawing her in. He was surprised by the strength with which she wielded the sword.

Over and over he drew her forward, before launching his own attack at her. Jacantha blocked him easily. She realised, that if he did not have magic on his side, she could easily defeat him in a fair fight. But the fight was not fair she realised. She landed a blow which should have sliced through his arm but the blade defected on contact with his flesh.

She drove forward again, pushing him back towards the edge of the clearing. They weaved in and out of each other's blows, an intricate dance, only his magic ensuring they were evenly matched.

Wend held up his hand and started laughing "My dear we could keep this up all night and all that would happen is you would have less energy for the marriage bed. Come now yield to me and be mine now."

She shook her head, reiterating that he must defeat her. "Maybe you need a little more incentive to claim your prize." She taunted him.

She stepped back from him and removed the leather armour covering her chest and legs revealing the scanty leather garment she had purposely worn underneath. She saw the lust in Wends eyes as she took up her stance again and once more began the contest.

****

Trywn had cleared the lower floor of the castle and now he, and the others, made their way up to the higher floors. Blood dripped from their swords as they dispatched all who crossed their path. A shout came from Fleura; she had found the chamber where the breeders were huddled together. Everyone stopped holding their breaths awaiting Trwyn's orders. He stepped into the room and looked at the women and children huddled there.

There were around twenty women, and fifteen children ranging from new-borns to around five years of age. Trwyn stopped to consider the options, Jacantha had trusted his judgement to do the right thing. They could be innocent, the women may very well be those that the people seeking sanctuary at home, had mourned as lost already. These babies brought up in loving homes could be good people but what if they weren't. Could he risk polluting Jacantha's castle with the depravity he had witnessed downstairs?

He walked up to one of the women grabbing her by her throat.

"Are any of these children his?"

She stared blankly at him not comprehending his meaning.

"Do any of these children have his blood?"

Anger seeping into his voice as he repeated his question.

Again, she did not answer, he threw her to the floor and grabbed the next woman repeating his question. She stammered a reply insisting that none of the children were Wend's. He grabbed the first child a baby and held it up examining its face for any features that would betray its parentage. It gazed up at him with big blue eyes. He passed the child to Fleura then repeated the process with each child in the room. When he had finished six babies and two toddlers were ensconced in the arms of his men. He ordered they be taken outside.

The women started screaming, convinced that these were the ones he had selected to destroy, believing themselves rescued. Only as he issued the next order did they realise their error. They threw themselves over the remaining, dark eyed children, desperately trying to protect them. They tried to use their bodies as shields, placing themselves between the cold hard metal of the swords and the soft innocent flesh. It was over quickly. Trwyn noticed the looks his men gave him. They had followed orders but he could tell they had not agreed with them.

Fleura re-entered the room and saw the carnage. She looked at Trwyn with questioning eyes, to have slaughtered innocent children was something she could never have suspected him capable of. She wondered now if he had made the decision or whether he was following orders from another, though she could not believe that Jacantha could ever have been the one to issue it either. Silently, she left the room and continued the search of the upper chambers.

****

Jacantha quickly realised that in skill Wend would not beat her. If she were to lose this contest, she would need to contrive to allow him to think he had defeated her. Wend had her on the back foot when she felt a root just behind her ankle and decided to use it to her advantage. She launched forward to gain a little space, then allowed him to force her backwards once more. She carefully measured each step until she was in position. Then she fell backwards allowing herself to trip on the root. As she fell she engineered that her grip on her sword should loosen and fall from her grasp.

Wend pounced upon her, pinning her arms by her side and using his weight to hold her immobile. He bought his face down to hers, hovering just above her looking down into her eyes. She could feel his breath on her face as it hung just inches from her own. She could feel his heart race in the thrill of his alleged victory as his chest pressed against hers. She braced herself ready for what was to come, but he remained still just gazing down on her. One hand now moved releasing her arm and began stroking her hair. For a moment she wondered what his intentions were then he spoke.

"Ah, my dear, now you are mine. You have no idea how hard it is for me at this moment. But I shall be patient. We will be joined immediately upon returning to my castle and then...then I shall take my leisure in exploring every crevice of your beautiful body. Until then a kiss will suffice. He leaned forward his lips pressing down on hers.

Her mind was swimming; she knew that it must be ended tonight. Her instincts refused to allow her to respond to his kiss, but she knew she must. She closed her eyes and allowed her free hand reached up cradling his head as she kissed him back. She felt the energy passing between them. A hum was audible in the air, as the energy started to build. She could feel the effect her kiss was having on him and slipped her tongue between his teeth snaking into his mouth feeling his body tremble at her response.

For a moment Wend forgot his intentions and released her other arm, his hand searching out her breast, as his tongue duelled with hers. His fingers now entangled in her hair holding her close as her nipple hardened beneath the fingers of his other hand. He felt himself hardening and he shifted his body position so she lay beneath him, his knees forcing her legs apart, as he pressed himself against her. Through their clothing Jacantha could feel him excitement and she gently rocked her hips against him inviting him to take his prize. Then suddenly he jumped up, pulling away from her and was on his feet.

He reached down and grabbed her by an arm, hoisting her to her feet. She sensed she was losing him, that he was managing to keep his composure better than she had expected. She twisted from his grasp and leapt out of reach of him. He advanced towards her but she raised her hand to stop him

"Stop! You want my people to follow you? Yes?"

He stopped, looking at her a puzzled bemused expression on his face.

"Yes, and you have already explained that by defeating you, they must accept this. Now stop the games, the sooner we get back to my castle, the quicker I can have my pleasure, and possibly, you shall have yours as well."

He stepped towards her again.

Again, she held her hand up and stepped back.

"It is no game, defeating me is only part of it. For our two kingdoms to be made one, the union must take place on the border of the two kingdoms. That is why I chose this place to meet as it straddles our two kingdoms."

She stood looking at him, then slowly removed the rest of her clothing until she stood naked before him.

"If you want my kingdom, you must make the union here and as we are already here why wait." She smiled at him and allowed her tongue to run across her lips,

"Unless of course you would rather wait, ride all the way to your castle be joined, then ride all the way back." She took a step towards him. "Your people already follow you, surely they would not dare question you doing what was required to bring them greater wealth. And if we are honest, and I believe we should be honest, I think you will find sitting in the saddle, rather uncomfortable at the minute."

As she spoke the last words, she allowed her gaze to settle on the bulge that had grown in the front of his leggings.

He laughed "Well if your people insist I take you here, on the forest floor, who am I to argue. And to think you call us the barbarians."

****

Trwyn was now sure there was no one remaining in the castle, other than his own people. The biggest resistance they had met was when the men had discovered the hounds shut in a room, two men had been injured before the beasts had been slain. They had destroyed the small bloodstones in the great hall but had yet to find what they were searching for. Celdwady had instructed him there would be a large crystal. It was imperative this be found and destroyed. He ordered his troops to split up now, every door should be torn down, cupboards smashed and every crevice searched.

Everywhere Trwyn went, he found further evidence of the depravity that had resided here. Ropes hung from ceilings, slivers of skin and traces of blood told the tales of their use. He found implements he could not begin to speculate on their usage only be sure that they had inflicted pain and misery. Once he was convinced the crystal was not to be found in the upper chambers, he ordered everyone back down to search the lower floors. Again they turned everything upside down in their search.

Trwyn was beginning to despair of success, when the shout came from the great hall. In ripping down the hangings, they had discovered the secret door hidden there. They had opened it but no one had entered yet, calling to Trwyn instead. There in the centre of the room it stood. A faint glow emanated from huge red stone. He moved closer and looked into it. Trwyn froze at what he saw there within it.

There must be another stone Wend had with him, he realised quickly. He looked in horror as he saw his wife, stood naked before Wend Y Mawr. He could only see her from behind. He watched in disbelief as she walked towards Wend and wrapped her arms round his neck in a lover's embrace. He watched as Wend's hands travelled over her body stroking those firm buttocks he had thought were his alone. He stood torn wanting to turn away but unable to do so.

There was a scuffle in the doorway and Fleura pushed her way into the room. She saw what had fixed his attention and drawing her own sword, she brought the hilt down heavily in the centre of the stone. There was a crackling sound and the picture faded. She repeated the blow, this time the stone shattered. Trwyn was thrown backwards fragments of crystal piercing both their bodies.

Fleura took control and ordered the others away from the door to continue the search, to be sure they had destroyed all the crystals. She turned to Trwyn, his face pale and his pain evident to her.

"Trwyn, listen to me! We have no right to judge her or question her. She has no choice in this. She is doing what she must to save us all. You must remember that."

He looked at her and nodded. He knew she spoke the truth but that did not ease the pain, no wonder Jacantha had refused to tell him or anyone else what must be done to fulfil the prophecy.

He called the men to order outside the castle. They were sure they had missed nothing but Trwyn needed to be sure. They had dragged the tables from the great hall into the hallway and the hangings they had torn down, making them into a bonfire. Trwyn dropped the torch and watched as the flames took hold. Only once he was sure that everything within those walls, would be consumed by the flames, did he give the order to mount up.

Despite their success in their mission, they rode silently, each knowing that it was not over yet. It would not be over until they arrived home and found their queen awaiting them. For Trwyn he was unsure it would ever be over, the images of what he had just witnessed, burned through his mind and it would take more than flames to cleanse them.

****

Jacantha pressed her body against Wend, a shudder passed through her as his hands moved over her flesh, but she ignored the sensation, pushing on in her mission. Her hands deftly removed his tunic, breaking contact between their bodies, only for the briefest of moments. Her hands traced the contours of his muscled chest and back her fingertips skimming lightly over his flesh. Despite her revulsion at what she must do she felt her body begin to stir as she pressed her lips against his.

This time she did not see it as a betrayal, it was merely doing what it needed to do in order to fulfil the prophecy. She did not attempt to hold back, she surrendered to the desires coursing through her veins, her nails digging deeply into his back, as the urgency within her built.

Wend felt a tremor in his power, he glanced towards his sword. The stone in its hilt seemed duller, less radiant than normal. He did not have time to dwell on the thought, as the hellcat in his arms dug in her claws. Maybe doing things her way was not such a bad idea. He reached down sliding one had between her legs. He forced his fingers into her expecting to meet resistance but they slipped in without hindrance. He considered this for a moment, trying to think straight as her hand reached down taunting him through the material still concealing his manhood.

He recalled a fragment of conversation, long ago, something to do with warrior women and their horses. Something about the riding from a young age breaking their barriers, this must be the reason. He lifted her from her feet now and laid her on the grass. He knelt over her, his eyes looking over her whole body, taking in her beauty.

He could feel the energy building, the blue sparks he was used to, now joined by white ones. He took this as a sign that he was correct that their union was meant to be. He bent his head to her breast and took her nipples between his teeth, tugging on it gently at first but then increasing the pressure, as she writhed beneath him. He trailed his tongue down across her flat stomach before burying his head between her legs. His tongue tingling, from the energy building up, as he made contact with her. He could feel the tension building in her, as she pushed his head down, forcing his tongue deeper into her.

Jacantha could feel her energy building, she knew she needed to reach deeper than ever before to ensure success. As his tongue probed her, she gathered her thoughts, relieved he could not see the look on her face. She had guiltily practised the skill of separating her mind and body during her lovemaking with Trwyn. Briefly his image flitted into her mind but she pushed it aside, focusing at the task at hand.

She glanced across at the sword. It was just within reach. She looked round now for a suitable rock. Releasing one hand from Wend's hair, she felt round in the grass until she found what she was looking for. It was smaller than she had wanted, but had a sharp point around one edge. She moaned, encouraging Wend to continue in his actions, as she moved her hand towards the swords hilt.

She tightened her grasp on his head, with the hand still twisted into his thick hair, as the other descended on the stone. A crackle snapped through the air as it split. Wend attempted to lift his head, he felt a change in the air around him, but she pleaded with him not to stop and he continued, now sliding his fingers deep into her, as her nails dug into his shoulders.

Jacantha smiled, the time was growing near. She gazed up at the moon, a red sheen was beginning to form over it. She pulled his head up to hers and rolled Wend onto his back, away from his sword. Now it was she who moved down his body, her lips fluttering against his skin, as they travelled over his hard chest muscles and down his stomach. She used her teeth to pull lose the ties that held his leggings. She teased him through the material before releasing his manhood. She let out an involuntary gasp at the size of him, he was far larger than Trwyn. She wondered now, whether she would be able to take him and not be distracted by the pain it would surely cause but her body trembled with longing, at the thought of him filling her.

She pressed her lips against the tip, letting her tongue gently play with him, as she considered her next move. She was supposed to be a virgin, she knew this was important to him, she must act naively now and allow him to believe he was in control. His hands now took hold of her head, as he coaxed her with soft words, to take him in her mouth. Then in a sudden move, he grabbed her hair tighter, forcing himself deeper into her mouth. She gagged struggling for breath and pushed away from him.

He laughed now.

"Do not worry, my beautiful queen, you will soon learn how to pleasure me that way. We have all the time in the world for me to teach you how to please me."

He pulled her up now, until her face was above his, then he rolled her over so she was back underneath him. He was back between her legs now, forcing them wider, as he reached down pushing his leggings out of the way, and adjusted his position.

"Now, this will only hurt for a moment or two, my love."

She tried to reply but he silenced her, pressing his mouth down over hers, as he entered her.

There was no gentleness, only raw animal instinct, as he drove into her. Rather than the pain she had expected, her body responded, driving her hips up to meet his. The air now exploded around them, tiny thunder claps of energy, burst into the air. As he drove into her harder and faster she saw the majority of these explosions were blue, emanating from him rather than her. She closed her eyes and allowed her mind to re-join fully with her body.

Immediately she was overwhelmed with sensations. Pain mixed with pleasure and somewhere deep inside, she was hungry for more. She pulled her legs up wrapping them round his waist. Her hands clawed at his back, fuelling him to plunge into her even deeper. Her back arched, as he threw his head back, he let out a roar like a wild beast, as he sought to satisfy them both. She could feel the moment fast approaching now, Wend seemed unaware of the changes taking place around them.

The air was heavily charged now with bright white explosions outnumbering the blue ones. She felt him struggle to catch his breath, he could not hold back much longer. She now focused her mind on the sensations rushing through her body, she fed them bringing herself closer to release, she knew timing was everything. She threw her arms round his neck pulling his mouth to hers, just as their lips met she pleaded with him.

"Now! Now! Come with me..." She felt his whole-body tense as he released himself into her. Her body clenched onto his. holding him deep inside, as she allowed her own release to overcome her. Then she lay still.

Wend had never felt such energy before, already his mind was racing ahead to the things he would do to her in time. Only now after his release, did he realise something was wrong. He could feel the energy around him but he did not feel it filling him as it had before.

He looked down at her laying beneath him now and saw the white light surrounding her body. He tried to lift himself up but found he could not move he was trapped in her energy, unable to pull away. She smiled up at him and reached out and stroked his face. The look on her face was angelic she had never looked so beautiful and serene as she did at this minute. He felt himself falling, his mind told him he was still but the sensation continued.

He was in limbo no longer in his body but floating above looking down at the sight of their entwined limbs. He realised he was not alone and looked round to see Nadredd stood beside him.

It was Nadredd who spoke first.

"I am sorry my friend, if only you had listened."

"What do you mean? What is happening? Why are you here?"

"I am your friend, who else would there be to meet you, you are dying, you wanted to much. If only you could have been content with what you had. She is beautiful you were right about that. And she was destined for you, her destiny was to be your downfall, she was born just for you."

"No this cannot be; I want to go back I cannot die!" Wend grew angry, he tried to force his way back to his body but the white energy barred him from returning.

"You cannot fight this. You have already lost. All you can do now is accept your fate and join me."

"Never! I cannot die! She cannot do this; I will not allow it!"

"This is your last chance if you do not come with me now you will be forced to stay here in between lives. Wend I am your friend I beg you join me now!"

Nadredd held out his hand but Wend. Sadness was etched on Nadredd's face as he drifted away leaving Wend alone floating above where his body still lay entwined with Jacantha's.

Jacantha lifted her head and placed her lips to his anchoring him, gently she kissed him. Then he realised frantically he tried to push his way back to his body that his energy was being drawn away from him. He watched helpless, as the bursts of blue energy faded becoming pale and the finally melting into the white that surrounded her. He felt himself weakening, shrinking, he was becoming transparent. The last thing he saw were her eyes brimming with tears, as everything went dark.

Jacantha lay still. The heavy weight of Wend's inert body holding her in place. She felt had felt his life force leave him. She had felt a terrible sadness that threatened now to engulf her. Had he chosen a different path he could have achieved so much more, in those last few moments she had felt his soul, he had been alone and frightened, and so sad. She had also felt his feelings for her in as much as he was able he had truly loved her, any hatred she had felt for him had melted away leaving only pity.

She glanced towards the trees, aware she was no longer alone. Two wolves walked towards where she lay. They took hold of Wend's arms and pulled him from on top of her. The wolf that she knew to be the Lady came to her now pressing her muzzle against Jacantha's face encouraging her to get up and move. She heard the voice in her head instructing her she must leave now, this part was over, soon they would be together. Nature would take care of what must be finished here. She rose to her feet unsteadily, she was aware a change had taken place, somewhere deep inside her soul.

She became aware now of her senses had been enhanced once again but this time she knew they would not fade again but remain with her. She looked towards the woods she sensed the other wolves hiding amongst the trees. She could hear their ragged breathing and she could feel their hunger. Fear now filled her senses and she realised the horses were foaming up. They too had recognised the scent of the wolves.

She turned towards where the Lady and her consort stood beside Wend's remains. She lowered her eyes and sent a silent message that she would leave now and await them at her castle. She knelt beside Wends body and closed his eyes then leant over and placed a last kiss upon his cold lips. She made to walk towards Wend's horse but the male wolf stepped between her and the beast. She nodded her understanding and returned to her own mount climbing quickly into the saddle.

As she turned and rode off towards home, she heard the dying screams of the horse, as the last tangible link with Wend was destroyed. The first part of the prophecy had been fulfilled, only time would answer whether the second part would also come to pass.

Chapter Twenty-Five

Jacantha passed most of her homeward journey in a trance. She tried to process what she had done and witnessed. The screams of the dying horse still echoed in her head. Her new senses overwhelmed her. Visual and audible sensations bombarded her from all directions. She tried to block them out unsuccessfully, she knew she would need Celdwady's help to learn to control these new powers. She could not imagine continuing a normal life with this clarity, surely if she could not control it, over time it would drive her insane.

She drew her horse to a halt as the castle came into sight. She knew the others would not be back until tomorrow morning at the earliest, but still she was reluctant to ride those final miles back to her home. She knew there would be questions and she was not sure she was willing to answer them, even in her own mind. She would have to lie to those she loved and respected the most. Only Celdwady would understand. Could she tell him all now?

The Lady had made it clear to her before what she could and could not share, but now that part was over, could she tell now? Could she unburden her guilty heart? No, she must not, there was more to come yet she knew, and this burden was one she must carry alone. She dug her heels in and spurred the horse onwards. She had faced her enemy, what could be left to face now that could be any worse.

Celdwady saw her approach from the tower. He had been waiting there since a few hours after she left. He had watched the moon change throughout the night. His hearted had skipped several beats as he saw the red mist envelop it. Only when he saw it clear and shine with a brightness he had not seen since his childhood, did he know for sure she had been victorious. The atmosphere now was charged with positive energy. It was so palpable he could almost reach out his hands and touch it.

He threw down the runes again, still the same confused messages. He was sure that they would have changed now but still they kept their secrets. He knew from things Jacantha had said, there was more to the prophecy than the events of the one night, but he had been convinced clarity would come, once the path was chosen. He hurried now down the stairs to greet her at the gate.

Jacantha saw Celdwady stood waiting for her, relief clearly etched in his features. He took hold of the bridle and led her up towards the stables. A young boy dashed forward to take her horse, a huge smile on his face at the sight of her. Then he looked at her face and his smile froze, the boy quickly averted his eyes and hurried away with her mount. She turned to Celdwady and looked him full in the face only to see the same frozen smile fixed there. "What is wrong? What has happened?"

Her first thoughts were of Trwyn, had something happened to him? Had they had news?

Celdwady shook his head and reached out to take her arm.

"Come, I will show you." She allowed him to lead her into the castle towards his chambers.

Everyone they encountered had that same expression as they looked at her face. She raised her hands several times, feeling for some sort of scar or brand, that would give last night's events away. As she entered his chamber she came face to face with Brawd. He let out a gasp as Celdwady guided her past him over to a crystal mirror set on the wall. She started at her reflection and her expression now froze as those of the people looking at her had. Her eyes, which had been the brightest of blues, were now a cold hard ice grey. She felt her knees weaken. Exhaustion overcame her and she slumped to the floor.

When she came around she was laying on her own bed. Celdwady sat guard over her. She could hear conversations taking place just outside the door. Trywn was out there, demanding entry. She could hear Brawd pleading with him to be patient.

Celdwady reached over and touched her brow. "Is there anything you wish to discuss with me, before that husband of yours breaks down the door?"

Weakly, she shook her head. She needed time to decide how much she should share and how much should remain secret.

"When I am ready I will come and find you, I promise but for now I just want to sleep." Celdwady nodded his acceptance.

He stood and crossed the room, as he reached for the door handle, he turned to her and smiled.

"Remember you do not have to bear everything alone, I am here for you, until the very end."

Again, she nodded, she could feel the tears welling up, she felt so weak and tired. They both knew that this was not over yet, and that her days were still limited.

Trwyn burst past Celdwady as he opened the door. Celdwady looked at him, Jacantha observed there was something in his face, that Celdwady was obviously concerned about. She thought that it must be how he would react to the change in her eyes. She looked Trwyn squarely in the face allowing him to observe for himself and waited for a response. He sat next to her on the bed. She could sense so many conflicts within him. He stroked her face.

She reached towards him, needing his arms around her. She needed to feel his embrace to put her heart at ease. Instead he pulled away from her, as if it would hurt her to touch her. He looked at her face, tears building in his eyes.

"You are tired I can see that. They have told me you must rest. I just needed to see you were alive for myself. I shall bed down in one of the spare rooms for now, until you are feeling stronger." He leant forward and kissed her on her forehead.

Then, as quickly as he had entered the room, he was gone. Jacantha fell back against the pillows and the tears began to fall.

The next time she was aware of her surroundings, Fleura was sat beside her. She could see she was not the only one to have shed tears recently. She reached out and took the girl's arm. Fleura turned towards her, she was the first one to look at Jacantha without her face wearing a mask of shock.

"How long have I slept?"

"Only a few hours." Fleura replied. She seemed to be considering her words before she spoke again. "I need to tell you something. But I don't know if I will be overstepping the mark. I think I have to tell you but I am so confused. There is so much going on and I am scared and I do not know how long I can remain here. I love you like a sister, you have been so good to me but still, I am unsure, you may hate me."

"Hush! Have no fear, nothing you can tell me will make me hate you. I can think of no reason you should ever leave here. What makes you think you could tell me anything that will make that necessary?"

"Has Trwyn been to see you? How did he seem to you?"

"Yes, he came when I first woke, why do you ask?" Jacantha fought back the tears that threatened to overtake her again. Now, a whole new batch of questions flooded through her mind. Had something happened between Trwyn and Fleura while they were away? Was that the reason for his behaviour towards her? She shook herself, no, that could not be it, neither of them would betray her that way. But why did Fleura think she would be sent away?

Fleura seemed to sense her struggle, and paused before continuing.

"Something happened, at Wend Y Mawr's castle. Well two things happened, the first is easier to tell. He killed the children, not all but over half and every woman in that place. Even those who were obviously held against their will. He looked like he hated them all. I am sure if he had found that chamber alone, before the others he would have killed every child. I have never seen him so filled with hatred and loathing, it was like he was possessed."

She paused then continued, explaining exactly what had gone on in the room. She explained how he had examined each child before deciding their fate.

Jacantha sat up now in shock. This was so unlike Trwyn, he was gentle at heart. The Trwyn she loved would have brought every child back, believing a loving home could undo any harmful influences on such young children. She looked at Fleura again.

"You said two things. What was the second?"

A flush rose over Fleura's cheeks.

"We saw you!" She waited a moment to allow this to sink in. "Only he and I saw. It was the bloodstone; it must have been linked to something that he had with him. We saw you, naked, offering yourself to him."

"What exactly did you see?" Jacantha's voice was stifled as she fought to swallow down the bile that rose in her throat.

Fleura described what they had witnessed. She told her the way Trwyn had stood transfixed by what he had seen. How he been withdrawn ever since. Jacantha nodded. She now understood why he had pulled away from her. He not only knew of her betrayal but had witnessed part of it. How could he live with that knowledge and still love her?

"Why do you not despise me for what you saw?" She asked Fleura.

"Because I know that you did it because you had to. I know you would never have taken such a course by choice."

"Yet you talk of leaving? You talk as if you trust me, as if you understand, yet would walk away, when you know I need a friend the most?"

Fleura looked at the floor, when she spoke her voice was barely audible, even to Jacantha's enhanced senses "I have no choice. There is no one else to blame only my own weakness."

Jacantha stared at her. She reached out with her mind and she knew.

"Is it because of the child you are carrying?"

Fleura looked up at her wide eyed. She opened her mouth to speak but she could not find the words.

Jacantha smiled at her "Do not worry. You are not the first nor will you be the last. You love my brother, he loves you. I will arrange that the binding be done immediately. A few will snigger but let them. I would say welcome to the family but right now I am not so sure that you would see that as a blessing."

Fleura threw her arms round Jacantha. Tears followed down both their cheeks as they clung to each other but each was enveloped in their own problems. Jacantha was the first to break away. She took a deep breath and took hold of Fleura firmly by the shoulders.

"Right, we must deal with these things. I need your promise, you will speak to no one, of anything that has been said here in this room. You will help me dress now then I shall find Celdwady and with his guidance all shall be dealt with as it must. I need you to put your faith in me and I know I can put my trust in you to protect my secret. Trwyn will not speak of it now, though in time as it eats away at him, he may give me away. I shall take steps to prevent this for his sanity and our love, as much as for the protection of us all."

Fleura nodded her assent and helped Jacantha into a simple gown. They walked through the castle together, sisters in heart until they reached the corridor to Celdwady's chambers. As Jacantha turned to leave, she looked at Fleura once more, reassuring herself she had brought peace to the young girl.

Celdwady was startled by Jacantha's appearance. He rose and moved towards her as she entered his chamber. She halted him with a hand gesture and moved to stand by the window. She poured out her heart to him once more.

She told him the story of her conversation with Fleura in her chambers, she now told him briefly of her enhanced senses. She cried as she him of her fears regarding Trwyn and his ability to deal with what he had seen. The only thing she withheld was what had happened after the orb had been destroyed. What was still to come she could not tell him as even she was still unsure.

Celdwady listened. His discomfort was evident to her as he shifted his weight in an attempt to refrain from pacing the room. This strong brave woman stood before him and he had never seen her look so vulnerable and defeated. He had searched through his scrolls looking for an explanation of the change in her eyes. Now he realised that the knowledge he had sought was not for him to know. Whatever had happened in that clearing was between her and the

Lady it was not for him to question what or why. When she had finished, she turned to him, her eyes imploring him for assistance.

He took a seat in the chair by the fire, gazing into the flames, ordering his thoughts before he spoke.

"Fleura will keep your secret, I do not doubt her. Her problem is easily remedied; I shall arrange the ceremony to take place in a few days. It will be as part of the victory celebrations. The problem of Trwyn, that is more complex. I could give him a potion which would wipe his memories of the last few days, but he would be aware that they were missing. It would be foolish to suppose he could believe that he had played no part in the attack. I propose a weaker draft that I shall prepare.

I shall take him on a little spiritual journey of his own and rather than attempt to change his memory, I shall endeavour, to persuade him that what he saw was a vision created by Wend to destroy your union. Once this has taken place, it shall be up to you to draw from him what happened with the children. I agree with Fleura, it is disturbing not that he killed them, many others would have done the same. But that it is so out of character for him. It maybe he was susceptible to the malign influences there, but there may be more to it, given he selected some to live.

You should go back to your chambers and rest, we will discuss the changes that have overcome you once the rest it taken care of. I suggest, rather than try to stop them, you experiment with them, find your limits, experience the sensations so we can have greater knowledge, when the time to explore them fully comes. I shall brew the potion now and Brawd will find Trwyn and bring him to me but he must not know you have been here.

Jacantha nodded and left the room returning to her chamber. Brawd slipped from behind the curtain that hid a second chamber at the back of the room. He looked at Celdwady. A look passed between the two that needed no words and Brawd left to find Trwyn.

Trwyn entered the room and looked around suspiciously. He could see no reason why he had been summoned here. Celdwady motioned that he should sit but Trwyn refused, pacing like a caged animal, his agitation evident. Celdwady looked up at him and considered his words. Brawd had slipped back behind the curtain, in the hope that his presence would be forgotten.

"Trwyn I have known you since you were a babe in your mother's arms. I have always known you to be one of the gentlest of men, as well as one of the most honest. I am going to ask you now, is there something you wish to tell me?"

"No! Should there be?" His reply hostile, a tone in his voice Celdwady had never heard before.

"Maybe, you would like to tell me about what you saw in the orb?"

Trwyn's face contorted "So that interfering bitch has been to see you?" He spat his words out.

"If you mean Fleura. then yes, but she came because of her own discomfort at what she saw. Did you ever stop to think about what the two of you actually saw? Or did you just think the worst of your wife?"

Trwyn's face froze, to have it thrown at him in accusation, was almost unbearable. He knew what he had seen, how could Celdwady think that he wanted to think the worst? What other explanation could there be?

"Come Trwyn, take a seat and drink with me and let us discuss this like two men who think logically, let us put emotion to one side."

Trwyn slowly moved to the seat Celdwady directed him to and took the glass. He took a drink, swallowing slowly not noticing, the other man did not put his own glass to his lips.

"What else am I to think? I saw her naked, offering herself to him."

"Ah, but did you? Did you see her face? Can you be sure it was her? Can you be sure even if it was she was acting of her own free will? Can you say for certain that she might not have been under a spell Wend Y Mawr had cast upon her?"

"Of course, it was her. I didn't need to see her face to know it was the woman who is supposed to be my wife!"

Trwyn was struggling to keep his temper under control. He wanted to go to her and drag her here, before this man who thought she could do no wrong and force her to tell the truth.

"And my other questions, can you answer those?"

"No but..." Trwyn faltered.

"I think you saw exactly what you were supposed to see. I want you to consider, and listen to what I am telling you. If you still want to believe the worst of her when I finish, then I shall arrange for your union to be dissolved."

Trwyn looked at the older man, dissolve his union? Was that what he wanted? No, he loved her. The thought of losing the one he had thought was beyond his reach for so long was unbearable. Did Celdwady know something he didn't? Had she already spoken of separating because he had stayed away from her? Or because of what had happened with Wend? His head was swimming. He felt tired, unable to focus his thoughts. He nodded that he would listen to Celdwady, what did he have to lose?

"I think you saw what Wend wanted anyone who looked into that orb to see. Consider, he went alone to fight a woman. What if he had been unable to defeat her? Do you think he would want one of his men to see that? We know from past experience that Wend had a vivid imagination when it came to your wife. We know he made a room full of people believe he was raping her on that device. Is it really so hard to imagine that he could not create a vision and store it in the orb?

If any of his men had wondered in there, what would they have seen? The defeated warrior queen, throwing herself at the feet of their triumphant leader. In short, they would have seen just what he wanted them to see, not what was actually happening." He paused waiting for Trwyn to react.

"Is that possible?" Trwyn struggled to remember exactly what he had witnessed.

Could he have been mistaken? He wanted to believe this new version of events. Could he have misjudged his own senses so badly? It made perfect sense Wend would not have wanted to risk his men seeing him lose, he would have been sure of winning but there was always the risk of defeat. Why else would the vision of been there if not for his own men to see, he had not been aware they would attack otherwise his men would have been ready to defend.

"Many things are possible. Some things that Wend knew are beyond my comprehension. I cannot tell you how he did it, because I do not choose to dabble in those dark arts in which he immersed himself. I can show you scrolls which will explain it to you, if you so desire, but I consider those arts dangerous, no good can come of them. Look what he has managed now, even after his death, he seeks to destroy your harmony. It may not have been his intention when he created his vision, but I am sure he would be thrilled with its outcome."

Trwyn stood abruptly, staggered and fell against the chair, Celdwady rose and helped him back to his seat. Trwyn was mumbling his words slurred together, Celdwady lifted the glass and put it to Trwyn's lips.

"Here just a little more. I know you want to go to her, but she is resting why not just have a little nap here, just a few minutes, and when you awake you can go to her. You will remember the truth of what happened when you awake. The truth is Wend created a vision for you to see, do you understand that?"

Trwyn swallowed the liquid Celdwady had poured between his lips. He weakly nodded as his eyes closed and his head dropped to his chest.

Brawd came out from behind the curtain. He collected both glasses and threw them into the fire the remaining contents causing it to spark and hiss.

It was dark when Trywn awoke. He found himself sat facing Brawd who was deep at study with a heavy looking book. Brawd looked up and acknowledged him. He explained that Celdwady was with Jacantha. She had developed a fever and was being cared for. Trwyn rose immediately still feeling a little groggy he went to leave the room but Brawd stopped him. He coaxed Trwyn back to his seat. He could see the suspicion in the warrior's eyes. He knew that few took him seriously, the mere apprentice but Celdwady had explained to him the importance of establishing a relationship with the important members of council now if he were to take over from Celdwady in the future.

He talked now of general castle life, the impending union of Arth and Fleura, the politics of pleasing all the elders. He discussed the feast that was to come once their queen was well, he knew Trwyn was still eager to leave but he continued trying to engage him and to occupy his thoughts.

It was nearing dawn when Celdwady returned. He found the two young men sat deep in discussion of castle politics. He smiled seeing his young apprentice finally stepping out of his shadows, soon he would be put to the test. Trwyn jumped to his feet seeking assurance his wife was well. Celdwady nodded she would be fine now but must rest. He could not say exactly what was wrong, he had never seen anything like it. He placed his hand on Trwyn's shoulder.

"Go to her, take a firm hand with her and make sure she does nothing but rest for the next few days at least. She is weak far weaker than she knows, or will admit to. I will not lie to you Trwyn, I fear for her, whatever magick took place to save the rest of us have drained her. I must rest a few hours and then I shall look for something to restore her, as much as is in my power to do at least. Prepare yourself for the worst and pray for the best."

Trwyn fled the room heading straight for her chamber. Brawd turned to Celdwady and threw him a questioning look, she had seemed fine earlier if a little tired. Celdwady shook his head.

"We shall talk when I wake, we will have much to discuss."

Trwyn entered their bedchamber as quietly as he could. Jacantha lay on the bed looking pale and fragile. He crossed the room, Fleura who had been sat by her, stood moving back as he approached. He climbed onto the bed beside his wife and cradled her in his arms. She opened her eyes briefly and looked up at him. He kissed her lips gently and held her as she slept. Fleura slipped from the room.

Trwyn had never put much faith in the Goddess before. He had believed, as he had been taught to that she controlled the world around him, but other than that, he had never given much thought to the matter. Now he dropped to his knees beside the bed and prayed for the Lady to give him time to make his peace with Jacantha.

Queen Of Ages: Ascension

Chapter Twenty-Six

Jacantha drifted in and out of consciousness for several days. Each time she opened her eyes she saw Trwyn by her side. She tried each time to speak but no sooner had she opened her mouth than a sweet liquid was poured into her mouth and slumber overtook her again. Finally, she awoke feeling stronger and as the liquid approached her mouth, she reached up and grasped the wrist bearing it.

Celdwady looked down at her and smiled. 'You had me worried for a while there my child.'

His words accompanied a flurry of movement within the chamber. Trwyn, who had been sleeping, his head resting on the bed, sat up abruptly Jacantha smiled to see him looking startled. She reached out her hand to him and he leaned forward taking her in his arms

"Forgive me?" He whispered in her ear.

She held him back at arm's length and looked into his eyes. "There is nothing to forgive. But there are things to discuss, now is not the time though."

The castle now bustled into life with the news that their queen was restored. Her brother came to see her in her chamber looking concerned and frightened. She rose from the bed to greet him, seeing not the man, but the child she had cared for standing before her. He broke down, pouring out his fears not only regarding his own abilities to rule, but to be a husband and father. She laughed as she thought back to her own doubts and sat him down. She told him about the night by their father's pyre when she had considered running for the hills. She told him of all the fears she had had and watched as her light dimmed a little in her brother's eyes and he saw her now with all her frailties and faults rather, than as the star he had placed on a pedestal from his infancy. She knew it caused him pain to see her as she really was but knew if he were to carry the kingdom forward after her departure, he needed this.

When they arose, they did so as equals, not queen and heir or chosen one and mortal but as brother and sister. She regarded him now, seeing him stand a little taller,

"Fleura will be a good wife, she will help you and give you good advice, be sure to listen to your wife, as much as the elders." He nodded before leaving her alone.

It had been decided that the wedding would take place as soon as it could be arranged upon her recovery. She felt guilty she had allowed the weakness to overcome her and place the celebrations on hold.

Tomorrow the feasts would begin, followed by her brother's wedding the day after. They would feast in the great hall until sunset, when the men would leave for her brother's enforced absence, and she would hold court for Fleura in the evening. She dreaded that as much as she had her own, she knew there would be questions about how she had defeated Wend. The older women would be fishing for any gossip they could grasp onto to get on up on their neighbours, and she wondered if her strength would hold up for such a long day and worried as weariness took over, she might give something away.

She ate in her room again with Trwyn, tomorrow would be soon enough to face everyone else. She and Trwyn had still not spoken of what had happened at the castle, she was wary of bringing the subject up and upsetting him so soon after Celdwady had solved the problem of what he had witnessed in the orb. She looked at him now, searching deep inside him, looking for a sign he was capable of what he had been accused of doing. She saw shadows deep behind his eyes and knew his actions were haunting him but did not know how to draw it from him. She sensed if she pushed he would retreat further from her. Once they had finished eating, she placed the tray outside the door so they would not be disturbed and knelt before him.

She reached up, touching his face, drawing it to hers and their lips met. She felt a hunger for him now she had not felt before, a need to prove to herself that their union was unbroken. She pressed herself against him, inviting him to take her. She felt his body stiffen and he pulled away, tears threatened to well up in her eyes but when she looked at him she realised, that it was not her that he was seeing, but he was reliving some other moment.

"Talk to me." She spoke softly as not to destroy his reverie. "I am your wife there should be nothing hidden, tell me what is haunting you."

"You know what I did. I know Fleura told you." It was a simple statement spoken without malice.

"Yes, she told me what happened. But I want you to tell me why..." Her voice trailed off as she saw him preparing to speak again.

"I need you to know I am not proud of what I did. But everything I saw there....it was tainted by him. Even those children, the innocence was gone from their eyes already. It is a poison in the blood, the evil corrupts no matter how much you think you can control it. No matter how much I thought I could control it."

He paused looking at the puzzled expression that was now showing on her face, she opened her mouth to speak but he continued, "I was born here as were both my parents but my great grandmother on my mother's side was not. She was one of those from the castle, she was a concubine, and Wend's grandfather was also my grandfather."

He stopped, letting the weight of what he had just told her sink in.

"When she found out she was with child she kept it secret, the first chance she got she ran. My father told me when she was dying she confessed to everything so she could go to her grave with her conscience clear. She knew that there were only two possible outcomes if she stayed, if she had a boy he would be taken and brought up without her, trained to fight and kill. If it was a girl, she would have been sent to work into the kitchens until she was old enough to serve in other ways.

Wend was already in his teens then, she had seen the way he took his pleasure with the younger girls. She was scared for her unborn child. She knew running was her only chance. My great grandfather found her alone in the forest, she was weak and threw herself on his mercy. He brought her here and was bonded with her, he told them she was from a different village out by the borders and that the child was his. No one thought to question it, he had relatives that lived out that way and had been visiting around the time she must have conceived, it all seemed believable. But do you understand, the blood that runs through Wend's veins, is the same as runs through mine. Deep down I am the same as him."

"No, stop there, you are nothing like him. You are kind and loving, you are everything he was not. That he could never be. It is not the blood that runs through you that makes you who you are, it is the actions you perform. "

"But I am, when I was there, in that place I felt no love only hate. I wanted to destroy them all, if the others had not been there I would have killed all those children. And what scared me the most...a part of me enjoyed it. I enjoyed their fear, I felt a thrill as they screamed and I silenced them, and you want to believe that I am a better man."

"I know you are a better man. It was not the blood that made you feel that way it was the place."

Trwyn turned away from her and she grabbed his face, turning it back to hers, as she continued.

"It was the energies he had built up in that place. That was what affected you and it affected you more because you are a good man. You have to believe me, I looked into his eyes, I looked into them as he died and there was nothing there I see when I look into yours."

She reached up and pulled his face down to hers, this time as their lips met he kissed her back. His arms sought her, pulling her to him, hands shaking as they each sought to remove the others clothing. Their lovemaking was frenzied, each desperate to banish their own demons deep within each other's bodies. Jacantha clawed at Trwyn's back, she looked up at him, searching his face with the new knowledge, she had to reassure herself that she had spoken the truth to him.

She knew now, why there had been times that she had recognised that look in his eyes. They were so like Wend's eyes but with a depth and warmth that he could never have possessed except just as death took him. Guilt swept over her that she had allowed him to enter her thoughts he was gone and could not be allowed to exist, even in her thoughts now. She buried her head into Trwyn's chest and allowed the pleasure of their union to overwhelm her.

The sun was rising as they awoke the next morning. Jacantha dressed carefully aware all eyes would be upon her. She wore the dress she had worn the day she was crowned it seemed a little tighter than previously but she thought no more of it as Fleura helped her pile her hair high on her head and set her crown in place. She took a deep breath and prepared herself to face them all

"Well we cannot avoid them all any longer." She turned to Fleura and they walked to the Great Hall together.

Trwyn was waiting for her just outside with her brother. He took her arm and the four of them entered together. The cheers were deafening. A lavish feast was already laid out, food that would be eaten during the course of the day filled the tables. Jacantha took her seat on the throne Trwyn to her right and her brother sat at her other side. Fleura stood hesitantly to one side, unsure where her place was, not yet family but unwilling to leave her lovers side. Jacantha smiled and motioned for an extra seat to be brought and placed at her brother's side. Fleura looked at her gratefully and sat.

It was Trwyn who finally stood again and called for silence. Jacantha now rose to her feet and addressed the room.

"My people, now is the time for celebration. We have defeated our enemy. His castle has been burnt to the ground, his army destroyed, along with all the souls his evil corrupted and polluted. The few innocents we could save, now have loving homes, here within our heart. Tomorrow we shall celebrate the union of my beloved brother and his betrothed and I know their union will be as happy as my own. Then we shall begin the difficult task of rebuilding these lands.

There will be long days of hard toil ahead but I know you are equal to the task. Messengers shall be sent out to the lands beyond Wend Y Mawr's kingdom and we shall announce the freedom from his tyranny to them. His lands shall now be our land but it will be any years before they recover to be of any practical use. The Lady shall aid in its recovery and we give thanks to the Lady and her consort for the victory they have given us and the prosperity which awaits."

She paused as the room lifted their glasses and drank the toast.

"I know questions are being whispered. I know you wish to ask of the prophecy."

She glanced at Trwyn knowing the question dwelt in his heart more than any others present. "I shall be amongst you for a little time yet. The prophecy is not yet fulfilled, but in time I must leave you. I do not wish to talk of this further at present there is time enough for that to be discussed. Today, I order you all to drink and make merry."

She raised her glass and emptied it in one deep draft. The room erupted into laughter and cheering.

She resumed her seat and turned to Trwyn she saw the pain in his eyes as she placed her hand over his and whispered to him

"Do not fear we have time yet and part of me shall remain with you I promise."

He nodded his understanding but his eyes still reflected his feelings. He had believed it was over now, her words confirmed his worst fear, that it was not.

The feasting began as always, with the consumption of a host of delicacies, Jacantha found the smells nauseating and sat picking at hot bread rather than sample the other delights. Celdwady watched her from across the room. He motioned to Brawd to follow him and the two men left the room together silently.

Back in his chamber Celdwady took up his runes. He cast them down and leant over studying the formation in which they had landed. Brawd looked down at them intensely, then the two men locked eyes.

Brawd was the first to say what was on the two men's minds. "A child? But whose?"

Celdwady ran his hand over the pieces of carve bone seeking for further knowledge.

"All I can say is with the child, balance shall be restored, the runes tell me nothing further, it shall be no normal child of that I am certain and it will be your place to guide her. You will be the guardian of the prophecy which is to come."

"What do you mean the prophecy which is to come? Has not the prophecy been fulfilled? Wend has been defeated what more can there be?"

"There is much more to come. And come it will, in only a few months all our lives will change and you must be ready to take my place, as I must be ready for the journey that awaits me. You have the mead brewed for tomorrow?"

"Yes, master but I do not understand, you speak as if you will be leaving us here."

"So I shall, as will our queen. You must be ready to take your place as guardian to her child and to advise and protect all. You shall start tomorrow by uniting Arth Dwyn and Fleura. It will be seen, as symbolic of you finishing your apprenticeship, and taking your place as my successor."

"People will question why you are not conducting the ceremony."

"They will speculate, they will not ask out loud, and they will know soon enough. Already they guess at what is to come. The prophecy spoke of sacrifice yet Jacantha returned. When she fell ill many expected her to die yet she survived although I believe that her body was fighting to save the child within. The child will be normal do not misunderstand me on that aspect but the pregnancy I think not. "

"How do you mean? Will she die in childbirth?"

"No Jacantha will live that I have seen, but the child will come early, it will be healthy and fully developed, though it should not be. We must pray and prepare for tomorrow but first we shall return to the feast and eat and be seen to celebrate for a short while. Never forget appearances are important and no matter what you feel you must conceal it and do and say nothing to give concern."

Brawd nodded as the two men headed back to the great hall, each deep in thought at the prospect of what was to unfurl in the coming weeks.

The festivities were beginning in earnest when they returned. Couples filled the dance floor and despite the early hour drink flowed freely. Jacantha sat upon her throne watching over proceedings, yet seemed barely aware of the activities taking place around her. Celdwady noted the glazed distant expression in her eyes and approached her. He offered her his hand and she allowed him to move her round the room. She nodded at those who spoke to her, acknowledging their presence with only the briefest recognition. He led her into the alcove where Trwyn had pronounced his love for her.

Celdwady looked deep into her eyes "You know what is to come?"

"Yes." She turned away as she continued. "I shall bear a child which will provide the balance in the world then I must leave. I will never know who is the true father to the child, not that it matters, the blood that runs through one, is shared by both."

Celdwady looked at her quizzically and she explained Trwyn's family history. How he and Wend shared an ancestor, therefore the blood that coursed through their veins was the same, only Wend's actions had separated them. With tears in her eyes she confessed her concerns that Trwyn might struggle to bring up the child alone, knowing how he felt about his heritage.

"Do not fear child, he will not be alone. Brawd shall watch over them both and advise him and do not forget your brother and his wife will be there for them. She shall have a little cousin to play with and they shall bring prosperity back to the kingdom. Everything is in hand, we have a few months in which you shall set them on the right path before we depart. All shall be well, I promise you. You should tell Trwyn soon and make the most of the time which remains."

"I shall tell him tomorrow after the ceremony but now I must get back, he will be wondering where I am"

Jacantha turned and re-entered the hall leaving Celdwady alone with his thoughts. Trwyn was at her side within moments, questioning her as to the reason for the private audience with Celdwady. She attempted to soothe him yet she could see his worry beneath the facade he put on.

The celebrations continued until an hour before dusk. The men took their leave, heading out of the castle for Arth's last night of single life. The women gathered round the fire. The banter was good natured and jovial as they teased Fleura of what was to come on her wedding night. Jacantha was relieved to see they had all accepted Fleura so readily and also that the amount of ale consumed throughout the day promised to keep the evening short. Jacantha did her best to join in with the conversations but her recent illness had left her drained.

As the night drew on she made her excuses and left the party to spend the night alone in the huge bed. In her chamber she stood at the window looking out at the moon. Her path was set before her, she knew what was to come, yet she felt a fear now that she had not experienced before. Her hand strayed to her stomach as she thought about the future, her unborn child would have without her. She knew how it was to grow up without a mother but to grow up never having known your mother at all seemed so cruel. She thought back to Celdwady's words 'she would have a cousin' could it be a daughter? How could he know?

She shook her head of course he could know, if she admitted it she had known before he told her. Her daughter. Would it matter who the father was? In the distance she heard the wolves howl as if to answer her unvoiced question. She must put her faith in the Lady once again and believe all would work out for the best, even if she was not to be part of her child's life. She climbed into bed and fell into a deep dreamless sleep.

She awoke early the next morning and dressed hurriedly. She had intended on helping Fleura prepare for the ceremony but as she arrived at her chamber she found her sat ready awaiting Arth's arrival. She smiled at the disappointment on Fleura's face as she saw who had entered the room, remembering her own wait. She joined Fleura at the window, looking for the tell-tale signs of dust on the roads from the horses hooves. They spotted it in the distance, she turned and hugged Fleura before leaving to take her place amongst the guests.

The men arrived at the gathering place to join the women a few minutes after Jacantha's arrival. Trwyn moved straight to her side, he took her arm. It struck Jacantha that he was holding onto her a little tighter than necessary but she pushed the thoughts from her mind. Fleura and Arth approached now, they looked so happy. Jacantha smiled at seeing her brother walking tall with his intended on his arm. He seemed to have gained in confidence since their discussion and she could not help but wonder how much Fleura had influenced this.

Brawd stepped forward and began addressing the congregation. She noticed a few looks exchanged at the fact it was the young apprentice conducting the ceremony rather than Celdwady himself. She worried about the wisdom of this, if Fleura's condition became known, then they would assume that this were the reason and she worried it might undermine the union.

Brawd was explaining now that his master was indisposed and that rather than cancel proceedings that he would officiate. He spoke of new beginnings and the future that would be built. That under the rule of first Jacantha, then Arth the kingdom would gain in strength and prosperity. Jacantha felt Trwyn's grasp on her arm tighten until his hold was painful. She carefully reached up, making sure that she was unobserved, and pulled his grip loose. She knew everyone would be turning his words over in their minds. Many believed she had come through her illness and the prophecy had been fulfilled, few had realised that the sacrifice was still to be made.

She stood and watched as Brawd conducted the ceremony bonding her brother and her friend with a heavy heart. She could see the happiness on their faces a mirror of her own a few weeks ago. So much had happened since then, so much had changed and yet more change was destined and no matter how much it hurt those closest to her, she could not change it.

The ceremony closed and she was the first to congratulate the newly joined couple. Trwyn offered his blessings through a forced smile and as the others made their way back to the castle to begin another day of feasting, he hung back, dividing Jacantha's loyalties between her duties and her husband. She knew her absence would be noted in light of Brawd's words, but she also was aware that there were things which must be discussed. She sat on a fallen tree stump and motioned for him to join her. He refused to sit pacing back and forth in front of where she sat, both waiting to see who would speak first. It was Trwyn who finally could hold back no longer, as his anger exploded within him.

"What did he mean Arth will be king after you? What is he saying? Are you going somewhere? What is happening, were you not going to bother telling me after all I am only your husband? I thought it was over, he is gone. You won and nearly died doing it, is that not enough? What more can there be? Tell me! Do I not deserve to know?"

She sat as he fired question after question in her direction, knowing the answers would bring him no peace but accepting he must be told the truth however painful the result.

"I am with child." She stated it calmly, watching the clouds appear behind his eyes as he processed the information. He began to open his mouth again but she continued before he had chance to speak.

"I shall bear a child I will not raise. You alone shall raise our daughter and I shall fulfil the prophecy and our daughter will live in a land of peace and prosperity, never knowing the strife we have endured. I warned you before we were joined that our story would have no happy ending, not for me anyway. I also told you a part of me would always be with you and so it shall or should I say she shall."

"Are you telling me you will die in childbirth? Surely Celdwady can fix this, he can prevent it? There must be something that can be done."

It was then she realised that she must take steps to make this easier for him. He would never be able to bear the pain of watching her ride away but how could it be achieved, he would only be able to move on if he believed she was dead. If he knew she were out there somewhere, he would search for her until it destroyed him. Her mind raced at possibilities, each dismissed as soon as it appeared but he was waiting now for an answer. She had allowed him to believe one lie, could another save him from more pain?

"Celdwady can do nothing. Even if he could, he would not. What is destined must be allowed to run as it will. You say I fulfilled the prophecy, no I did not because I am still here, there has been no sacrifice. Our daughter will bring the balance the world needs, I understand that now, she is a balance of my blood and yours."

She paused while the meaning of her words reached Trwyn.

"Therefore, she is a balance of my blood and the blood that you shared with Wend Y Mawr, however unpleasant that fact is to face. If I remain the balance is thrown again too far in one direction."

"But it will be in the favour of good, how can that be wrong? How can that not be allowed by the gods for good to outweigh bad? I do not understand! I do not understand why you will not fight it to stay with me, to stay with our child! You of all people know what it is like to not have a mother."

"Trwyn, it is not for us to choose where the correct balance lies, we put our faith in the Goddess to guide us and watch over us. She alone understands what is needed for life to prosper. We kill for food, does that make us good in the eyes of the deer we hunt, no, of course not. Yet we both exist in harmony. I want a world for our daughter where she knows freedom, where she can grow up without worrying the day she turns sixteen she will have to draw blood on the battlefield.

Look around you, look at what we have here and think what it would be like, for it to all be torn away. Compare it to the lands you saw that Wend ruled over, the destruction. The devastation of both the land and people. If I do not fulfil the prophecy, that is what I sentence, not only our daughter to but every other person who lives here. Yes, I am your wife and I love you but I am also Queen.

My people will always come before my personal feelings. I have a duty to them which I was born to, which comes before all else I have chosen for myself. I know you love me and want me to stay with you. And if...if I could I would but ifs, will do neither of us any good.

We have a few months left together; the child will come early but will thrive. It is up to you to decide, whether we spend the precious time we have remaining in arguments and recriminations, or whether we make the most of each moment. Now I am returning to the hall, you should decide before you join me, which you intend to do."

She did not look back as she strode away from him to the castle. She knew how badly he was hurting but her words could bring him no comfort he must find his own way to deal with the events which could not be forestalled. She would seek out Celdwady tomorrow and discuss her flight with him. There had to be a way to convince them all she had died, at least until she was far enough away to prevent them seeking her out.

By the time she reached the great hall, celebrations were beginning in earnest. The food had been brought out and everyone was indulging in the overeating that only peace would allow them to indulge in. Her brother threw her a questioning look as she took her seat at the head table. Heads turned subtly towards her, noting Trwyn was not at her side. Fleura passed her a glass of the mead the couple had been brought to toast their union, but Jacantha pushed it away. She piled up her plate from the delicacies within reach, knowing despite her lack of appetite, it was important she eat now, if not for herself then for the child she was carrying.

She had made little progress in forcing the food down when Trwyn appeared. She watched his progress across the room as people halted him with questions half hidden in concern. She watched each gesture, searching for clues as to his decision for their short future.

Eventually he disengaged himself and took his seat beside her. Neither spoke instead he reached over and took the glass of mead she had earlier refused and lifted it to her lips before draining the rest in one. He took her hand and led her to the centre of the room. As they stood facing each other, the musicians started playing and he took her hand and began the dance. They moved as one, performing the intricate steps twisting and turning still not a word spoken. She understood he would make the most of their time but the only way he could do so was to block out the truth of what was to come.

Chapter Twenty-Seven

Time passed quickly, days merged into weeks, then into months. The business of rebuilding was well under way. A constant stream of people journeyed to and from the castle as new villages sprung into being, radiating further out towards the borders once again. Jacantha spent days shut away with Celdwady making preparations for what must happen, while Trwyn worked with the others rebuilding, crafting tools for building and farming.

As she looked out of the window, she rested her hand on her swelling stomach. The last few months she had been happy, at times blissfully so but always in the back of her mind remained a voice, counting down the days that she had remaining. Trwyn had not brought up the subject again but she knew it played on his mind. She saw him looking at her sometimes, tears swelling in his eyes. She regretted that she must leave him with a lie but to let him live with the truth would be unbearable for him. They had planned so carefully, everything was ready only Celdwady and Brawd knew of her plans and were working tirelessly trying to find a solution to the one problem that remained, how to convince everyone she was dead.

. The birth was only days away, she smiled to herself, it was one advantage to being part of the prophecy, she knew exactly when her time would come and that her child would survive.

Fleura had given birth to her nephew only two days ago, the child had been small which had been fortunate, given they had passed the child off as arriving early, to cover her brother's indiscretion prior to his union. She had helped in the delivery chamber, holding Fleura's hand, as the new life had made its way into the world.

She had held her breath waiting for the child to announce its presence. Even though Celdwady's words had assured her the child would be healthy, she had not been satisfied until she heard him let a hearty bawl. Watching Fleura had helped her prepare for the act of giving birth but as she watched Fleura's face as the child was placed in her arms, she knew she must come to terms with the truth of her feelings.

Dusk was approaching as she headed from the castle. She wore her cloak its hood pulled over her head. Up close she could not disguise who she was, but from a distance, she hoped Trwyn would not spot her. Once through the outer gates, she left the path seeking the shelter of the trees, as she slipped deeper into the shadows. Only when she was sure she had escaped the castle unnoticed, she slowed her pace.

She moved through the trees until she found a place that allowed her space to lower her body to the ground. She rested for a few minutes before pulling the moonstone from her pocket. She had not used it since she had returned from her confrontation with Wend. She could only hope that she could achieve what she intended. She held the milky orb cupped in front of her body and began to chant.

The words flowed from deep within her, she could not answer how she knew the words to say, yet they poured forth. As she continued, the orb began to glow, a faint sheen at first but building in intensity with each repetition of the words, until finally if shone as brightly as the moon had on the night her journey truly began, the night she had sat by the fire consuming her father's remains. She lifted her eyes from the orb and looked into the eyes of the wolf standing only feet away from her.

The Lady shook off her guise and rose to stand above her. Jacantha bowed her head as the Amante approached and settled on the ground beside her. She slipped her arm around her daughter and held her as tears flowed from them both.

"I feel your pain my child. I feel your fear. Know only that what you shall do, is what must be done. Only by doing so, can your people be free to follow the destiny that awaits them and you to follow yours."

Jacantha fought to rein in the tears, as she told her the plan she had to disguise her leaving. She explained the one difficulty that they had not yet overcome, creating a false death was one thing, but she had not thought of a satisfactory way to avoid the pyre that her body must be seen to lie upon and be consumed by. Amante sat in silence listening to her, absorbing each word, formulating a plan to help her daughter do what must be done. Finally, she reached deep with her robe and pulled out and ancient, torn parchment.

"Take this and give it to Celdwady when they time is right, he will be able to read it and perform the enchantment required. I must insist it returns with you, when you come to join me next. This is not knowledge for this world, and under no other circumstances, would I allow it to pass to mortal hands."

She rose to her feet pulling Jacantha along with her. She took Jacantha's face gently in her cupped palms and looked deep into her eyes. She could see the pain and sadness buried beneath the surface, a tear rolled down her cheek, mirroring the one making its way down her counterpart.

"We are one, I feel your pain, I feel all you have endured and must still continue to, in a few days our daughter will be born and leaving her will break your heart, but only by doing so, can she be what her destiny requires. We each must play our part, yours is to join those who watch, as other take their turn. Soon, you shall rest a while safe in my arms."

She leant forward and kissed Jacantha's forehead and as she did so a wave of tranquillity and peace flowed from her lips throughout Jacantha's body. Slowly she turned and walked away, as she reached the cover of the trees, she looked over her shoulder, her eyes unflinching as her body shifted and the wolf was unleashed.

Jacantha remained where she stood, breathing in the forest air. It was tempting to stay here, to think of her daughter born to nature here in its glorious confines. Yet she knew that her duty required her to return. She must ensure to fluid transition between her rule and her brothers. She must be sure that no one would search for her. She walked slowly back to the castle retracing her earlier steps. As she placed each foot careful to avoid stumbling, she did not notice the trail of newly sprung flowers left in her wake.

She had barely passed through the gate, when Trwyn came rushing towards her. Panic etched lines on his brow as he berated her for leaving the castle grounds alone. She smiled reassuring him that no harm had been done, she had simply wanted a walk, all the time she was conscious of the scroll hidden beneath her cloak. He walked her back towards the castle and for a brief moment Jacantha wondered, if things had been different, whether he would still be treating her this way.

The last few days his attendance upon her had been constant, only leaving her side when she chided him for neglecting his duties in helping in the forge or delivering supplies to those rebuilding the surrounding villages.

As they drew closer and the solid stones loomed above them, she made an excuse to send him on an errand. Yet another lie passing her lips, as she expressed a desire for fruit, and he hurried away to the kitchens to procure it for her. She slipped quickly along the corridors to Celdwady's chamber. He was deep in consultation with Brawd when she entered. As she passed him the scroll and delivered the Lady's message before hurrying away to her chamber before Trwyn could discover her duplicity.

Celdwady carefully unrolled the scroll. The parchment protested as he tried to smooth it down, eventually he anchored its edges with crystals as he began to survey its contents. He could only make out a few words at first. They made no sense to him, this was like no enchantment he had ever seen before. The words that he could decipher called for certain items to be placed together in a crucible. He urged Brawd to gather them, as he sought amongst the strange script for clues as to what he was about to do.

His head told him not to proceed, if Brawd were to create a charm without being aware of its full consequences, he would have scorned him and let him feel his full anger. This was different, it was from the Lady, this was a test of his trust. The Lady could have no interest in their plans failing, he could see no reason why she should. As he began to follow the few instructions he could read, he became aware of Brawd hovering by his shoulder. He knew he would not be able to shield Brawd from the implications of his actions.

He motioned he should join him at the table as he carried out the complex preparation of ingredients. He had never seen a spell or potion as complicated, even with the few instructions that were decipherable. Once he had completed all that he could read, he stepped back. The two men's gaze fixed upon the crucible bubbling away. It was then they noticed the words on the parchment move. The ink swam across the page, the words that had been readable a few moments ago, gone new ones now appeared in their stead. These were instructions not for further ingredients to add or actions to take, but a dismissal.

Brawd looked to Celdwady watching to see what the older man would do. He leant forward and rolled the scroll up, they would do as it instructed and reopen when the time was right.

It was three days later when Jacantha felt the first pain. She sat at her window sewing as it passed through her body. She took a deep breath, she was aware this could last for hours and had no wish to summon assistance before she had to. She looked out the window and saw Trwyn heading towards the door.

She knew he would be coming back to check on her and picked up her sewing moving to the edge of the bed and seating herself, hoping she could hide the pains. Another seized her just as Trwyn opened the door, it caught her off guard and she could not keep him from noticing. He turned running down the hall raising the alarm.

Celdwady was dozing when the news reached him. Brawd ran about grabbing the equipment they would need to deliver the child, while Celdwady took down the scroll and spread it across the table. He waited as the words shifted and settled, then gathered the new items he would need, adding them into the bag with the normal necessities. He rerolled the scroll and took the bag. Brawd would join him with the crucible once Trwyn were out of the way.

When he entered the room Jacantha was lying on the bed. Trwyn hung over her, holding her shoulders down as she protested that she would prefer to sit. Celdwady smiled, he had seen so many men go to pieces worrying about their beloved. He gently took hold of Trwyn, steering him towards the door,

Trwyn protesting as he was forced from the room. Jacantha felt guilty, she knew she would not see him again. She longed to call him back for one last embrace, but knew that normal appearances must be maintained, she must do nothing to arouse his suspicions.

Jacantha settled herself down on the bed, while Celdwady moved around the room making preparations. A couple of the older women came to the door and he sent them hurrying to fetch fresh bedding and plenty of water. Jacantha closed her eyes and tried not to think of Trwyn pacing the great hall waiting for news. She was thankful that custom prevented him from staying close at hand and required only the Guardian be present at the birth of an heir.

Her brother would take over the crown but only until her daughter reached sixteen, when she would take her rightful place as leader. Her mind drifted as she sought to block out the pain, wondering who her daughter would resemble. How would she look as she accepted the crown and became a queen in her own right?

So many mixed emotions flooded her mind, she closed her eyes lost in her own thoughts, as she clung to the knowledge, that her actions ensured her daughters future. She listened to the voices as they brought things into the room only once silence filled the room did she open her eyes.

Brawd and Celdwady were gathered huddled over the scroll. The final words had formed, revealing the true intent of the enchantment. Celdwady shuddered contemplating the magic they were about to perform. This, as he suspected, was no mortal spell, rather it was the magic of the Lady herself, the magic of the gods. He turned to look at Jacantha, his face drawn and serious. The magnitude of what they were about to do real to them all now. At that moment, a pain gripped her body, stronger than the others and it was Brawd who came to her side and began preparations for the birth, while Celdwady prepared the ingredients, adding them to the crucible in silence.

Brawd mopped at Jacantha's brow, frequently he glanced across at Celdwady, they were only minutes away from the time the child would be born. Finally, Celdwady joined them and took his position to deliver the baby. Jacantha now moved to the edge of the bed, bracing herself ready to push. She gripped Brawd's arm so tightly she threatened to rip it from its socket. On Celdwady's word she pushed down hard, pain ripping through her body.

In between pushes, she swallowed deep breaths, before almost immediately the next wave tore through her and she bore down again. She saw the tears in the old man's eyes as he watched first the head then the shoulders appear. As he lifted her daughter she fell back on the bed waiting to hear the cry that would signify all was well.

It seemed an eternity before the babe let out a small cry but fell silent almost straight away. Jacantha struggled to sit up again to look and see what was happening but Brawd pushed her back down. She knew she could overpower him easily but fear paralysed her, she laid staring at the ceiling offering up silent prayers to the Lady. She had accepted that she must be sacrificed, but that her daughter should be, was not part of the bargain.

Celdwady looked down at the child, it was perfectly formed. Yet something was wrong, the child did not announce its presence with a hearty cry, rather a mere whimper. The runes had shown she would be healthy and grow to be a great queen but as he looked at her laying limp in his arms, he could not help but wonder how he had got it so wrong. Jacantha called now from the bed for her child, he wrapped a sheet around it as he passed it to her.

Jacantha propped herself up to receive her daughter, moving the sheet aside to look down on her perfect features. She pressed her lips to the baby's brow and closed her eyes. She reached one hand up under the pillow and pulled out the moonstone. As soon as her fingers closed around it, it began to glow brightly. She brought it round and placed it under her daughter's hand. Her lips still pressed to her child's brow, the circle between them complete, she waited eyes closed. Time stood still as she reached out with her mind through the child's body warming it, stirring the life force deep inside. Finally the child let out the hearty cry they had been waiting for.

Celdwady now roused himself, they had very little time to complete and execute their plan, the sound of the cry would have alerted those in the hallway that the child had been born and news would fly quickly to Trwyn. He quickly cleaned Jacantha as he helped her from the bed. She sat on a bench feeding her child while Celdwady took the afterbirth and placed it in the centre of the bed. Brawd brought him the crucible and they both repeated the incantation as they poured the liquid over the bloody mess. Immediately it began to bubble and take form.

Jacantha watched, wide eyed, as she saw it stretch and grow. Limbs began to reach out across the sheets, features forming becoming a face until she saw herself laying there. Brawd now reached for the child and Jacantha felt her heart break as she handed her over. She grabbed the bag she had hidden earlier and threw her cloak around her shoulders, she moved towards the door but could not resist turning and placing one last kiss on her daughter's lips. She reached out to Brawd with tears in her eyes she opened her mouth to speak but the words choked in her throat. She pressed the moonstone into his hand her eyes saying what her lips could not. He nodded his understanding as she turned and fled from the room.

She hurried down the corridors until she reached a secret passage and slipped into it. Only then did she stop and catch her breath. She stood, back pressed against the cold stone tears, flowing down her cheeks. In the silence she heard a blood curdling cry and she knew that Trwyn had been fooled. She could not bear to hear the noise for a second longer and slipped further along the passage to prepare for what still awaited.

Chapter Twenty-Eight

She crouched in the passage waiting. She had dressed once she could no longer hear the noises from within the castle, now weak from blood loss and emotionally drained, she waited to make her next move. She longed to lie down and press her forehead to the cold damp stone and let the darkness engulf her. Ahead she could see the entrance to the passage which led out to the rear of the castle. The light was starting to fade, under cover of darkness, she would creep out and make her way from her home for a final time.

There was a rear gate, it was small and usually guarded but tonight she knew there would be no one there. Tonight, while she slipped through the darkness, everyone would be gathered in the courtyard, as they lit the pyre to consume, what they believed was her body. It had been arranged that Celdwady would perform the ceremony, then he would depart on a spiritual journey, leaving Brawd to take over and crown her brother tomorrow.

Tears threatened to overcome her again as she thought about Trwyn sat by the pyre watching the flames flicker and dance around what he believed was her body. She could not allow herself to think of her daughter, her only consolation that a wet nurse would not be needed, she knew Fleura would step up into the mother role and complete what she could not. Her daughter would have a mother, if not in name, then at least in actions.

Celdwady stood over the body looking down at Jacantha's features. Even though he knew that is was an illusion, his heart was heavy. Trwyn had burst into the room only minutes after she had left, that she had escaped through the corridors unseen was a miracle. Trwyn had been bursting with joy and pride, as his eyes first greeted his daughter in Brawd's arms, then the realisation had come that Jacantha lay unmoving on the bed. He had flung himself over her, cursing the gods and begging for her return. It had been hard to witness the grief that had ripped Trwyn's heart from within his chest and extinguish all hope of salvation. Trwyn had turned on him blaming him for not saving her, for failing her.

Celdwady could not hold it against him, he had not approved of Jacantha's scheme. Now he understood her reasons though, she was right Trwyn would never have allowed her to walk away unchallenged, he would have spent his life trailing them. Jacantha would have been unable to go to her resting place with him at her heels, this way, in time they would both find peace. In other circumstances Trwyn would have been the one to prepare the body, but in his grief, he could not bring himself to do anything other than cling to her hand, pleading for a miracle.

He had allowed Fleura to assist Celdwady in washing and dressing her. Once as she brushed and braided Jacantha's hair, he had caught Fleura looking puzzled. She opened her mouth as if about to say something, then she thought better of it and remained silent. His heart had skipped a beat, as the realisation, that she was not fooled sank in. Now the bearers were approaching, ready to carry their queen to her pyre, he reached out and touched Trwyn on the arm.

        The young man looked up at him and nodded. Everyone must do their part even in the depths of his grief Trwyn knew this. He must do what was needed now for her, for his love for her, he must be strong, and do, as he knew she would wish. As her body was lifted, he gathered his thoughts and lifted their daughter from the crib in the room, she would see her mother's spirit soar and tomorrow they would find a way to live without her. Fleura and Arth fell in at either side of him, Fleura holding her own child tightly in her arms and the three of them followed the bearers carrying the body through the silent corridors. They all watched as Jacantha was placed upon the carefully upon the logs. Trwyn did not hear Celdwady's words as they floated across the courtyard nor the sobs from those stood around him. The only noise he heard was the long low howl of a single wolf out in the distance.

    Celdwady passed him the torch and with tears in his eyes he lowered it to the kindling. He threw the torch onto the pyre and looked down at his daughter who had begun a soft whimpering. His lips pressed against the same spot which her mother's lips had blessed her earlier and Trwyn realised that Jacantha had not left him part of her remained here within his arms. Reluctantly he passed the babe to Fleura to take indoors while he settled for his vigil by the pyre.

Chapter Twenty-Nine

Jacantha slipped towards the gate, as she had expected it was unattended. She opened it only enough to slip through and pulled it closed behind her. Now on foot she made her way deeper into the wood to await Celdwady at the spot where they had arranged to meet. Dressed in simple warrior clothing, she rubbed dirt into her face to aid her disguise. She pulled the cloak closer around her as she found the spot and hid so that she could observe the road unseen.

Celdwady returned to his chambers he had already packed a bag with the personal things he required, as well as another with provisions he suspected he may require. It would be a day's ride before they could stop to obtain anything else and be sure she would not be recognised. He had secured a horse for himself earlier before the silence had begun to mark Jacantha's passing.

Brawd had taken on the burden of gathering everything for him and making sure that all was ready and loaded onto the saddled horses. It was Brawd who had come up with the plan for him to take extra supplies, on the pretence of delivering them on route, giving him the excuse to take an extra horse to bear the burden. Though Jacantha would not doubt, have preferred her own steed that was not possible it would have aroused suspicion and he doubted Trwyn would have allowed it, it was a part of who Jacantha had been. He did however have her sword and crown hidden deep within the bags. He had taken the liberty of copying them months ago, knowing they may be needed. He had ensured the copies were the ones placed upon her as she was prepared for the pyre.

He now performed a last-minute check to be sure everything was in order. He stood looking round his chambers that had been his home for so long. The pain he felt at leaving was nothing to that he knew Jacantha must be feeling, but he had inhabited these rooms for nearly a century, now he left them in Brawd's hands.

He had no doubts Brawd would fulfil his duties well, over the last few months he had watched as the apprentice gained in skill and confidence. Yet there was knowledge the young man must learn on his own and he had packed away a few of his books along with the scroll to take on his journey. It was time to leave, satisfied all was in order he made to exit the room only to find Fleura waiting outside his chamber.

She was agitated and though Celdwady knew the cause, he was at a loss as how to comfort her without betraying his Queen. Fleura slipped past him into the room, pulling the door closed behind her to assure they were not observed, speech was by custom forbidden during mourning, and as she looked round the room, he wondered whether she would speak given the circumstances. Instead she picked up a quill and dipping it in the ink etched a few words on a piece of parchment. She wrapped something in the folded paper before writing on the outer fold 'Jacantha'.

She hurried back to him, fearful of being discovered here and pressed the paper into his hand before opening the door and running away down the corridor. He buried it deep in his pocket without looking at it and closed the door behind him heading for the stables. Jacantha had chosen well in her brother's match.

Brawd met him outside the stables the reins of the two mares in his hand. No words were exchanged between the two, each knew this was farewell but needed no words, their eyes conveying all that was required as Celdwady mounted his horse. As he rode out through the courtyard, Trwyn's eyes turn to watch him. He could still see remnants of the bitterness that had filled the young man's heart a few hours ago as he had fallen beside the bed overcome with grief. Trwyn gave him a brief nod, as if to convey he held no grudge, as the older man passed by and out of the castle gates.

He carried on along the main road for a few minutes then after checking he was not being watched, he turned the horses through the trees towards the smaller track where Jacantha waited for him. As he drew nearer he scanned the road for signs of her waiting for him, breath held as no sign of her emerged. He reached the appointed place and halted, still she did not appear.

Slipping from the saddle he cautiously called out to her. At first nothing, then the merest whisper.

He moved towards the sound and found her crumpled on the grass. Gently he helped her to her feet, half carrying her to the horse. As he helped her up he noticed how pale she looked, the exertions of the birth then her flight were now evident as she sat precariously in the saddle.

They moved off again slowly, Jacantha swaying in the saddle. They had intended to ride through the night to maximise the distance between them and the castle before daylight, but looking at her now, Celdwady was unsure how far she would make it. After riding for the first two hours Celdwady called a halt. Jacantha could barely remain in the saddle, he took her reins and led the horse deep into the woods beside the road. He assisted her from the horse settling her against a tree stump while he cast a shielding spell around them.

He moved quickly, lighting a fire and digging deep within the bags for supplies. He placed a small cauldron into the flames and poured in some broth he had taken from the kitchens. As it heated he watched Jacantha slumber, her eyes had closed as soon as she touched the earth. The rest would help her heal physically but he knew she needed to come to terms with the emotional anguish of what had happened, before they reached their final destination.

At full speed it would have taken three days to reach their final destination now, it would be closer to four. He had thought long and hard about which direction they should go in but the Lady had included her own plans within the scroll, directing them to a distant corner of the land. The place she had chosen for them to meet her was secluded, unlikely to be disturbed by anyone but it was also difficult terrain to traverse especially for Jacantha in her weakened state.

They had another day and a half travelling along roads, with one or two small hamlets where they could take on extra provisions but the last part of the journey would be tiring and as he looked down on Jacantha now, he doubted she could handle it. He let her rest until the food was ready, then before waking her, he poured out a dark liquid into her dish, pouring the broth over it and mixing it in. He may not be able to take away the heartache but he could help her regain strength and help ease the bleeding that accompanied childbirth.

He lifted her carefully, putting the bowl to her lips letting the liquid slip into her mouth and down her throat. Gradually she seemed to come around a little and took the bowl in her own hands but she had no interest in drinking the broth. Celdwady chided her as if she were a child, coaxing each mouthful past her lips, only once it was finished, and she moved to return to her slumber, did he pull Fleura's packet from his pocket and hand it to her.

He watched in silence as she unfolded the paper, catching a glimpse of gold in its centre. She read the note over and over, clutching whatever had been contained in her hand out of sight. He watched the tears roll down her cheek then sat stunned, as she threw the paper into the fire, watching it curl as the edges caught a flame. She now sat looking at her open palm Fleura's locket resting in the centre. He waited to see if she would open it but instead she slipped the chain over her head and tucked the locket down her tunic out of sight. She laid back and closed her eyes.

They rested a few hours, the moon was still high as he roused Jacantha and put out the fire. A little colour had returned to her cheeks after her rest, but she was still week and silent. They mounted the horses and set off back to the track. They rode in silence, watching for any other travellers on the road. As the sun rose they turned south heading further away from the castle.

It had been many years since she had travelled this way and many of the sights stirred memories of a childhood trip with her father. She could not help wondering if Trwyn would bring their daughter to explore her future kingdom as her father had brought her. The tears threatened to rise again as she realised she would never even know her daughter's name. Her hand strayed to her chest tracing the outline of the locket, a gesture which did not go unnoticed by Celdwady.

They now approached the first of the hamlets, Jacantha kept her hood up covering her face and her head bowed. No one paid any attention to the old man and the bent woman, riding through but still they were more content when they passed out the cluster of cottages and put them behind them unrecognised. Celdwady reached into a bag passing Jacantha a lump of bread to eat as they rode along, after last night's delay he was unwilling to stop again until night fall. She chewed slowly upon each mouthful as the miles passed by.

Finally, as the sun set behind the hills in the distance, they made camp by the side of the road.

They were now far enough from the castle that she would not be instantly recognised but they still needed to be cautious, Celdwady once again cast the shield spells while Jacantha built up a fire. They dined on cold meat, bread and cheese she ate a little more now and willingly drank the liquid that was proffered towards her. She disappeared behind a clump trees taking a flask of water to cleanse her body with before redressing in fresh clothing.

She threw the soiled clothing into the flames and watched as the fire spluttered and destroyed them. Still she seemed unwilling to speak and Celdwady did not wish to pain her by questioning her. Instead he told her tales of the Lady, stories she had heard as a child for Jacantha rather than soothing her it only reminded her all the more of what she had left behind and she curled up, willing sleep to take her away from the pain. Celdwady's concern grew as he watched her sleep, he needed her to break through the barrier pain was causing her to put up, but knew this was something she must do for herself, he could not help her in this.

The next day was passed in much the same way as the previous one, with the exception of their journey through the hamlet. Celdwady made a point of pausing in the village and buying more bread and cheese. He enquired after the latest news and discovered as they had thought, news of the Queen's demise had not reached here yet. To the people here, her reign meant very little, they knew what had happened on the other borders and that they owed much to her for the peace that gave them prosperity but they would not recognise her if she rode down the main road. He thanked them and smiled and they moved on their way again. They ate again in silence that night and slept well. Jacantha now well on the way to physical recovery, only the Lady could ease her mind Celdwady decided.

The next morning, they set out on the final day travelling. They left the main track and now followed smaller rougher paths until they reached the base of a mountain. They now picked their way up winding tracks, unused for many years until the horses could go no further. They unloaded the packs, taking with them all they could carry then set the horses loose. They would head back towards the castle instinctively but Jacantha doubted they would get that far, some lucky person would find himself in possession of the two fine horses that had strayed onto his land.

They carried on now on foot, picking their way between the boulders the path rising steadily upwards. About half way up they found the cave. The sun was setting and they decided to spend the night sheltered within its confines. They gathered kindling and wood for a fire as best they could but it was a small blaze they sat round. As night fell the temperature dropped and they both pulled their travelling cloaks about them.

After a while Jacantha rose and moved to sit next to Celdwady. She removed her cloak and slipped inside his pulling hers over them so they now had a double layer of cloth wrapped about them and each other's body heat to fight off the cold. She laid her head against his chest, and the gloom of the cave, the words came at last. Tears fell as she poured out her heart, only when there were no more left to come, did she pull out the locket and open it for the first time.

Inside a tiny dark curl of hair nestled against the gold, her daughter's first lock that Fleura had snipped and slipped to her, a smaller piece of paper fluttered to the ground, Jacantha picked it up and read it.

"Kallisa, her name is Kallisa."

Exhausted and drained, she rested against his chest, the locket clutched tightly against her chest and slept.

The Lady visited Celdwady in his dreams, giving him his final instructions to guide them on their final steps. In his dreams he saw the castle and knew the dream was not his alone he looked and saw Jacantha stood beside him sharing his vision. Trwyn sat with his daughter in his arms, tears still ran down his face but they were tears of joy at the gift he had been left with. In his old chambers he saw Brawd sat by the fire still studying the ancient volumes.

In the great hall Arth sat with his wife and child by his side, his face strong and compassionate, as he spoke with those present about the legacy he had inherited and plans for continuing the kingdoms growth. They saw the kingdom now as if they were soaring above it. They saw the rebuilding of homes, families reunited as those who had fought by her side returned home to live in peace. In her sleep Jacantha smiled, knowing her pain and suffering had not been in vain.

They did not speak of the dream the next morning, they had no need as they looked at each other, they saw the peace reflected in the eyes. They followed the cave through to another exit on the opposite side of the mountain. They found themselves on a ledge above a small valley. It was a steep descent but they found themselves hurrying downwards, some inner voice urging them forwards. They moved through the trees at the base of the rocks until they came to clearing. A spring bubbled into a small pool, the water crystal clear and cool. In the centre stood a lone tree. A huge oak whose branches spread wide and whose trunk was divided at the base forming a hollow that a person could walk through.

Celdwady began the preparations for the ceremony which would take place at sunset while Jacantha prepared the fire and set about making her last meal. They still had bread and cheese she searched now to add berries and wild fruits. Once their preparations were complete they sat and ate together the mood finally lifted and a sense of peace and contentment filled them both.

It was still early when Jacantha slipped into the cool water and bathed in the spring, she felt her cares rinse away with the dirt, until Celdwady announced it was time for her to dress. The double had been sent to the pyre wearing her wedding dress but now Celdwady pulled from his bag the dress in which she had taken her crown. She pulled it on surprised it fit considering she had given birth only a few days ago.

She pulled a comb from her bag and sat allowing Celdwady to comb her hair braiding sections and pinning them before he placed the crown upon her brow. He picked up her sword, handing it to her and then stood back. She looked every inch the queen as she stood before him. They had barely finished their preparations when the sunset behind the mountain.

She turned startled by a noise, and saw a group of men approach, the men all wore the same ceremonial robes as the one she was familiar seeing Celdwady wear. She watched as he stepped forward to greet them, he met them as one met old friends, with warmth and love. One by one they moved forward, kneeling before Jacantha and pressing their lips to her hand. While no words were spoken she was aware of their voices engaged in conversation and found with very little effort she could hear them clearly. They made enquiries of Brawd's progress and she understood these were the Guardians who normally resided in their hidden grove preparing the younger ones to accept their calling. She felt their urgency grow and realised it was time for the ceremony to begin.

Jacantha knelt now before the altar that had been set up as Celdwady called on the elements and then called forth the Lady and her Lord. The other Guardians formed a circle around the clearing as they waited, the air shimmered around them and the Lady stepped forward from the ether smiling. The lord followed, and then came others, all shimmering and incredibly beautiful. The light that shone from them was almost blinding. Celdwady fell to his knees besides Jacantha as did the other Guardians. He watched spellbound as the Guardians who had come from the spirit world approached Jacantha, the moonstone in her crown now shining as brightly as the light emanating from them. They raised her to her feet each embracing her in turn as they propelled her towards the Oak. There she stood now with the Lady, mother and daughter as one by the gap in the mighty tree.

The Lady took her hand and led her between the great roots into the cavernous chamber created within the trunk and bid her to lie down. From where he knelt Celdwady watched Jacantha rest herself upon the ground and the Lady lean down whispering to her as she placed a kiss on Jacantha's forehead. The Lord now joined them embracing his daughter warmly, placing a moonstone in her hand to replace the one that she had left with her daughter, as soon as her fingers touched it, the light filled it. The Lord and Lady now knelt over their daughter hands clasped above her head and whispered an incantation, Jacantha's eyes closed and the light within the moonstone dimmed to a faint glow.

Celdwady waited, he expected them to leave now and that he would remain here until the eternal slumber took him to be reunited with his ancestors. Now the Lady came to him, he felt her gratitude as it flooded his body, she held out her hand to him and led him to take his place by his Queen. As he lay down it was made known to him his journey was not finished, he would rest now by Jacantha's side, his return to the spirit would be postponed for the present.

As they slipped into a sweet dreamless slumber, the Lady moved a hand across the trunk, bark spread across the gap sealing the entrance. The mortal Guardians bowed low to the Lady before turning to depart. The Lady took her Lords hand and they began a slow dance around the tree with each foot step plants sprung up filling the clearing. One by one as the clearing filled with new growth, the figures of the other Guardians faded and vanished until only the Lady was left.

"Sleep well my children." She whispered before she too faded from sight.

Deep within the protection of the ancient oak trunk, a faint glow emanated from the moonstone clutched in a pale hand, Queen and Guardian slept awaiting the call to waken.

About The Author

Born in Leeds, currently living in Huddersfield, Paula Acton decided, when she turned forty, to stop dreaming about writing and do it. Having been published in online journals, and featured in the charity anthology Lupus Animus, her first collection of short stories was published in August 2015, Disintegration & Other Stories explores when the love story goes wrong and happy ever after is no longer an option. Her second short story collection Voices Across the Void is an alternative to traditional ghost stories where in many cases the ghost tells their own tale.

You can find out more on her on her social media sites

Website - http://paulaacton.co.uk

Facebook - https://www.facebook.com/Paula.Acton.Author

Instagram - https://instagram.com/paulaacton/

Twitter – https://twitter.com/Paula_Acton

Also By This Author

Paula Acton

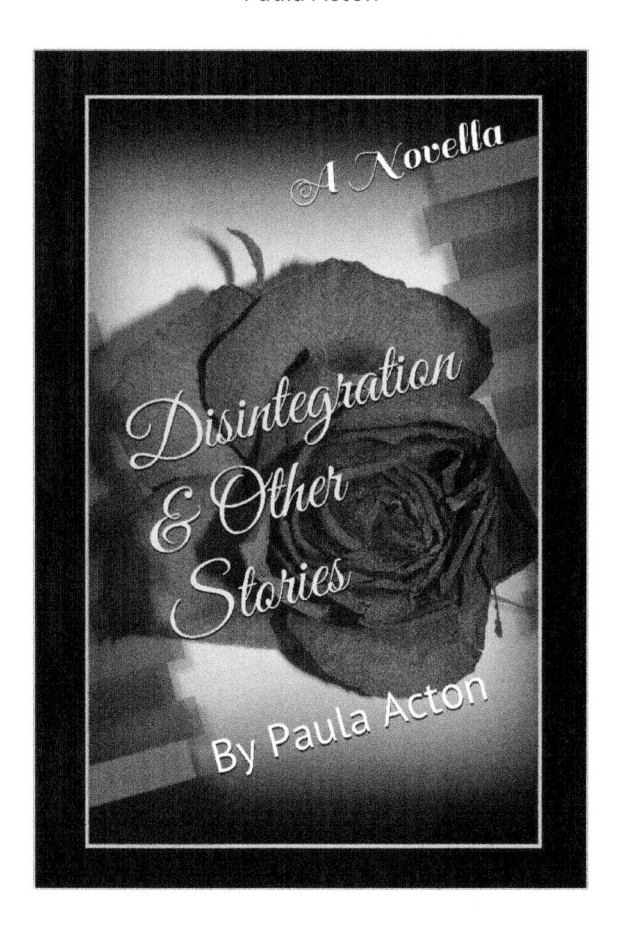

A series of short stories about when the fairy tale ends and everything falls apart. Love,death and revenge all feature in these tales where not everything is as it seems. The phrase till death do us part takes on a different meaning in both Disintegration and Empty, while Table For One and Deuce examine the more humorous side of betrayal.

5 ou*t of 5 stars* Amazing

Queen Of Ages: Ascension

By Amanda on 2 January 2017
Absolutely amazing. I loved it. Each story has the possibility to become its own novel. Wonderful work. Can't wait to read more.

5.0 out of 5 stars Great selection of short stories with twists you won't expect.
By Helen on 11 July 2017
A selection of short stories based around divorce/separation and the reasons behind it. Even though each tale is short in length, they all have enough in them to make you invested in the tale. I thoroughly enjoyed them.

Voices Across The Void is a collection of ghostly tales, not all ghosts are friendly but they all want to be heard, this collection is told many from the other side, with as many emotions as they displayed in life they want your attention now, so the question remains, are you listening?

5.0 out of 5 stars Worth reading.
By Dave on 13 August 2016
Well written book of stories by a new authoress, some with a real twist. Hope to read more written by her.

5.0 out of 5 stars Excellent read
By Gill 7 May 2017
Paula is a talented writer and I would recommend this book for everyone. Great read. Don't miss it. Excellent book.

5.0 out of 5 stars This was a good book
By Kim 29 December 2017 - Published on Amazon.com
Format: Kindle Edition|Verified Purchase
If you're into mystery, suspension, with a touch of scary, then Voices Across The Void, is the book for you. This book will give you all of that, and some surprise emotions as well.

There were several stand-out stories for me; The Cottage was one of them, this was a story about redemption, closer, and self evaluation. At least, that's how I felt while reading. The Hospital was another mind bender, though tragic, it was also beautiful at the same time. Finally; The Bluebell Woods, I don't have enough words to express how this one story touched me. The emotions I felt while reading, surprised, and shocked me. I went from fear to anger so fast, that I had to take a break, and stop reading. The Bluebell Woods is my worst damn nightmare! To read it; had me crying, feeling bitter, laughing, and towards the end rejoicing.

This was a great book; it kept me entertained during the holidays and on these cold, and blustery days and nights.

Queen Of Ages: Ascension